Judith Logan worked as a legal secretary for many years before becoming the administrative assistant to an assistant chief judge of the Provincial Court of Alberta.

After 28 years in the Provincial Court system, she retired and immediately began writing her first book, *Monkey on Her Back.* This true story was published as an e-book on both Kobo and Amazon Kindle books. That book was the rebirth of a lifelong love of writing for Judith.

She no sooner self-published her memoir, and soon she began writing her second book, *Not Another Word!*, a totally fictional mystery novel very different from her memoir. This novel was published on Amazon Kindle Direct Publishing on May 14, 2017. Judith then immediately began writing the sequel, *Shadows of the Missing.*

"My only regret," says the author, "is that I didn't follow my dream of writing many years ago. I have more stories left to write than my age may allow, although I will never give up as long as my imagination doesn't fail me!"

Judith and her husband are retired and live on a ranch in Alberta.

For Gayleen
Thank you for reading
my stories!
Judi Logan

This novel is dedicated to my husband, Bruce. It can't be easy, living with a wife who wanders around in a fog, her every action dictated by the voices of literary characters echoing in her head! My dear husband not only accepts the workings of my quirky imagination, he calmly sits and discusses the evolving plots to my stories as if they are real to him as well! For always being there, for constantly encouraging me with your love, patience, understanding and acceptance, you have my undying love and gratitude!

Bruce Logan, this one's for you!

Judith Logan

Shadows of the Missing

Whatever Happened to Lloyd?

Austin Macauley Publishers™
London • Cambridge • New York • Sharjah

A CIP catalogue record for this title is available from the British Library.

ISBN 9781788233996 (Paperback)
ISBN 9781788239516 (Hardback)
ISBN 9781788239813 (ePub e-book)

www.austinmacauley.com

First Published (2020)
Austin Macauley Publishers Ltd
25 Canada Square
Canary Wharf
London
E14 5LQ

I wish to acknowledge my many friends and family members who have supported me throughout the time it took me to write this novel. Without all their support, I am not sure I would have been able to finish what I started, which would have been a real shame. I also wish to commend the employees of Austin Macauley who continue to work tirelessly during the COVID-19 pandemic, at home and at the office. Stay safe!

Note to Readers

This story takes place in the provinces of British Columbia and Alberta, Canada. Accordingly, Canadian units of measurement have been used.

Table of Contents

Recapitulation

In the previous novel, *Not Another Word!* At the tender ages of 14 and 9 (nearly 10!), siblings Braden Lloyd Jordan ("Lloyd") and Lacey Colleen Jordan began a difficult journey

Where were the parents, you ask?

Their father, Paul Martin Jordan, was in prison, serving a ten-year sentence for embezzling funds from the company that he worked for.

Where was their mother, Anna Marie Jordan, you ask? With only bare-bones high school education, Anna had partied her way through school, barely passing her subjects during her last year in high school. She worked as a cleaning lady. She also did laundry and ironing in her own home for regular, steady customers. Struggling hopelessly to make ends meet, it increasingly seemed as if "the harder she worked, the 'behinder' she got."

Finally, Anna made the most agonisingly difficult decision of her life. After deep soul-searching and weighing of very limited alternatives, she chose to abandon her children. In her heart, she truly believed that they would be better off in the foster care system, where they would at least be warm and fed. She snuck away when her children were in school, leaving only an ambiguous note behind. There was no way to trace her.

Devastated by their mother's action, Lloyd and Lacey carefully planned and successfully executed a visit to the prison in British Columbia to see their father. With the blind faith of the very young, they fervently believed that with his monetary assistance, he would be able to help them remain in their home and look after themselves until either their mother returned or their father got out of prison.

However, at the end of the visit with their father, they were apprehended by two social workers. The children were returned to the Province of Alberta and taken to the home of foster parents, George and Martha Schmidt.

During the short duration of their stay at the Schmidt place, one of the foster girls, Charlotte Ford ("Charley") was sexually assaulted by George Schmidt. Charley ran away.

Lloyd and Lacey were next placed in a wonderful, caring home. Henry and Harriet Greschner loved and cared for the children as if they were their own biological son and daughter. Susanna was their daughter by birth. Susanna and Lloyd were the same age. However, tragic, unforeseen circumstances occurred and once again, Lloyd and Lacey were moved.

Foster home #3 – Simon and Bertha Savard cared for a total of eight children including Lloyd and Lacey. While Mr and Mrs Savard ate like royalty, the foster children were fed barely enough to keep them alive. Lacey and Lloyd were 11 and 15 years old. One of the girls at this home, Amelia Anderson, also ran away. She disappeared in the same manner that Charley had disappeared, that is, without a trace.

Foster home #4, the farm of Bart and Gladys Bourke – first-time foster parents, only Lloyd and Lacey were cared for in this home. At this time, Lloyd was 15, Lacey was 11. Bart Bourke worked Lloyd hard. When Lloyd was 17 and Lacey 13, a completely unforeseen circumstance once again necessitated a move.

Foster home #5, living in the home of Peter and Elsie Petrie until they were 17 and 13 years old, this was one of the worst placements. Foster child Annie Barcley was 16. She, too, ran away; disappeared like a snowy owl in the light of day.

Events at the Petrie house escalated from bad, to worse, to god-awful. It was during this placement that Lloyd decided to take matters into his own hands and go searching for the missing girls. Lacey was left behind to cope with her life as best she could.

In a final placement, Lacey went to live with Stumpy and Hilda Somers. She was their only foster child. As wonderful and caring as these foster parents were, Lacey was lonely and desperately missed her brother.

Impulsively married at 16, Lacey continually pined for Lloyd. There had been no word from him since he left. Despite efforts on Lacey's part to ensure that he would be able to find his sister when he was ready, the plot continued to thicken.

Not Another Word! Was never intended to require a sequel! The characters became alive in the imagination and the mind of the author, and they dictated the conclusion of *Not Another Word!*

And thus begins Book #2, the sequel, *Shadows of the Missing: Whatever Happened to Lloyd?*

I trust you will enjoy reading the adventures as much as I enjoyed writing them!

Judith Logan, Author

Chapter 1
The Journey

Excerpt from *Not Another Word!*

Lloyd could wait no longer. He would take matters into his own hands. Wednesday evening, he snuck out of the house and went to the mailbox. There, he double-checked that the original information was still there. He left another piece of paper in the hiding place, right beside the vehicle information.

Thursday morning, Lloyd held back while Lester and Lacey got on the bus. As usual, they were busy chatting with friends and didn't notice when he waved the driver on and then ran towards the ditch where Annie had last been seen.

Not long after the school bus was out of view, a vehicle came up the road. Lloyd held out his thumb and the truck stopped.

The driver's face was hidden by a five-gallon cowboy hat. His hair was long, sticking out from beneath the hat, further obscuring his face.

"Going somewhere, fella?" the driver asked in an intentionally deep voice.

"Yes, how far are you going?" Lloyd asked.

"Vancouver."

"Great! That's where I'm going also. Thanks for stopping."

Lloyd threw his backpack in first and climbed into the cab of the 1-ton, pumpkin orange truck with a shell covering the truck box, with black and green lettering on the doors that read *ZO'S HAULING.*

Without even a glance at the driver, Lloyd breathed, "I'm ready."

"Well then," said the driver in his normal voice, "Let's roll!"

For several minutes, Lloyd simply sat and looked out the side window of the pumpkin orange delivery truck. He neither spoke nor looked at the driver. He simply stared blindly out of the window.

Finally, he turned his head and observed the man behind the wheel.

The driver appeared to have very long legs which ended in a pair of scuffed, black-and-tan leather cowboy boots with worn-down heels.

Black T-shirt under a black and grey plaid flannel shirt. Sleeves rolled up above the elbows. Rugged face. Longish black hair. Very dark eyes. Pale, smooth skin.

Lloyd had absolutely no idea of the guy's age. Twenty-five would be his W.A.G (Wild-Ass Guess).

His large, calloused hands spoke of a lot of physical labour, something other than a truck driver. From the little Lloyd knew about truck drivers, they seemed to wear gloves for protection when doing anything involving their trucks.

Finally, Lloyd spoke up. He said, "My name's Lloyd. Thanks for stopping. I appreciate the lift."

The man didn't ask what Lloyd's last name was. He either respected Lloyd's privacy, or he simply didn't care.

"Nice to meet you, Lloyd. My name's Adam, Adam Draper. I'm happy to have the company. It's a long drive to Vancouver and the time passes quicker with someone to talk to. I just fill in as a temporary driver and so I never really get used to the long haul with anyone other than myself to talk to!"

Inwardly, Lloyd moaned. The last thing he felt like doing was chit-chatting for the next eleven or more hours!

He glanced in Adam's general direction and mumbled a barely coherent "Nice to meet you too," before turning and once more gazing out the window. He focused his mind on what he might find on the journey ahead.

Near the Alberta/British Columbia border, Adam pulled off the road into a weigh scale area. He waited until the attendant in the small building was finished with another truck driver. Opening his door, he jumped out, turned back to Lloyd and said, "Back in a flash" before striding over to speak with the attendant.

As Lloyd pretended not to watch, he nevertheless observed Adam hand the scale operator a small wrapped box. In return, Adam was handed what looked like a roll of bills which he hastily stuffed into his shirt pocket. At this point, Lloyd leaned back in his seat and pretended to doze. He feigned a startled jump when Adam opened the door.

"Sorry, kid," Adam said as he fastened his seat belt, "I didn't mean to disturb you. Just making a delivery is all."

He handed Lloyd a thermos lid, filled with hot chocolate. It was nearly cold, but Lloyd gratefully drank it quickly and then handed the container back to Adam. Adam tightened the lid on the original thermos container and threw it into the back.

Releasing the parking brake, he smoothly guided the truck back on to the main highway and continued driving west. Lloyd once again leaned his head against the window. Within a couple of minutes, he was soundly asleep. A few minutes later, he was dreaming…

A man and two women, one of the women no longer young, stood at the edge of the water. The late morning sun glistened brightly on the gently dancing waves of the emerald green lake. Their craft waited expectantly, tied to the jetty.

The man helped both women settle comfortably in the canoe before he climbed in and picked up his paddle. They glided smoothly along on the cool water, headed for the small island that beckoned in the distance. Reaching the land, the man positioned the canoe alongside an old jetty. While his wife held the canoe steady against the side of the jetty, the man helped the older lady out of the craft. He then turned to assist his wife but she was already out. He reached in and removed a wicker picnic basket and four folding lawn chairs from the canoe.

It was beautiful on the shore of the island. A cool autumn breeze heralded the coming winter but today, the sun shone brilliantly and warmed their cheeks as they sat on the beach. The man pointed skyward.

"Look," he softly said. "See them? There are only five. One must have lost its love. Trumpeters mate for life, just like you and me." His wife smiled and patted his hand.

Some time passed. His wife fretted. She said worriedly, "He should be here by now. He promised he would be here."

"We can wait a little longer," her husband said. "We'll wait as long as we can."

They waited for two more hours. Finally, the man gently told both women that they would have to return the canoe to the rental agent. If they didn't leave now, it would be dark and the rental booth would be closed. They quickly packed up the remains of their picnic and returned to the jetty. The husband reloaded the canoe, then helped the women back into the craft.

Reaching the centre of the small lake, the man stopped paddling. His wife leaned back and he put his arms around her. The older woman trailed her hand in the cool water, watching the ripples grow larger until they disappeared. All three quietly watched in the distance as a young deer drank from the water's edge, in the same spot where they had sat only a few minutes before. After one last lingering look at the island, with tears wetly rippling down her cheeks, the elderly woman reached to the bottom of the canoe and brought up a wooden container. She kissed the box and then gently lowered it over the side of the canoe.

Utter silence. Not even a bird trilled. The five Trumpeter swans floated in place, their beauty reflected in the stillness of the water. Time stood still. Each lost in their own separate thoughts, the three people deeply appreciated the peace and the quiet. They fully realised that all too soon their busy lives would drown out their memory of this blissful silence and this beautiful lake.

"I'm sorry he didn't show," the man gently said. After several minutes more, the man picked up his paddle and continued rowing back from whence they had come…

His heart pounded. The blood and sweat poured down his forehead, stinging fiercely when they reached his eyes, blinding him as he raced at full speed, stopping only when his feet hit the water. It was not a long distance, probably no more than five hundred metres from the main shoreline to the small island. Gasping for breath, he dunked his head beneath the water to clear his vision. He then began to swim towards the shore of the island.

(At this point, Lloyd shivered in his seat, thrashed around. He moaned loudly, but did not awaken.)

Exhausted, he reached the rocky beach. He swore as he slipped while trying to throw himself up on to the jetty. He caught himself but not before his knee banged painfully against the side of the ancient wooden structure.

He attempted clumsily to untie the equally ancient wooden canoe but his bleeding fingers were stiff with cold. Finally, the knot broke free. He lunged into the craft, picked up an oar, prayed that the canoe would float. He began to paddle hard. Rounding the end of the island he spied the other canoe in the distance, already nearing the far end of the lake. He called out, but the wind direction and the exhaustion in his entire being made it impossible for his voice to carry that far. Tears of frustration, heart pounding with anxiety and disappointment, he turned the canoe around and headed slowly back to the jetty. He collapsed on the shore and, chest on fire, he breathed raggedly until his breathing evened out.

He fell asleep. When he awoke, it was dark but he knew he had to keep going. Leaving the canoe, he walked into the water and began a slow swim back to the mainland. A few strokes later, he felt something sucking him down towards the bottom of the lake. He tried to kick harder, to swim faster but still, he kept on sinking…

Lloyd awoke with a strangled cry!

He glanced wildly around, wondered where he was. His heart pounded. He was sweating heavily, wringing wet. His chest hurt; he couldn't catch his breath.

Glancing to his left, he finally realised where he was, in the pumpkin truck on his way to Vancouver. The driver, Adam, was not in the vehicle.

Lloyd tried to peer through the darkness. They were parked in front of a dilapidated, ancient trailer. It was very dark outside so it was difficult to see much more. Only one faint light came from inside of the building.

Puzzled, Lloyd debated whether or not he should get out of the truck. Before he could make a decision, though, Adam appeared at the driver's door, opened it and climbed in. He glanced over at Lloyd, appeared to be surprised that his passenger was awake.

Casually, Adam asked, "Have a good sleep?"

"I guess so," Lloyd answered. "Didn't realise I was so tired. Sorry I haven't been much company. Where are we?"

Without thinking, Adam replied, "Hope, British Columbia." He hastily added, "Just making a regular stop. We'll be on our way now. Want some more hot chocolate? There's some in that thermos if you want it."

"That would be great, thanks, Adam." Reaching towards the console, Lloyd picked up the small thermos, poured the liquid into the lid and thirstily drank the contents. Shortly after, he was once again sound asleep.

The distance from Hope to Vancouver is only 152 kilometres but Adam made several stops between the two centres, delivering packages at each stop. Lloyd slept deeply the entire way, not even stirring when the truck stopped for several minutes at each delivery location before Adam would return, jump in and continue on the journey.

The next thing Lloyd knew he was being tapped on the shoulder, not so gently. Groggy, he sat up straight and looked over at Adam.

"What's up, Adam?" he asked. "Is something wrong?"

"Nope," Adam replied. "But this is as far as I go in Vancouver. I have to turn around and head on back from here."

"Oh," said Lloyd. "If you will just tell me where in Vancouver I am, I'll take it from there." He looked around the area through the truck's windshield. He had never been to Vancouver before, so he didn't have a clue about his surroundings.

"You're in East Van," said Adam. "Here's a map. Not too far down the street, there is a homeless shelter. There are a lot of hostels and homeless shelters in this area of the City. I've heard nothing but good things about one at Hastings and Gore. It's got lots of beds, at least 60 or more. It's operated by some sort of church group. You should be able to get a bed there if you go right away. All the shelters tend to fill up by early to mid-afternoon. Now I really have to hit the road. Grab your gear. Good luck to you, young fella."

Lloyd obediently grabbed his backpack and stepped out of the truck. Before he could even thank Adam for the ride, he was gone, with only a quick wave and a brief toot of the horn.

Chapter 2
The Streets of East Vancouver

Left standing on the edge of the road, Lloyd stared after the departing pumpkin truck, his mouth agape. A honk from the horn of a passing bus had him leaping off the road and onto the sidewalk.

Looking around, he noticed a park – a sign identified it as *'OPPENHEIMER PARK'*. Spotting a vacant park bench, he practically staggered as he walked over and sat down heavily.

He didn't feel right. His head ached; he felt disoriented. His stomach rolled and grumbled but he didn't feel hungry. He was terribly thirsty. Although he had slept nearly all the way to Vancouver, he felt like he hadn't slept a wink. If he didn't know better, Lloyd would think he was badly hungover, or at least what he figured a large hangover would feel like. He knew that couldn't be the case, the main reason being he didn't drink!

Frowning, he tried to think back. The only thing he remembered drinking was the hot chocolate. Through his fuzzy brain, something was nagging at him. Thinking hard, he suddenly realised that both times after he drank the hot chocolate, he fell asleep almost immediately. Was it possible that Adam had put something in the drink? But why would he do that? What would be the purpose? Adam dropped Lloyd off in Vancouver just as he had said he would. He couldn't possibly think that Lloyd knew anything about anything bad; or could he? Lloyd sort of recalled a surprised look on Adam's face at the wreck of a trailer when he saw that Lloyd was awake. He had quickly offered Lloyd more hot chocolate. Lloyd had drunk all of it thirstily.

Lloyd tried harder to remember where they had made stops along the way. He vaguely remembered the first stop – at the roadside weigh scale near the Alberta/British Columbia border. It was just before they left that roadside stop that he drank the first lid full of hot chocolate. He even more vaguely remembered a dilapidated wreck of a trailer. *Hope B.C.* echoed through his scrambled thoughts but he wasn't sure of its significance or why it buzzed around the back of his brain like a pesky mosquito.

Lloyd knew that they had stopped briefly at several more places but he had been too out of it to awaken fully enough to assess the reason for the stops. He gave himself a mental shake. Reflecting out loud, he called himself an idiot for being so suspicious. After all, Adam was driving a delivery truck. ZO'S HAULING was a delivery outfit. Of course, there would be stops along the way.

He thought, *All this thinking is making my headache even worse!*

He looked down at the jumble of papers that Adam had given him. On the first sheet of paper was an address for a homeless shelter on East Hastings Street. There was a note on that page saying the shelter had 60 beds – 40 for men and 20 for women. Three meals a day were provided, as well as counselling, assistance with finding permanent housing and employment.

The second sheet of paper was a map. The location of the shelter was circled on the page. Adam had scribbled a comment – *'You should go early to the shelter if you want to get a bed. They fill up by mid-afternoon/early evening. Best of luck. ADAM'*

Lloyd dug into his backpack, looking for his watch. His dad had given Lloyd the watch for Lloyd's last birthday before his father had gone to prison. Lloyd kept it with him but rarely wore it. Pulling it out of the pack he checked the time, put it on his wrist. Ten-thirty, time to check in to the shelter. He looked at the map, noted the address and stood up shakily. Still fuzzy, he couldn't seem to get his bearings.

He saw a man coming out from behind a tree, zipping up his jeans.

"Excuse me, sir," Lloyd called out. "Can you please tell me which direction I need to go to find the shelter that is run by some church group?"

"Just new in town are ya, new in town?" the man asked. Not waiting for Lloyd to answer, he pointed and said, "You go that way, (he waved his arm in a westerly direction), but you better get a move on because they fill up real fast, they fill up real fast."

"Thanks!" Lloyd said. "You sound like you know a lot about the place. Is that where you are staying?"

"Nah," said the man. "I got kicked out, kicked out. Those shelters have strict rules about booze and drugs, booze and drugs. I thought I could sneak some into my room but I got caught, I got caught."

"Oh!" Lloyd said. "Where do you stay, then?"

"Wherever I happen to be when I get tired, when I get tired," the man said. "I carry my sleeping bag with me, bag with me. Last night I was lucky, I was lucky. I found a big wooden shipping box in an alley, in an alley. Someone had already dragged it from beside the dumpster to under a fire escape, under a fire escape. Protected me from the rain showers we had, showers we had. For once, I was nice and dry and warm, nice and dry and warm. First thing this morning though, some guy who had his office in the building run me off, run me off. I told him to have a nice day anyway, nice day anyway. I left right away, right away. Don't want no trouble if I want to continue to live in this area, to live in this area."

The man reached into the plastic garbage bag he was carrying, pulled out a mickey of cheap booze. He waved the bottle at Lloyd.

"Want a slug, want a slug?" he asked before taking a tiny sip himself. The bottle was only about one-quarter full.

Lloyd couldn't imagine depriving the poor man of his nourishment. Who knew when he would be able to get some more liquor!

“No thank you, sir,” Lloyd said. “I really better make my way to the shelter to see about getting a bed for tonight. I’m not as fortunate as you. I don’t have a sleeping bag.”

“Well, young fella,” the man deferentially tipped an imaginary hat towards Lloyd, “You have a great day now, have a great day now. It’s a beautiful morning, a beautiful morning. Just look at the beauty that God has made, God has made.”

Whistling a merry-sounding tune, he wandered away, stopped at a nearby garbage bin, and climbing over the side, he began to scavenge the contents.

In less than a minute, the man’s head popped out of the bin, holding a partial sandwich in his hand. “Bingo!” the man cried, waving the sandwich at Lloyd. “Breakfast!” Chomping on the find, he climbed out and headed off, presumably to the next garbage bin. Lloyd felt sick.

Checking the map once again, he headed down the street towards the shelter. Besides feeling ill, Lloyd was feeling completely overwhelmed. For the first time since his impetuous decision to leave the foster home to try and find the missing girls, he wondered if he was doing the right thing.

He arose from the park bench and ambled off in the general direction of the hostel. In less than five minutes, he approached a long, two-storey building. The basement level was covered with steel (he presumed) bars. A set of steps led up to the main doors.

Looking around, Lloyd noticed a large church towering behind the shelter which, he assumed, was the church affiliated with the shelter. (He was to eventually find out that he was correct). To the left of the shelter, several very old buildings perched, huddled close together and very close to the edge of the road. What sidewalk there was, was badly crumbled. He noticed that a Chinese grocery store occupied one of the buildings; a Dollar Store another, and some other kind of store. Lloyd wasn’t sure what it was because all the writing was in Chinese. There was, however, a picture of a pair of eyeglasses painted on the window. There appeared to be apartments above some of the stores.

Several people, shabbily dressed, were mingling in the immediate area. One fellow muttered to himself as he picked cigarette butts off of the ground and carefully put them in his shirt pocket. Unfortunately, his shirt pocket had a large hole in the bottom and as fast as he filled the pocket from the top, the butts fell out the bottom! The poor fellow didn’t even notice. Although Lloyd thought about mentioning the fact to the man, he decided it best not to interfere.

Another fellow sat on a ragged, rolled up sleeping bag, leaning against the sides of the stairway leading up to the main doors. He sat motionless, stared dejectedly at the sidewalk, said nothing.

An elderly woman bumped into Lloyd’s back with her heavily-laden, wonky-wheeled grocery cart. “Get out of the way, boy!” she snarled. Lloyd apologised for blocking her way. She accidentally pushed the cart off the sidewalk, tipping it over, spilling everything on to the street. Swearing like a drunken sailor, she struggled to right her cart before a vehicle could come along and crush all her earthly possessions.

Lloyd gently put his hand on her shoulder. "Please, ma'am, let me do that for you. After all, I was in your way."

"Don't break nuthin!" the old woman huffed. "That's valuable stuff you know. You be careful you hear? Them things in that cart is everything I has in this *#%* world."

She stood glaring balefully at Lloyd, never taking her rheumy eyes off of him as he hurried to replace the belongings that had been in her cart. When he was done, he hoisted the front end back up on to the sidewalk, walked to the back and lifted up the rear end of the cart. He then rolled it to the far side of the sidewalk, safely out of the way of other folks who, like himself, foolishly stood in the middle of the sidewalk to do their gawking.

"There you go, ma'am, good as new!" he said to the old woman. Despite her best efforts to appear sullen, she smiled at Lloyd, revealing a mouth full of gaps where once had been teeth.

"Thanks, young fella," she said. "You'll do. Have a good 'un." That said, she shuffled off down the street, her heavily-laden cart weaving crazily around obstacles, heading for Heaven knew where.

"Wow, boy!" a voice behind Lloyd commented. "I see you broke the ice with BeeBee. That's something. She's colder and more crotchety than a witch with haemorrhoids riding a broken broom."

"BeeBee?" queried Lloyd, turning around to see who was speaking.

"Well, we residents of East Hastings Street call her that – short for Belligerent Bessie. If you say 'black', she'll swear it's white; if you say 'hot', she'll swear it's cold. That kind of personality, you know the type. Must tell ya though, that's the first time I ever seen her smile or say thanks to anyone."

The man Lloyd was facing was short and stocky. It was hard to guess his age, but judging by the thin grey hair, probably in his mid-to-late 50s. He had the purple, heavily veined and swollen nose of a copious drinker. No sooner did that thought cross Lloyd's mind, then the man reached into his back pocket and pulled out a mickey. Unlike the bottle of the first man Lloyd spoke within the park, this bottle was nearly full. Holding out his arm and waving the bottle around precariously, the man raised his eyebrows.

"Drink?" he asked Lloyd.

"No, thanks, sir, I don't drink," Lloyd answered. *Good grief!* Lloyd thought. *That sounds pretty pompous!*

He quickly said, "Thanks anyway, Mister. You have a good day, sir. It was very nice to meet you. I need to go into the shelter now and arrange for a bed. Hopefully, I'll see you again sometime soon."

Lloyd turned away and quickly climbed the stairs to the main doors.

At the top, one hand holding on to the doorknob, Lloyd turned and took another quick look at the street. A motley crew, but no one seemed terribly unhappy. They seemed very accepting of the positions they were presently in. Lloyd would love to hear some of their stories. *Perhaps I'll get a chance to hear some,* he thought as he opened the door.

As the door opened, a bell jingled somewhere behind a reception area. No one was at the desk. There were several chairs. Lloyd sat down on one of them, prepared to wait.

He did not have to wait long. In just a couple of minutes a door behind the desk opened and a matronly woman appeared. Not noticing Lloyd at first, she sat down and started to open a pile of mail.

After a few minutes, Lloyd stood up, walked across the waiting area to the desk, nervously cleared his throat. She raised her head, noticing him for the first time. "I'm sorry, young man, I didn't see you. What can I do for you?"

The woman wore a bright yellow name tag. It read, *'MONA GRACE FORD'.*

Lloyd explained that he was in Vancouver on a mission. At this time, he did not go into any details.

"You do realise, do you not, young man, that this is a shelter for the homeless? You certainly don't appear homeless to me."

Lloyd sputtered in a very bitter tone of voice, "That's where you are wrong, ma'am, I am definitely homeless and very much unemployed."

Mona Grace Ford studied the young man in front of her. Something in the tone of his voice worried her.

"What's your name and how old are you?" she asked. She continued speaking before Lloyd could reply. "You know, Vancouver has youth hostels. They are set up for young people and are very inexpensive. You can get a bed at a youth hostel for as little as $15.00 a night."

Ignoring the information she had just provided, Lloyd spoke. "My name is Braden Lloyd Jordan, but everyone calls me Lloyd." He crossed his fingers behind his back as he answered the second part of her question. "I'm nineteen." *That wasn't really a lie*, he thought, *I'll be nineteen in only a little over a year from now*. He was afraid to tell her he was only 17.

Mona Grace laced her fingers together, rested her joined hands under her chin, sceptically murmured, "Hmm." She then asked, "How much money have you got in your pockets, Mr Lloyd Jordan?"

Lloyd hung his head, ashamed that he had to answer, "I've got $50.00 cash. About $5.00 of that's in change."

"That's it?" asked Mona Grace Ford. "How long are you planning to stay in Vancouver and how long do you think you can survive on $50.00?"

He raised his head and stared straight into Mrs Ford's eyes, anxious for her to believe him. "I don't have a clue, to tell you the truth. It was a spur of the moment decision. I guess – I mean, I KNOW that I wasn't thinking very clearly when I left Alberta." Lloyd looked behind him before continuing. "It's a long, long story and I see other people are waiting to speak with you."

Turning to his right, Lloyd took two steps back towards the exit. "Sorry to have bothered you." His voice was husky and his eyes were threatening tears.

"Hold on a second, Braden Lloyd Jordan. Did you hear me say I didn't have a bed for you?"

She stood up.

“Tell you what, Lloyd,” Mrs Ford said. “You have a bed for tonight at least, on the condition that you will speak with one of our counsellors.”

She continued speaking as if reading from a prepared script. (Lloyd figured it was part of the job training – to memorise all the details regarding the shelter). “You see, other than free beds, we also provide free counselling services, three meals a day, and assistance with finding employment for those people who are able to work. We do hope, though, that once a person gets on his or her feet, that they consider making a donation to our shelter. It costs a whole lot of prayers and a whole lot of money to run a homeless shelter, especially a shelter this size. We are always looking for financial assistance. If you can’t provide money, then we always welcome volunteer helpers. Now, come along. I’ll show you where you will sleep tonight.” She turned and faced the waiting area. “Be back in just a minute, folks. Sorry about the wait!”

As they walked down the hall towards the men’s dorm, she filled Lloyd in on what was expected of him for as long as he stayed at the shelter.

“You are required to make your own bed and keep the area around your bed clean and tidy. There are enough lockers at the back of the dorm for the number of beds in the dorm room. Each locker has a number that corresponds to the number on the foot of each of the beds. Each locker has a combination lock. Your bed is #10 so your locker will be #10. I will give you the combination for the lock. Keep #10 locked at all times that you are not within sight of it. Meals are served between 7 and 8:30 for breakfast; between 11:00 and 1:00 for lunch and between 5:00 and 7:00 for supper. You are expected to scrape off your dishes and put them on the conveyor belt when you are finished. Put your empty tray on the cart that is next to the conveyor.”

She turned to the left and they entered a very large room. A prominent sign on the door dictated, *MEN’S ONLY DORM. NO WOMEN OR PETS ALLOWED.*

“There are 40 beds in this dorm,” Mona Grace said. “There are also 40 storage lockers. Anything you do not take with you every day must be kept in your locker. If you don’t keep your locker locked, be prepared to have everything stolen when you come back to the dorm. Nothing can be stored under the bed. Unless you have a counselling appointment with one of our counsellors, you have to be out of the building before 9:30 am. This allows the cleaning staff to do a proper clean-up of the entire building. If you need the bed for another night you must check-in at the reception desk and let them know before you leave the building. If you forget, too bad. Unless the shelter has an extra bed, you will, more than likely, end up sleeping on the street. It is a rare night, indeed, that the beds are not full. There’s a registration book on the desk in the lobby. Be sure you sign it, including your name, bed number and time you are signing in. You can eat your meals downstairs in the cafeteria. You can check back in in to your bed after 4:00 p.m. You can only stay for a maximum of 30 days. This is to encourage folks to get out and try to find employment and a permanent residence. Also, of course, it’s to allow new guests to access our facility and our services. One hard and fast rule – there are absolutely no liquor or drugs allowed in this building. If you are found with either booze or drugs on you, then you are ordered to leave the building immediately. No excuses, no arguing. Except under exceptional and very rare circumstances, you cannot come back." Mona Grace stood still, hands on her hips, staring intently into Lloyd's eyes. She liked what she saw.

"That's not a problem, Mrs Ford. I don't smoke, drink or do drugs. At least not knowingly," he enigmatically added.

With a quizzical look, Mona Grace turned to Lloyd. "Any questions?"

"Just one for the moment, Mrs Ford," Lloyd answered. "What about some of those poor souls wandering around outside, either blind, drunk or stoned? Does that rule mean they can't get a bed here?"

Mona Grace smiled sadly at Lloyd. "No, but they are not allowed to bring any drugs, smokes or liquor in with them. Some of these people come in. They are housed in a temporary detox area where they are kept under medical supervision for at least one night. If they become seriously ill while drying out, arrangements are made to transport them to a hospital for immediate attention, and then to an actual full-time detoxification centre."

"I see. Thank you, Mrs Ford," Lloyd said quietly. "No further questions right now."

More soft-hearted than her brusque mannerisms indicated, Mona Grace patted Lloyd on the shoulder. "When you check-in at the desk tomorrow morning, honey, there will be an appointment with a counsellor arranged. Ask the gal at the desk about it if she doesn't give you an appointment card when you check out for the day."

She looked thoughtfully at Lloyd, then added, "Young Lloyd, I have a good feeling about you. I think you are going to accomplish your mission, whatever that mission might be, and be back home before the 30 days are up here. Good luck. See you around from time to time."

She looked up at a large clock on the wall, quickly finished her instructions. "Your combination lock code is on this slip of paper. Memorise it, then return the combination code to the desk. Put whatever you don't want to take with you while you are out into your locker and then you have to leave for the day. I'll check you out."

"Whoops, I nearly forgot. There are signs directing you to the cafeteria. It's in the basement. Unless you want to spend that $50 in a hurry, I suggest you be back in time for lunch and again for supper!"

She walked over to the reception desk, loudly asking, "Okey-dokey, friends, sorry about the wait. Who's next?"

Lloyd returned to the dorm, put his entire backpack in his locker and then left the building, wondering what in this world he was going to do for the rest of the day.

Standing outside at the bottom of the steps, Lloyd looked around. Although there were a lot of garbage containers in sight, they were all overflowing. The street in front of him was littered with trash. The air smelled of a curious mixture of sweat, stale booze, bad breath and human desolation. Trying not to breathe too deeply without being obvious, he walked towards Oppenheimer Park. As he walked, he wondered where the derelicts who could not get accommodation for the night were sleeping. He soon found out.

A large sign at the entrance to the park proclaimed, *Park benches are for sitting, NOT for sleeping on all night. Please be considerate of others and leave them a place to sit.*

Lloyd slowly wandered through the park, thinking he would find a bench, sit down and plan his day. Although there were a lot of benches throughout the park, under each and every bench a man or woman lay sleeping on the ground. Some of them had a tattered blanket wrapped around them. Some slept on a piece of cardboard. Still others slept on the bare ground. Their belongings were either crammed tightly under the bench with the occupant, or a metal shopping cart was resting against the front of the bench, held in place by an arm or a leg wrapped tightly around a cart leg. In this way, if someone tried to seal the cart and its contents, the unfortunate "cart owner" would wake up immediately. Lloyd couldn't begin to imagine how they could get a sound night's sleep.

Emerging from the trees at the far side of the park, Lloyd spotted an empty bench at a bus stop. He jogged quickly over to the bench and sat down. He noticed a pamphlet on the ground beside the bench. Picking it up, he noticed it was about Stanley Park, a place he had heard about, read about but of course, had never seen in real life.

The map inside the brochure showed that it was about a 3.5-kilometre hike; approximately a 43-minute walk. With the amount of time he had to kill before being allowed back into the shelter, Lloyd decided to walk to Stanley Park.

A beautiful, mostly blue sky promised a clear and sunny day. Not wanting to spend any of his meagre funds on a bus ticket, he headed out on foot.

Chapter 3
Stanley Park

Checking his watch, Lloyd was surprised to see that it was only shortly after 10 o'clock! Keeping the Stanley Park brochure open to the map, he got up from the bench and started walking briskly in the direction he needed to go. He knew he wouldn't be back in time for lunch but maybe he could use a bit of his precious money to buy a cheap lunch before he actually arrived at the park. He was pretty sure that food within Stanley Park would be expensive.

Not wasting any time, he jogged for several blocks, slowed down to a walk to catch his breath, and then jogged some more.

In a hurry to reach his destination, Lloyd paid little attention to his surroundings. He did notice, however, that the closer he got to the park, the more affluent the area seemed to be. There were definitely more tourists and business people in this area of the city than the poor wretches that tried to live in East Van!

A block or so away from the entrance to Stanley Park, Lloyd spotted a hot dog/hamburger food wagon. Reading the menu, he gulped. Five dollars for just one small hot dog and that was the least expensive item on the menu!

He had to eat something, however, and so, he stepped up to the window of the food wagon and ordered one regular dog "fully loaded". The white-haired lady who took his order looked intently at Lloyd as he painfully counted out $5.00 in change.

"Anything to drink, dearie?" she asked, handing him his receipt with the order number in the top corner.

Lloyd blushed and shook his head, staring at the ground as he mumbled, "No thanks, ma'am, just the hot dog please."

Several minutes passed. The white-haired lady called Lloyd's number. She handed him a tray containing a delicious-looking foot-long smokie, a large order of fries and a bottle of Coke.

"I only ordered a regular hot dog," Lloyd said. "This must be someone else's order."

The woman winked at him and said, "Nope, this is your lucky day. That order is all yours, sweetie."

Before Lloyd could protest, she said, "Just pay it forward one day when you can. That's all the thanks required, young man. You have a nice day now, hear me?" She waved the person standing in line behind Lloyd up to the window.

Lloyd just stood there with his mouth open until the customer behind him not so gently shoved him out of the way.

Shaking his head, Lloyd carried his lunch over to a wooden table. He sat down and hungrily gobbled down his lunch. One thing he knew for sure, even though he hadn't met too many of them yet, there were certainly still some wonderful people in this world. He would definitely return the favour one day, hopefully soon. He would not forget the kindness of that kind lady!

As soon as he finished eating, he waved thanks to the white-haired lady. Then, belly too full to jog, he walked on slowly towards the entrance to the park.

Awed by the beauty of his surroundings, Lloyd began to wander through the piece of heaven that was Stanley Park.

Along the seawall, hi-rise apartments, white fluffy clouds, and Stanley Park reflected shiny, mirror-clear in the calm water.

Pedestrians shared the seawall promenade with bicycle riders, teenagers on rollerblades and parents pushing babies in strollers or carriages.

Downtown Vancouver falsely appeared to slumber peacefully, protected by the majestic North Shore Mountains. There was no hint of the busy turmoil that was the city's downtown core.

Many different types of boats were moored in marinas across from the park. A large number of these vessels were sailboats.

Lloyd looked further to his left and clearly saw the solid white sculptured sails at Canada Place. He knew it was strictly his imagination, but he could have sworn those sails were fluttering in the breeze against the brilliant sunny sky. The sails at Canada Place were probably one of the most identifiable viewpoints in Vancouver. Lloyd couldn't get enough of them and spent a good half hour just taking in the view.

Once he began to walk again, Lloyd stopped and watched as a beautiful young model balanced precariously on one foot on a low stone wall dividing the pavement and the water. Her photographer called out instructions as he frenetically snapped picture after picture.

Colourful wooden First Nations totem poles towered above passers-by.

Not far from the stately totems, he spotted a large bronze statue, a monument to Harry Winston Jerome, one of the greatest Canadian Track athletes of all time. Lloyd waited for the crowd around the statue to thin and he then stepped up to the statue. The bronze depicted a runner, perfect in physical body shape and running form, befitting of the top athlete that Harry Jerome was. A plaque at the site reads, in part:

HARRY WINSTON JEROME
Born September 30, 1940
Died December 7, 1982
British Columbia's Athlete of the Century. Lloyd noted that in 1971, Harry Jerome received the coveted Order of Canada.

Not very athletic himself, short-legged and underweight for his frame, Lloyd nevertheless greatly admired the athleticism of others. He thought to himself that Mr Jerome was certainly someone to look up to.

He continued walking for perhaps an hour or more, reluctant to leave the serenity of his beautiful surroundings.

Sitting on a bench to rest, Lloyd pulled out the brochure and read it once again. He was certain that he would spend as much time as possible exploring the rain forest that was an integral part of Stanley Park. He fervently hoped that sometime soon he would be in a financial position to tour the park on a bicycle, in a horse and buggy and a two-kilometre stretch on the miniature train that ran for both children and adults alike.

He wanted to eat at the Fish House, a Vancouver favourite with great views of English Bay (when he was working and making good money!)

He wanted to visit the Vancouver Aquarium.

He read that the Lion's Gate Bridge is iconic. Rather than just look at the bridge, you can walk over it, all the while enjoying terrific views of Vancouver. He noted that there is easy access from Prospect Point in Stanley Park. Walk down one side and back on the other. All that was asked of the walkers was that they watch out for cyclists and follow the signs about which side of the path you should be walking on.

Yet another thing for Lloyd's bucket list.

With a heavy sigh, he knew he must not lose sight of his main objective in Vancouver which had become two-fold: finding the 3 missing girls, and secondly, hopefully, finding his parents. This second part of his mission was known only to himself. He had not ever mentioned that ambition to Lacey. No point in building up her hopes. Lloyd knew that it would be nearly impossible to find out what happened to their father and mother. If he did find out, he would tell his sister. If he did not, then he had spared her further anguish.

He rose from the bench and started to walk back in the direction of the hostel, with far less enthusiasm than that with which he had arrived.

Chapter 4
The Whistling Man

By the time Lloyd reached the hostel, he was famished. It had been hours since he had eaten his lunch. He hadn't thought to take his backpack with him, and he certainly hadn't thought to fill the water bottle that he always carried in his pack.

Dumb move, he thought, *I won't make that mistake again. My backpack will go with me wherever I go from now on.*

Checking the time, he realised that he had only about 30 minutes before they quit serving supper. He quickly ran up to the dorm, grabbed his towel and facecloth from his locker and went to wash up.

The cafeteria was not very full this late in the day. Most of the homeless ate their supper as soon as the cafeteria opened. Lloyd guessed that it was so they would have more time to stake out a good sleeping area for the night. He idly wondered if most of the diners were lucky enough to have a bed for the night in the hostel.

He joined the small line-up for food. The food looked pretty good. He had a choice of stew, fried chicken or fish and chips, with the option to go back for a second helping if he wanted. He chose the stew.

Holding his tray in both hands, Lloyd looked around for a place to sit. He spied an empty table near the back of the room and headed for it. No sooner had he seated himself and begun to eat, when a middle-aged man sat down across from him.

"Hello, young man, we meet again, we meet again! Hope you had a wonderful day, a wonderful day?"

Lloyd looked up and over at the man. For a second or two, he couldn't place him but the light soon dawned. It was the gentleman who had found his breakfast in the dumpster; the cheerful, whistling, dumpster-diving man from this morning!

"Yes, sir, thank you. I had a very good day – walked all the way to Stanley Park, walked around a good portion of it, and walked back here. How was your day?"

"Pretty fair, pretty fair," said the whistling man. "Can't complain, can't complain. I wouldn't normally eat my supper this late, eat my supper this late, but I lucked out today and my friend Georgie is holding my place under my park bench for me, holding my place under my park bench for me. My lucky day, my lucky day!"

Lloyd was puzzled by the man's repetition of everything he said. He didn't stutter, but he certainly repeated himself.

The whistling man finished eating and went back for more.

He returned to the table without a plate, but his pockets bulged almost to the point of ripping open. Noticing Lloyd's quizzical expression, Whistling Man explained. "Got to take some food for Georgie, food for Georgie. Holding my sleeping place, my sleeping place. Gotta go now, young man, gotta go now. I got chicken for Georgie in my pocket, in my pocket. Bye now, bye now. See you again, again." Trying to hold his crammed pockets together, he whistled happily as he tried to hurry without dislodging his friend's precious meal. Lloyd could hear his melodic whistle for several minutes after Whistle Man had left.

Chapter 5
The Groper

Although Lloyd was still slightly hungry, he realised that he was more exhausted than anything else. He checked his watch. Only eight o'clock, but in Alberta, it was already nine p.m. Lloyd had got up very early Alberta time, and so despite this early hour, he was off to bed as soon as he signed the Register at the front desk (and checked off the column that confirmed he wanted to stay another night).

Minutes later, he crawled into bed #10, turned out the lamp attached to the wall above the headboard, and was asleep practically before his head hit the pillow.

Five hours later, something woke him. The dorm room was pitch black. Pushing the light-up button on his wristwatch, Lloyd noted it was one a.m. The room was quiet. What had awakened him? Bewildered, he rolled over and sat up, trying to get his bearings. A hand suddenly groped his shoulder, caused him to shudder and call out loudly. "What the heck!"

"Sorry, mate, didn't mean to scare you," said a simpering, disembodied voice. "I'm late getting in and just trying to find my bed in the dark. Just checking to see if this bed was empty." The grip on Lloyd's shoulder tightened. The syrupy voice continued, "How about if I just share this bed with you? Save me stumbling around looking for my empty one? Keep each other warm on a dreary, lonesome night?" He tittered suggestively. He did not release his most unwelcome grip on Lloyd's shoulder.

Punching blindly at the invisible hand that now stroked his shoulder, Lloyd whispered viciously, "Get lost, man. I'm not sharing this bed with you or anyone else, so just get away from me!"

"Okay, okay, okay! Jeez, some guys are touchy!" The voice became fainter as the man finally shuffled away from Lloyd's bed.

Now fully awake, Lloyd nevertheless lay down once again. Unable to sleep, he lay motionless, wanting to be sure his imprudent visitor did not return.

Now, minus the presence of "The Groper", Lloyd realised that the room was not nearly as silent as he had originally thought. A cacophony of snores reverberated from several beds, while harsh coughing echoed from others. Somewhere down the row, a man muttered something unintelligible in his sleep. A minute later, someone cried out harshly, obviously in the throes of a frightening dream. What Lloyd did not hear was anything from the intruder who had woken him up and who now kept him awake and on guard.

Lloyd lay there for what seemed like a very long time before he wriggled down further under the covers, wrapped himself up into a protective (he fervently hoped) cocoon and finally fell back into a wary, fitful sleep.

Morning sounds pushed back the curtain of sleep. Lloyd lay quietly for a time, listening to men coughing, moaning and groaning, passing gas and scratching as they prepared to face the day.

Some beds were already made, their occupants gone. Some beds were in the process of being made, albeit sloppily and hurriedly. The man who occupied Bed #9 next to Lloyd came back into the room and sat down on his bed. Looking over at Lloyd, the man shrugged his shoulders and said softly, "Bathroom line-up. Should have got up half an hour ago." With a weary sigh, the man lay back down on his bed to wait for the line-up to lessen, saying nothing more.

Lloyd allowed himself the luxury of lying in bed for another few minutes to disperse the cobwebs from his tired brain before he crawled wearily out. He threw his jeans and T-shirt on. He made his bed quickly but neatly, grabbed his toilet kit and bath towel from his locker and joined the line-up for the bathroom.

The line-up was almost comical. It was so diverse. Some men, like Lloyd, were dressed as they waited in line for the shower. Others just had their towels wrapped around their waists. One particularly rotund man's towel reached only halfway around him. Holding the ends together, he seemed totally unaware that a goodly portion of his privates was exposed.

One man, in particular, stared at Lloyd until he caught Lloyd's eye. Tall, well built with curly blond hair, glassy blue eyes. Long curly eyelashes that Lloyd's sister, Lacey, would kill to have, this man stood in the middle of the line-up, stark naked! He gave Lloyd a broad grin and winked at him broadly. "Good morning, Bed #10." He spoke loudly and lasciviously. Lloyd could feel his ears burning, the blush creeping slowly up his neck towards the rest of his face. The Groper continued, "If you get lonely tonight, I found my bed. It's #13." With a flit of his rear end aimed at Lloyd, he turned around and moved forward with the line.

Oh, dear Lord, it's The Groper! Lloyd thought. *Now, what do I do?*

The man in line behind Lloyd was the man from Bed #9. "Don't worry about that creep, he's harmless." His neighbouring bedfellow continued, "If he thought you were really interested, he would turn tail and run screaming from the building. It's been proven by tricksters time and time again. They call his bluff and he ALWAYS runs."

"Thanks." Lloyd stammered weakly. "I'll keep that in mind in case he should decide to take another 1:00 am walk around the room."

The shower stalls were on ten-minute timers. It was the only way that the 40 men could complete their ablutions in the morning and still make it to the cafeteria in time for breakfast.

Finally, Lloyd reached the front of the line. As he opened the shower door he looked down at the floor. He threw his facecloth down, stood on it and decided then and there that he had to spend a bit more of his meagre funds on a pair of rubber shower shoes. Although he knew that the entire building was scrubbed clean every day, Heaven only knew how many men had hit that shower stall before Lloyd did. From the sounds of 'horking' (noisy, throat clearing/spitting phlegm), sniffling and snorting that came from the other stalls, Lloyd could barely manage to force himself to step into the shower and clean himself up.

Feeling only partially clean, he returned to the dorm, hung up his towel and then proceeded to the cafeteria for breakfast.

The comfortably small crowd that was in the cafeteria at supper time was no more. This morning's line of both men and women extended out into the hallway as they waited for breakfast. Doing a quick headcount, Lloyd figured there were at least 55 people in the cafeteria. With a mental shrug, Lloyd got in line and waited his turn.

Considering the line-up, it was surprisingly quiet, very unlike the noisy school lunchroom that Lloyd was used to.

Waiting in silence, he swallowed the lump in his throat as he imagined himself getting on the school bus with his sister and other foster siblings. Close to tears, he knew he would have to get hold of Lacey soon. *She must be frantic*, he thought, *how unfair of me to just get up and leave on the spur of the moment as I did.*

He knew that the only way she would forgive him would be if he found the missing girls. Trouble was, he had no clue about where to start looking.

At the end of these dark and negative thoughts, he, at last, reached the front of the breakfast line-up. He chose scrambled eggs, sausages, an English muffin and a container of milk for his breakfast. He also took a carton of apple juice, a bottle of water, an apple, a banana, and a bran muffin to take with him in his backpack in case he couldn't make it back in time for lunch. With the cost of buying something to eat in Vancouver, he was unwilling to take a chance on having to buy his lunch again.

Shouldering his pack, he stopped in the reception area to sign out for the day, and check the column that would ensure he could stay for a second night in the hostel.

Chapter 6
The Counsellor

Just as he turned to leave the building, a voice from somewhere behind him called out. “Lloyd, can you please wait at the reception desk for a minute? I will be right out.” Lloyd sat down to wait.

In a very few minutes, Mona Grace Ford stepped out of the door behind the reception desk, walked over to Lloyd.

“Good morning, Lloyd,” Mrs Ford said. Without waiting for his reply, she continued, “There has just been a cancellation in a counselling session for this time slot. I know you are anxious to get on with your agenda for today, but if you are agreeable, it would be nice if you could fill in the spot.”

Anxious to get outside and begin his searching in earnest, the last thing Lloyd felt like doing was suffering through a counselling session, but when he looked up at Mrs Ford, standing over him with her hands on her ample hips, he didn’t know how to say no. Therefore, trying not to sigh, he stood up. Mona Grace Ford turned and began walking towards a short hallway to the right of the desk. Lloyd followed behind.

Reaching a doorway on the left side of the hallway, Lloyd read the sign on the door. It simply announced:

MONA GRACE FORD
Guidance and Life Skills Counsellor

Mona Grace unlocked the door to her colourful, cosy, cheery office.

Glancing around, Lloyd noticed a small desk in one corner. The wall behind the desk was full of built-in bookcases. Every section was completely filled with books. Against the wall opposite the desk and bookcases were two very comfortable looking leather swivel chairs. The chairs faced each other, separated by a small coffee table. A beautiful area rug housed both the chairs and the coffee table. A tall cupboard stood angled in the corner behind one of the chairs. Cups, glasses, a coffee pot and a tea kettle sat on the bottom two shelves. A small bar fridge nestled underneath the bottom shelf of the cupboard. A ceramic cookie jar with a rainbow design perched in the middle of the top shelf.

To the right of the tall cupboard, a coat rack stood. Mrs Ford gestured towards it. “Hang your backpack up there, Lloyd, and have a chair.” He hung up his backpack and then just stood, waiting.

When Lloyd made no move to sit down, she waved her hand towards the chair closest to the door.

She picked up the receiver of a telephone sitting on the desk, spoke into it. "Hold my calls, please, Mary, I'm with a client."

She hung up the phone and then opened the fridge, took out two bottles of water and set them on the table between the two leather chairs. She then placed the cookie jar, lid removed, in the middle of the coffee table, within easy reach of Lloyd.

Lloyd was still standing but beside the chair. Suddenly, realising what was happening, Mona Grace sat down first. Lloyd seated himself once he was sure Mrs Ford was comfortable.

"Well, thank you, Lloyd! Your manners are excellent. I appreciate it."

"Both my parents were sticklers for good manners, Mrs Ford. Dad always said that good manners would get a person further in this world than rudeness would."

Detecting a note of despair, Mona Grace leaned back in her chair. "Hmm, sounds like your parents were very intelligent, caring people. Tell me a little bit about your family, Lloyd. I'd like to hear about them."

Lloyd stared at Mrs Ford for a full minute, debating what and how much, if anything, to tell this woman, a stranger less than twenty-four hours ago.

The Counsellor simply leaned back in her chair as if she had all the time in the world to wait him out.

Making his decision, Lloyd took a deep breath and prepared to give her a minimalistic version of the life and times of Braden Lloyd Jordan, but only after he learned a few things about the outwardly crusty, inwardly compassionate woman seated opposite him.

Lloyd asked, "What do you want to know?"

"Anything you want to tell me, Lloyd. This is your time."

"Can I ask you something first?"

"Of course. Fire away."

"When I came to the shelter yesterday, you were the receptionist. I didn't know you were a counsellor. Why didn't you tell me that's what you do?"

Mrs Ford smiled wryly, softly answering Lloyd's question with one of her own. "Would you be sitting in that chair now, do you think, if I had said anything?" She stared intently at Lloyd. Lloyd stared back, looking straight into her eyes.

"Anyway," she continued, "The subject didn't really come up, did it? Other than I did tell you that we offered counselling services to our guests. I think I might even have mentioned that it is a requirement if you plan to stay more than a day or two. We wear quite a few hats here, Lloyd. Yesterday I was the receptionist. The day before that I helped clean the building because one of the regular cleaners was ill and couldn't come in. Today, I'm a counsellor. Who knows what I'll be tomorrow? Anyway, it's all God's doing. I'm here to do His bidding. If that means cleaning the toilets, so be it. As you know, this shelter is owned and operated by the Church. We all do what we are required to do in order to help the people who enter these doors. Now, before you ask, let me tell you that I do have a University education. I have a Master's Degree in Psychology. Presently, I am working on my Doctorate. I am writing my thesis on mental health issues and solutions of the homeless. I am not only interested in the problems associated with the homeless, but I am interested in finding out how many are able to eventually overcome their issues and go on to live productive lives. I want to find out just what the difference is between the temporarily homeless and the permanently homeless."

Mona Grace leaned back in her chair once again and started to laugh, a deep belly laugh that seemed to begin at her toes and work itself all the way up to and out of her mouth. Lloyd stared at her, his mouth open. What was so funny? Surely nothing was funny about people being penniless and living on the streets of Vancouver. He sat up straighter in his chair, ready to bolt.

"Nice work, buddy. You succeeded in completely distracting me and turning the focus on me instead of you. The cool thing is, I'm supposed to be the professional and you turned the tables before I even realised what you were doing!"

With one last half-chuckle/half-giggle, she settled back, and said, "Your turn, Lloyd, your turn now."

Chapter 7
The Weight of the World

Mona Grace simply sat back in her chair, prepared to wait for however long it took.

Lloyd leaned forward in his chair, staring at a point beyond Mrs Ford's right ear, clearly struggling. He took numerous deep breaths. His hands clenched and unclenched. *Where do I begin?* he thought. *Will Mrs Ford even believe me if I do tell her everything?* Seconds ticked by. The seconds turned into minutes. Mona Grace simply continued to wait.

Five minutes became ten. Ten minutes became twenty. Still, Mona Grace waited. Still, Lloyd continued to struggle with his thoughts and emotions.

Finally, after a full thirty minutes, and with one extra deep breath, Lloyd began to speak. He fully intended to give the counsellor only a brief overview of his and Lacey's lives from the times their father went to prison and their mother walked away. However, once he began to speak, he couldn't stop. He talked and he talked and he talked.

He didn't notice Mrs Ford getting up and bringing more water to the table. In fact, he didn't even realise that he had drunk an entire bottle as he was telling his story.

He most certainly didn't notice Mrs Ford's expression when he began talking about the missing girls. She turned positively ashen. Her mouth opened and closed, not unlike a fish in a net, gasping for air. She seemed determined to interrupt Lloyd, but at the last second clamped her mouth shut. Instead of speaking, she made a brief note on the pad of paper that rested on the coffee table in front of her.

Finally, after more than a solid hour of talking non-stop, often trying to catch up to his brain with his racing mouth, Lloyd ran out of steam. Ending with his hitch-hiking journey from Alberta to Vancouver with Adam Draper, he leaned back in his chair and shut his eyes, exhausted, relieved.

Mona Grace Ford could not sit still. Being careful not to disturb Lloyd, who appeared to be asleep, she began to quietly pace back and forth, from the corner cupboard to the door. From the door back to the corner cupboard. Over to the bookshelves. Picking up a Swiffer duster from the top of one shelf, dusting already dustless books and shelving. Back and forth, to and fro.

Finally, and against her better judgement, she could wait no more. She sat down heavily in her chair, sighed audibly. Cleared her throat. Whispered,

"Lloyd?" then louder "Lloyd?" and finally in a semi-hysterical voice she yelled, "Lloyd!"

Lloyd leapt to his feet, his head turning wildly in all directions, hollering, "What, what, what! It's okay, Lacey, it's okay!"

Feeling terrible for awakening Lloyd in such a startling manner, Mona Grace spoke more calmly and quietly now. She reached over and held both of Lloyd's hands in hers. "I'm sorry, Lloyd, for waking you up so rudely. Are you okay?" She squeezed his hands even more tightly. Lloyd winced. Seeing his face, she promptly dropped his hands. Her heart thumping crazily in her breast, she just gawked at Lloyd. She could not stop trembling.

Finally recovered enough from his long, long tale, Lloyd became aware that his counsellor did not look well. She was shaking visibly and appeared to be extremely short of breath. Worried, Lloyd reached for Mrs Ford's hands, this time he being the holder, she being the held. "What's wrong, Mrs Ford? Is it something I said?"

"No! Yes! No! I mean, indirectly you did, but unknowingly you didn't. I didn't know either, I mean – Oh, Dear Lord, I don't know what I mean. Help me, Jesus, please."

Mona Grace Ford slid out of her chair onto the floor, leaned her head down on the coffee table and wept. Lloyd looked at her in horror! What could he possibly have said to evoke this sort of reaction from the counsellor? He thought to himself, *I really don't remember everything I said. What do I do?*

He chose, wisely, to simply sit quietly, holding Mrs Ford's hands until she calmed down enough to talk to him.

After a few minutes, calling on all the inner strength she possessed, Mona Grace sat upright and gently pulled her hands from Lloyd's grip.

Excusing herself briefly, she stood up and went into the washroom. He heard the water running and Mrs Ford blowing her nose lustily. Soon the door opened and she walked over and sat in her chair once again. Although still pale with red and swollen eyes, she appeared to be in control.

Looking directly into Lloyd's eyes, she asked him, "How old was Charley?"

"Fourteen when me 'n Lacey met her."

"Was Charley her full name? I mean, did she have a middle name or a surname? Well, she must have had a surname!"

Trying to figure out just what was going through Mrs Ford's head, Lloyd replied, "Her name was really Charlotte, but she went by Charley." He stopped, still hoping to discern some clue as to what was going on here.

"What was her middle name?"

"If she had one I either never heard it or she didn't say. I never asked, to be honest."

"One more thing. Please, Lloyd, tell me, what was her surname?"

Lloyd got as far as 'F o – –' before realisation struck. Mrs Ford was nodding maniacally, unable to speak but waiting for Lloyd to put a voice to the discovery.

Awed, Lloyd practically whispered, "Her name was, IS, Charlotte, or Charley, Ford."

“Please, Lloyd, what did she look like? What was she like?” Mrs Ford waited, holding her breath, fearfully waiting for Lloyd to confirm her suspicion.

Wrinkling his brow in deep thought, Lloyd said, “Let me see, she was fourteen when she left our terrible foster home. At that time, she had shoulder-length silky blond hair; long, way down past her shoulder blades, almost to her waist, actually. She had dyed the bottom third or so of her hair a really bright pink colour. Sounds terrible but on her, it looked pretty. She wore very heavy makeup, but I’m pretty sure that was just to annoy our foster mother. Without her makeup on she was beautiful. She was already tall, thin. She was very protective of the younger foster kids and did not hesitate to order anyone to help her if she needed it.”

Lloyd looked directly at the counsellor. “I really like Charley, Mrs Ford and I don’t know how but I am not giving up on finding her and the other girls. I never will.”

Staring woodenly at Lloyd, his counsellor said nothing. Finally, Lloyd did.

“Is Charley your daughter, Mrs Ford? Is that why you are so upset? She’s your daughter and she’s missing? Don’t worry, I won’t give up on her, EVER!”

Mona Grace knew that if she was ever to help Lloyd, she must now tread very carefully. After pouring his guts out to her, baring his soul, wrenching his heart wide open for her, she must tell him the truth. She feared that once he heard her story, he would want nothing to do with her. She couldn’t have that happen. This young man was determined to find out what happened to the three missing girls. One of these girls was Charley! Yes, she must tread very cautiously. She felt a renewal of hope, an emotion that she would have sworn she had lost when Charley went into foster care. Lloyd deserved to know the entire story.

Lloyd, on the other hand, thought to himself that it was one thing to be searching for the girls himself, but now he had yet another person depending on him. Suddenly Lloyd felt the weight of the entire world now landing squarely and heavily on his young shoulders. Nevertheless, he sat up, prepared to listen to Mrs Ford’s story. His stomach growled loudly. Mrs Ford got up, refilled the cookie jar, handed it to Lloyd. She returned to her chair.

Chapter 8
Mona Grace and Domingo

"Yes, Lloyd, you are correct. Charlotte is my daughter."

Seeing that Lloyd was about to speak, Mona Grace held up both her hands to stop him. "Please," she implored, "let me tell you my whole story before you interrupt me; and especially before you judge me. And please don't interrupt me until I'm done. If I don't tell it all at once I probably won't tell it at all."

Lloyd simply nodded. He sat on his hands, leaned back in his chair, prepared to listen without interruptions.

Taking a large gulp of water, Mona Grace also leaned back in her chair. She stared at Lloyd as she spoke, but didn't appear to see him; she was travelling back, back, into her past. Shakily at first, but growing more resolute with each sentence, she began…

"I was raised here, in East Vancouver. My father was the head janitor at a hostel, actually. He met and married my mother when he was eighteen and she was only seventeen. A school drop-out, he nonetheless was hardworking, capable of a lot of things. He had already been working at the hostel as a janitor trainee for a couple of years. He worked there until the day he died of a heart attack. My mother was convinced that he died of a broken heart. She couldn't fathom that someone could die of a heart attack so young. My father was only forty years old."

Mrs Ford looked at Lloyd briefly before continuing. "They were poor as the proverbial church mice but they adored one another. Mother did what she could to help with the family finances by looking after neighbourhood children. Incomes were, and still are, very low in this part of the city, so although she looked after up to six children in one day, she hardly made any money. Sometimes she got paid with homemade baking or produce from someone's garden in exchange for child care. While the extra food was very welcome, Mother did not even make enough money to feed and clothe all the kids. Now, I know you are probably thinking that if they were so poor, and she didn't make any money babysitting, why did she take in more kids when she had a large number of children of her own. My Mama had a soft spot for children and single parents. She simply could not turn her back on a destitute parent who showed up at her door with a little one in tow.

"Nine months practically to the day after my parents were married, my eldest brother Stevie was born. Everyone had assumed that Mama was pregnant before they got married. Hah! Stevie's birth finally put an end to that piece of gossip! Every year for the next six years, another new baby was born. I'm the seventh and last child in the family.

"Seven kids and only one steady but minimum wage job did not make for a comfortable or easy life, that's for sure, but neither of my parents complained. I never once heard them say that they wished things were different, or if they had a smaller family they might have an easier time. They put their faith in the Lord and believed unequivocally that He would look after them and their large family. They truly believed that the Good Lord had blessed them with seven children.

"The small, ancient two bedrooms, one-bathroom bungalow they rented from a slum landlord grew more and more crowded. My folks simply moved the furniture around and added another air mattress to the floor if need be. Usually at least two of my siblings, sometimes three, shared an air mattress. My folks had one bedroom. The second one was used as a playroom/nap time/storage area for the day home children my mother babysat.

"My older brothers and sisters were left to reluctantly look after me as best they could because my mother had her hands more than full. Suffice it to say that I didn't get a lot of attention at any one time. What I did get was pretty meagre. More often I would get, 'Don't bother us, Mona Grace. Play by yourself!'

"When I was old enough to understand, my father told me that when my brother Stevie turned eleven, he began to spend more and more time away from home. He also began bringing home more and more money. Stevie's story was that he was working after school and on weekends at a local supermarket. To give proof to his story, he would bring home food at least once a week.

"I would hear my parents talking late into the night. They sounded worried, but I couldn't make out exactly what they were saying, or who they were talking about. Mind you, I was only about five years old at the time, so I certainly sensed when things weren't right, but of course, I really didn't fully comprehend their worries.

"One night, it was very late, a knock sounded at our door. Everyone was asleep and at first, no one heard the knock. It got progressively louder until everyone was awake.

"My father yelled from their bedroom at the back of the house, 'Do NOT open that door, kids! I'll be right there.' Seconds later he emerged from the back, still pulling his T-shirt on over his head. Motioning every one of us kids to stay still and be quiet, he opened the door.

"Two policemen stood there. The youngest looked extremely uncomfortable. I remember thinking that he was just a kid like us. I remember thinking that the young policeman seemed very sad.

"The older policeman asked my father if he was related to Stevie. My father said yes, he was his father.

"The younger officer sounded like he was choking. He said, 'I am so sorry sir, but we need you to come with us.'

"I remember my father crumpling to the floor, then calmly (it seemed to me, but in retrospect, I imagine it was the shock, he wasn't calm at all) looking up at the young constable. He simply queried, 'Is it, my son?'

"The young policeman simply spoke in a tortured voice, 'We're pretty sure but we need you to identify him.'

"I was too young to remember the rest of the night. I do remember my mother sobbing. My older siblings were crying. I remember my father trying to spare my mother the agony of identifying Stevie's body, insisting she stay with us kids. That was not about to, nor did that happen. Both my parents left with the officers. All of us kids just sat on our air mattresses, waiting for our parents to bring our brother home."

Mona Grace took a long drink of water, sighed, stretched her neck from side to side, then continued.

"I really don't remember what our parents told us when they came home without Stevie that night.

"The very day that I turned thirteen years old, they sat me down and told me that now that I was a teenager, I was old enough to know what had happened to Stevie. They were trying to put the fear of the Lord into me, I think. Although I was only thirteen, I was already strong-willed and somewhat rebellious. They told me in no uncertain terms, omitting no gory details, that the night Stevie had died he had lied to our parents. He told them he had to work at the supermarket. In actual fact, Stevie didn't even have a job there, never had. He had been running drugs for a neighbourhood gang known as 'The East Van Devils'. He was just a little kid with an angelic face. He was so flattered that these older boys paid attention to him and actually paid him money to deliver packages for them. I honestly don't think Stevie knew what he was delivering; at least I have always chosen to believe that he didn't.

"He was at an age where he hero-worshipped the wrong people. He thought the Devils were so cool. He thought they genuinely liked him. Stevie couldn't wait until he was old enough to be initiated into the East Van Devils.

"Anyway, I digress." Another drink of water, another sigh. Mona Grace once again began to speak.

"My father and mother sat me down at the kitchen table to tell me about that night. I remember how sad they looked as they talked to me.

"The night Stevie died, as I already told you, had started with a lie. Apparently, there was a rival gang known as 'The Dopers' that had been trying to infiltrate the Devils' territory for quite some time. This particular night there was a rumble scheduled between the two gangs. The members of both gangs had all agreed to meet at a certain place, at a certain time.

"My brother had implored the leader of the Devils to let him come to the rumble. If they wouldn't let him fight, he pleaded that could he at least watch from a safe place. He was told that he could NOT be anywhere near that location that night, that there would be no safe place for him to watch. (This was brought out later, in a trial where the leader of the Devils was on trial for the murder of the leader of 'The Dopers'. Incidentally, the Devils' leader got off on a technicality!)

"As you have probably already gathered, Stevie did not listen to the leader. At the appointed place and time, he stood a block away, on a corner that looked right down the street to where the members were congregating. His field of vision was unobscured but he figured he was far enough away that he would be safe while he watched the battle. Remember, my brother was only eleven years old. Young, impressionable, optimistic. Foolish as most eleven years old kids, head-strong, impulsive.

"Stevie didn't have a chance to see anything. As the two rival gangs gathered across from each other, one of the members of 'The Dopers' couldn't wait. He prematurely fired his handgun towards the rival gang. The bullet ricocheted off a brick wall and struck my brother right between his eyes."

Mrs Ford pressed her hands to her forehead, rubbed as if trying to erase the memory. "Sorry," she murmured, "I know it's a long time ago, but telling you is making it fresh again."

Once again Mona Grace took a large drink of water before resuming where she had left off.

"My parents were much more vigilant after Stevie died. I was too little to either have a job or go out unsupervised.

"I guess that let me eventually slip through the cracks of parental supervision because when I was fourteen, I met a guy and I fell head-over-heels. He was the love of my life. I would have done anything for this man.

"His name was Domingo Sanchez. I thought he was the proverbial prince from every fairy tale, tall, dark and very handsome. He was ten years older than me. I didn't care about the age difference. To me he was perfect.

"Domingo told me that he was a salesman for a pharmaceutical company and that the swanky car he was driving was a company vehicle. He dressed rich, right down to the thick gold chain with a large diamond in the centre of the crucifix attached to the chain. I was too awestruck to question anything he told me; too naïve to see beyond the glitter or his silver tongue.

"He was also a sub-leader of the East Van Devils, although I didn't find that little gem out until later.

"He treated me well. He paid endless hours of attention to me, something I never got at home, something that I craved. He bought me beautiful clothes, expensive gifts. He told me he loved me, that as soon as I turned sixteen, he was going to ask my father if he could marry me.

"He was so smooth. I never once thought to question him about why he had so much time to spend with me or to ask him when did he work. He sure didn't leave me during the day to go work somewhere. The old adage 'love is blind'? Well, I say it was deaf, dumb and blind!

"Looking back, we were together nearly every day. He didn't go to work, so often I didn't go to school! We didn't have a telephone so the teachers couldn't call my folks to let them know I was absent from classes. Even though I played hooky a lot of the time, I was able to keep up with my assignments. Although my marks weren't great, I was passing every subject. I made sure that I was at school on days when there were exams to be written. I had friends who would tell me what my homework assignments were, so I could complete the homework.

"Not wanting to face questioning from my parents, I kept the clothes and gifts from Domingo in my locker at school. I guess deep down, I knew something was not right, but I was too 'in love' to care.

"Things progressed smoothly with Domingo for a couple of months, until – you guessed it!

"Returning from the medical clinic in the neighbourhood, I excitedly told Domingo that I was pregnant. He just stared at me, horrified. Finally, he spoke. 'You'll have to abort it,' he said to me. 'I ain't ready to be no daddy to no little rug rat. Besides, I'm sub-leader of the Devils. I'm next in line to be the leader, the big Poo-Ba! The leader can't have no ties, especially an underage girlfriend and an illegitimate kid. Don't worry, I'll talk to someone, who knows someone, who will get rid of the problem.'

"'But, Domingo!' I wailed, 'This just means we can get married sooner. I know my parents will give their consent. What's wrong with that? It only means we can be together sooner!'

"He just stared at me. I'll never forget the expression on his face. He looked disgusted. He looked at me as if I was dirt! He opened the car door, and said calmly, 'Get out, Mona Grace. When you get rid of the problem, maybe I'll see you again. In fact, I'll come to see you tomorrow with the information and the cash you'll need to get rid of it.'

"I got out of that fancy car and practically before I had the door shut, Domingo roared off down the road. He had dropped me off several blocks from home. Dropped me like a piece of used chewing gum, garbage, on the side of the road. Left me a weeping mess to walk home and face my parents."

Mona Grace was so far into her past that Lloyd was pretty sure that he couldn't interrupt her even if he wanted to, which he did not.

Still more water, more Kleenex. After pacing for several minutes, she continued once again.

"I can tell you that one of the hardest things I have ever endured in my entire life was walking into that little crowded bungalow and waiting for my father to get home from work. I had decided to wait until supper was over and the rest of the kids were either in bed or out somewhere before I talked to my folks. At suppertime, I couldn't eat a single bite. My mother asked if I was feeling sick! I certainly was, but not in the way she was thinking.

"Finally, the chaos of ordinary living in our house settled. I asked my parents if they would please stay sitting at the table; that I had something to tell them. They looked quickly at each other. My Mama reached for my father's hand, and then for mine. No words would come out. My dad looked at me and said quietly, 'Mona Grace, there is nothing you can tell us that would make us love you any less. Just spit it out. Whatever it is, we will deal with it together.'

"With much weeping, wailing and histrionics, and in between uncontrollable sobs, I finally got my story out. I told them about Domingo's reaction. I assured my parents that there was no way that I was going to abort this baby. I wanted to keep it, even though I didn't know how I was going to support myself and a child. I guess I was hoping that my mother would offer to look after it while I finished school.

"My father squeezed my hand, told me that he was relieved that I wasn't going to have an abortion. Said he believed abortion was a sin. My mother said that as long as I continued to go to school and passed every subject, that they would look after the baby. But before school, after school, and on non-school days, that baby was my responsibility. Their child sitting ended right after school. If I didn't live up to my end of that particular bargain, I would have to leave and take the baby with me. They did add, though, that if I found a part-time job, they would look after their grandchild, as long as I didn't work so many days that I had no time to pay attention to the baby.

"I didn't think that they would enforce their stipulations, but I wasn't worried about it. I was just so happy that I still had a home and understanding parents. I was luckier than a lot of classmates, I knew. There was one girl in my class at school who, when she told her parents she was pregnant, got kicked out of the house. Her parents didn't ever want to see her again! She got so depressed that she committed suicide before her baby was even born.

"Looking back," Mona Grace said pensively, "I regret so much the anguish I caused my mother and father." She paused briefly, lost in her own thoughts.

"Anyway, I quit skipping school. I put my nose to the grindstone so I could catch up and improve my average. My plan was to finish high school and somehow go on to college and become a Social Worker."

Here, Mona Grace gave a weary, self-deprecating chuckle.

"I did all of that eventually, but it wasn't as simple or as black-and-white as I envisioned at fourteen years old! By the time I finished college, I was thirty years old, but with the help of Our Lord and my blessed parents, I did it! I now have a job at the hostel that I truly love.

"I can see, young Lloyd, the wheels turning in your brain, wondering about me and Charlotte. All in good time, my man, all in good time. I just need to get Domingo out of my story so I can continue.

"I thought Domingo would show up early the next day. I was sure that when he arrived I would be able to convince him that this pregnancy was meant to be, that it just meant that we could be together sooner. I still hadn't figured out that Domingo was all about, and ONLY about, Domingo.

"True to his word, but not until late the next evening, Domingo showed up at our door. My father had been waiting even more anxiously than I, and when the knock finally came, Dad made a move to answer the door. With difficulty, I managed to hold him off. I said I wanted to talk to Domingo first and then Dad could have his say if need be.

"I opened the door and slipped out, shutting it firmly behind me. I sat on the top step, and, looking right into Domingo's eyes, I patted the empty space beside me."

At this point, Lloyd noticed that Mona Grace's face was a brilliant red. The heat from her blush was almost palpable. Lloyd felt worried, sorry for the counsellor. It was obviously, even after all these years, a very painful recollection for her. Lloyd said nothing to Mona Grace. He just sat motionless, quiet, waiting for her to resume.

She continued.

"Domingo wouldn't sit down. He wouldn't even look at me after I tried to get him to sit beside me. I must say, I embarrassed myself. I literally fell down on my knees, threw my arms around his legs, begging him not to leave me and the baby. He just shoved me aside, threw an envelope on top of me and turned to walk away. I crawled after him. He kicked me away and left me lying on the sidewalk in front of the house like a broken, abandoned toy.

"My father had heard the commotion and opened the door. When he saw me lying there, and Domingo swaggering away, he ordered Domingo to stop. An insolent sneer on his face, Domingo turned around and stared. My father told him that he was a poor excuse for a man, that he should pick up his envelope and go away.

"That handsome man that I was so sure I was in love with, and who I was so sure loved me back, glared at me before he looked at my Dad.

"He spoke towards my father but he looked right at me when he said, 'Just consider it payment for services rendered.' With a truly terrible laugh, he walked away, leaving the envelope behind.

"My father lifted me up as if I were only the weight of a feather, carried me into the house. He put me on the sofa and sat next to me. My mother sat on the other side. They both hung on to me for dear life until I could calm down.

"Finally, after a long time, I was exhausted, all cried out.

"My father handed me the envelope that Domingo had flung at me. Inside was a name, phone number and an address. Knowing this to be the information regarding the abortionist, I crumpled the paper up and threw it on the floor. Dad picked it up and stuck it in his pocket. Also in the envelope was a bundle of bills totalling $10,000.00! I had never seen so much money in my life. I offered it to my parents in exchange for babysitting while I continued with my schooling. My father looked at my mother, who then spoke. 'That money will see you through school and college, Mona Grace. We will put it in the bank and you can withdraw what you need for school, as you need it.

"We haven't the money to send you to college. What we can do for you though, is have you live at home while you go to school. That way we can watch the baby for you. These two things will save you a lot of money and hassle."

"I started to protest," Mona Grace told Lloyd. "But my mother shushed me, saying, 'You know that we would do the same for all of our children, not just you. Do not waste this chance to improve your life, daughter. Stay here with your little one. Let us help you out in the only way we can."

Mona Grace looked blankly at Lloyd, but he knew she wasn't seeing him.

As if reading Lloyd's mind, she quietly said, "I never saw Domingo again. I don't know what my father did with the abortionist's name, address and phone number. I never asked. My father never said. I just know that when I needed money for college, it was there. My parents never talked about that night after Domingo walked away. All I know for sure is that I was determined to right my wrongs and make my parents proud."

Glancing at the clock, the counsellor excused herself for a moment. She picked up the phone and spoke into it. "Can you please bring two dinner trays to my office? I'm in a counselling session and we won't be able to get to the cafeteria before they quit serving. Thank you so much."

"Let's take a break, Lloyd," Mona said. "Our dinner will be here in just a few minutes. We'll eat and then I'll tell you what happened with me and Charlotte. I know you are anxious to hear, but I really need to take a bit of a time-out here."

"Not a problem, it sounds good to me!" Lloyd said. "I could sure eat anything. Thanks for thinking about dinner!"

Almost as an afterthought, but definitely not intended to be, Lloyd added, "I really appreciate hearing your story, Mrs Ford. I have a feeling that it will help me quite a bit. It will make me push even harder to find out what happened to the girls. Oh, man! This dinner looks really good, let's eat!"

Mona Grace laughed at the sight of the teenager digging into his dinner with such enthusiasm. She picked up her fork and joined in, her appetite nearly matching his after the long story she had unleashed from her innermost self.

Chapter 9
Mona Grace and Charlotte

When they finished eating, Mona Grace picked up the tray and put it on the floor in the hallway.

She closed the door and then, taking her seat once more, she sat back, and rhetorically asked, "Now, where was I? Oh yes, I never saw Dominic… I mean, Domingo, again." With a self-deprecating grin, she shook her head. "See?" she said sheepishly. "Not only did I never see him again, I nearly forgot his name! I must tell you, Lloyd, that I rarely either thought of, or think of, that self-absorbed, cowardly person.

"I continued going to school while I was pregnant. I wasn't the only young teenager in that same leaky boat. The teachers were very understanding and did what they could to make sure that their 'in-trouble' students got any extra help they needed.

"I surprised myself, I think, even more than I surprised my teachers and my parents. I knuckled down, studied hard. My marks showed it. I was so determined to make my parents proud that I surged ahead of the rest of the students in my class. I found that I loved school and I especially loved the feeling of accomplishment I got when I got an Honours mark on a completed assignment. Who'd'a thunk it, huh?

"The day that Charley was born started out like any other day. I got up, got dressed, ate a light breakfast, kissed my mother goodbye, and went to school. That's where the 'like any other day' came to an abrupt end! I had just finished writing a quiz in my math class. I was feeling a bit out of sorts, with quite a sharp ache in my lower back, but I just ignored it. I'd had this pain off and on for a couple of days already and, although it hadn't gone away, the pain in my back wasn't any worse, so I tried to ignore it.

"As I stood up to hand in my paper, something warm and definitely wet ran down my leg. I was, in turn, horrified, embarrassed, perplexed and scared to death! I was still only fourteen years old and a very naïve fourteen at that. Neither my mother, our family doctor, nor any other living soul had bothered to explain pregnancy, labour or delivery to me. I was totally ignorant of what lay ahead of me. I thought maybe my baby was dying or, even worse, that maybe I was dying and then who would raise my child?

"Terrified, I promptly sat back down, praying that none of the other students had noticed the puddle under my desk. I waited for the bell to ring. As the other students gathered up their belongings and dropped their quiz papers off at the teacher's desk, I sat with my head down, totally mortified.

"Luck was certainly with me because no one noticed me. Just as my math teacher was heading out the door, she stopped and looked right at me. 'Oh, Mona Grace, I almost didn't see you,' she said. 'Why are you still sitting there? Don't you have another class to go to?'

"By this time, tears were running down my cheeks. I was unable to speak. I could only shake my head. As the teacher stopped speaking, she began to walk over to my desk. I stood up and pointed at the floor beneath me, still unable to utter a single word. 'Aah!' Cluing in, she told me to hang on while she called the school nurse to come to the math classroom.

"While we waited for the nurse, she asked me if I had any pain or discomfort at all. I pointed to the puddle beneath my feet, pointed to my lower back.

"Taking a deep breath, I managed to croak out my most urgent questions – was I dying, was my baby dying, or worst yet, were we both dying?

"I have to give my math teacher her due; she didn't burst out laughing at my ignorance. Instead, she took my hand and explained that it sounded and looked like my labour had begun.

"The nurse arrived, took one look at the situation and locked the door to prevent any students from walking in on us. Upon being informed by the math teacher that my water had broken, the nurse asked me if I could manage to walk with her to her office. 'Don't worry,' she said, 'I've brought a blanket. We'll wrap it around you and no one will notice that your clothing is wet.'

"My teeth were now chattering, more from fear than anything else, but I managed to stammer out that I could walk to the nurse's office with her.

"My math teacher knew my mother and knew she would have a problem finding someone to care for her day home charges. She said her classes were finished for the day and she would drive me to the hospital and then she would go and stay with the children so my mother could be with me. She even telephoned our family doctor and told him that I was in labour and on my way!

"God Bless that woman. To this day I am so grateful that it was her class that everything began in. She was an angel in disguise! In fact, I was so grateful that I named my baby girl Charlotte, after that math teacher, Mrs Charlotte Whitby.

"At the hospital reception, I didn't know what I was supposed to do, so I just took a seat in the back of the waiting area to wait for my mother.

"In what seemed like hours, but was probably more like only a half-hour, my mama came rushing in, looking frantic and looking for me. I stood up and waved at her. She scurried over and practically fell into the chair beside me. I asked her how she made it to the hospital so quickly. She said that Mrs Whitby had piled all six of the children that she was looking after that day into the back seat of her car, drove my mother to the hospital, and then drove all the children back to our house. She then looked after them for the entire day and most of the night until my folks were able to get home. See what I mean by an angel?

"Anyway, once my mother arrived, she registered me at the hospital reception desk. We then were taken up to the Maternity Ward. By this time, I was in strong labour, so strong that I could hardly walk in a straight line, so they put me in a wheelchair.

"To be honest with you, the rest of that day and most of that night is pretty much a pain-filled blur! I remember the doctor coming in from time to time, patting me on the leg, saying it wasn't time yet, disappearing, leaving me in a field of agonising pain.

"My mother stayed with me throughout. My father came in once, took one look at me, turned pale as a sheet on a summertime clothesline and almost ran out to wait elsewhere. Heh, heh, even after going through labour with my mama seven times, he still couldn't handle it. Guess that's why the Good Lord made us so it's the women that do the birthing!

"Anyhow, finally, way into the middle of the night – well, I guess it was more like early morning, they took me into the operating room to do a Caesarian section. The doctor told my parents that my young, fourteen-year-old body, couldn't stand the strain of labour anymore and that the C-section was the safest way to keep both me and my baby alive.

"The next thing I knew, I woke up in my room with my parents both beside me, smiling like that Cheshire cat in Alice in Wonderland. A nurse popped her head in the door, saw I was awake, disappeared briefly and then came into the room carrying a tiny bundle wrapped in a pale pink blanket. She placed that teeny tiny little thing on my chest, well away from the incision on my stomach, unwrapped the blanket and showed me the most beautiful blond, blue-eyed miracle that was my daughter."

At this point in her story, Mona Grace stopped to wipe her eyes. Looking over at Lloyd, she smiled shyly and whispered, "Now that is a true miracle, the miracle of birth.

"I felt a tug at what could only have been my heartstrings and tears of happiness sprung from my eyes, skipped down my cheeks. I looked down upon that delicate little branch of my family's tree and softly said, 'Hello, baby Charlotte. I'm going to take such good care of you!' I then kissed the downy peach fuzz that was the hair on the top of her head, handed her to my father, and I went to sleep, dreaming about the miracle that was born from my body, and about the fun that she and I would have as she grew to adulthood."

Mona Grace looked at Lloyd, raised her eyebrows as if to question whether or not she should continue. Mute, Lloyd nodded his head, made himself more comfortable in his chair, then looked at the counsellor, urging her by his expectant posture to continue her fascinating life story.

"Should have been a 'happily ever after' story the way I have told it so far, hey Lloyd? Well, it was, for the first three years of Charley's little life. It wasn't easy, going to school, working a part-time job as a waitress at a nearby hamburger joint, and still finding the time and energy to bathe my daughter, play with her and read her a bedtime story before I tucked her in.

"My mother loved Charley too; said she was the best-behaved child in the family, and certainly better than any of the children she babysat! Of course, my mama was kind of prejudiced, being as Charley was her first grandchild and everything!"

Here, Lloyd observed a very noticeable change in Mona Grace's demeanour. Her breathing became shallow. Her eyes watered, threatening to overflow and course down her cheeks, but she determinedly batted them away, took a gigantic deep breath, and continued.

"One evening, after my shift at the burger joint and after a particularly long and trying day at college, I walked home, so tired that I stumbled almost every other step. As exhausted as I was, I was looking forward to spending a bit of quality time with my three-year-old baby girl, even if only to lay down beside her for a brief cuddle, and to kiss her goodnight as she slept.

"Turning in to our front yard, I knew something was wrong. Every light in the house was blazing. My parents never wasted electricity, especially late in the evening – they just didn't have the money for frivolous waste.

"Just as I reached the door, an ambulance pulled up in front of our house, sirens blaring, lights flashing. Two attendants leapt from the cab of the truck and raced to the front door. A third attendant struggled to get a stretcher from the back of the ambulance. The first two, in their hurry, brushed me to the side, nearly toppling me off the front step. Following on their heels, I also raced into the house.

"My father lay sprawled on the floor of the living room, unconscious, his clenched fist stiff on his chest, on top of his heart. My mother lay prostrate beside him, smoothing his hair and sobbing brokenly as she whispered in his ear.

"I knelt down beside my mother, put my arms around her, pulled her gently out of the way of the EMTs, who needed to save my father. 'What happened?' I asked her. Her explanation was unintelligible, the words caught in between each of the harsh, gut-wrenching sobs spewing out of her mouth. 'He came home from work late,' my mother finally explained. 'He said he felt unwell, that he might have eaten something bad for lunch. It wasn't his stomach though. I knew it wasn't because he suddenly clenched his chest in the vicinity of his heart and he simply keeled over. Thank the Good Lord he was on call at the hostel. He had his pager on him and he was able to press the button as he collapsed. Sally from the hostel called 9-1-1. You know the rest.'

"I tried to block my mother's view of the EMTs and my father. They were desperately performing CPR. I could hear ribs cracking. Finally, one fellow whispered to the other, but I heard him. He whispered, 'He's gone.'"

Lost in her memory, Mona Grace sat quietly for several minutes before she looked at Lloyd and said calmly, "Forty years old and dead of a heart attack. My mother was never the same after that. She could barely navigate around that small house and look after herself. Oh, she tried! For a few months after my father died, she kept looking after the children but the environment was far from healthy for any of them. Mama would sit in my father's chair and let the children run wild throughout the tiny place. Sometimes she would feed them, that is if a little one would come up to her and tell her that they were all hungry. Sometimes she would tell the child to wait a bit and she would feed them, but she would forget.

After a couple of months, I visited the parents of the children and explained to them that my mother was no longer capable of babysitting and they would have to find someone else.

"I don't know what those parents did but I had no one to care for Charley. It wasn't safe to leave her with my broken, torn mother. My brothers and sisters lived too far away to help me. No one in our neighbourhood could help me out. I had to finish college or I would have wasted all that money that Domingo had thrown at me.

"I was desperate, Lloyd," Mona Grace said brokenly, "I got hold of Child Services, met with them in person and asked them flat-out – if I turned Charley over to them, would they find her a decent, loving home until I could graduate and look after her myself? They assured me that they would do that.

"So, I signed the papers. I went home and packed all of Charley's things – clothes, toys and books. I kissed my baby goodbye and watched them pick her up and carry her to the car. All the while she was holding out her little arms to me and screaming 'MaMa!!!' at the top of her little voice.

"I was so sure that I would get my baby back in a short time. I had two more years of college left in order to get my degree in social work. Even allowing time to find a job in my field after I graduated, I figured I could easily get Charley back before she started Grade one.

"But," Mona Grace said, "life has a funny way of kicking you in the butt sometimes, you know? I kept going to college and working part-time at the burger joint, as well as making sure my mother ate supper, showered and went to bed at a reasonable hour. I generally tried to manage everything. Hah!

"I came home late one evening and found my mother eating cereal out of one of my shoes! She was sitting on the floor, eating from and talking to a shoe! I couldn't manage her anymore. I called our family doctor and she found a placement for my mother in a long-term facility that catered to patients with severe dementia. In only a matter of weeks after she moved in, she didn't even know who I was when I went to visit her. The little bit of money that I had managed to save went to buy clothes for my mother, as well as small treats when I went to visit her in the long-term care facility. She was there for six months and then she died. The death certificate said she died from pneumonia, but I think she died from a broken heart, just like my father."

Momentarily overcome, Mona Grace swallowed hard before continuing.

"Time passed. At Christmas time, Easter time and Charley's birthday, I would drop off gifts for my little girl with Child Services, together with a note asking them to please ensure that Charley got my gifts. I think that, deep down, I knew they wouldn't reach her, but I tried. Every single year I dropped off gifts and a note, but never did I get a reply.

"I graduated from college, got my present job at the hostel. By this time, I was firmly convinced that it was too late for me to get Charley back – too much time, too much water under the bridge. I convinced myself that she was in a loving home, with a family who could give her everything that I could not. I was convinced that even if I found her, she would hate me for giving her up. With everything I had been through, I knew I couldn't handle the rejection. I chose to believe that leaving her with that (mythical) loving family was the kindest thing to do for Charley, and so that is what I chose to do.

"I was actually at peace with my decision until the day I turned on the suppertime news and learned about three missing foster children. When the picture of Charley came on the screen, my heart bent like a willow in the wind, then snapped back and slapped me in the face. She looked just the same as the last time I saw her when she was three years old, just older! Who had I tried to fool all these years? I now had a teenaged daughter that no one could find, a daughter that had run away from an evil foster home. There was no mythical, magical, loving home that Charley had been placed in.

"Dear God, Lloyd, she deserved to be loved, happy and well cared for! I was so certain I made the right decision! Now, look what's happened. You have to track her down, Lloyd, you simply have to! God has sent you to help me, despite my failings as a mother. I have to believe that."

Totally spent, Mona Grace leaned against the back of her chair and closed her eyes.

Lloyd simply sat perched on the edge of his chair. Not only was he deeply moved by Mona Grace's story, but he had a brand-new perspective about the actions his own mother had taken so long ago. That recollection of his and Lacey's lives clearly needed revisiting!

"Mrs Ford," Lloyd spoke quietly, not certain if Mona Grace was awake. "Mrs Ford, are you awake?"

"Yes," she replied, not opening her eyes, "I'm awake."

"I'm going to find her, Mrs Ford. I'm going to find out what happened to Charley, no matter how long it takes me. Charley and I are the same age and…"

Here, Lloyd let out a gasp, staring over at the counsellor, aghast that he had inadvertently let slip that he was younger than he had told her he was.

Mona Grace smiled at Lloyd, her eyes now wide open. "I was pretty sure you weren't as old as you said you were, Lloyd. But don't worry because, knowing you and my baby girl are the same age, I just know it will be easier for you to find her. I just know it."

"I need a bit of air," Lloyd said. He looked at his watch. Quarter to seven! It would have to be a short bit of air if he was to make it to supper before the cafeteria closed.

Lloyd stood up. "I think my 'counselling session' time is long over for today, Mrs Ford. I want to thank you for a very eventful day though. I learned so much today, including the fact that perhaps I have been hating my own mother for something that she felt she simply had no choice in, that abandoning my sister and me was just something that she had to do. Thank you for that. I hope you and I can talk again soon."

With a brief wave, Lloyd turned and left the office, heading for the front door and some fresh air to clear his head.

Chapter 10
The Poor and the Homeless

Lloyd stood on the top step outside the front door of the shelter, ostensibly surveying the area but seeing nothing. His mind was in a turmoil; in fact, it almost felt like his brain was bubbling in its efforts to absorb all of Mona Grace's story.

After standing there for several minutes, Lloyd slowly descended the stairs and began walking towards Oppenheimer Park, mindful that it was getting dark, mindful that the cafeteria would be closing soon. He reached the park entrance, was surprised to find a vacant bench. Although it was only early evening, most of the derelicts would most likely have already found their sleeping spots and would be bedded down for the night. Lloyd felt fortunate to find the vacant seat and he sat down wearily, pleading with his overloaded brain for just a few moments of calm, of peace and quiet.

As Lloyd began to unwind from the emotionally charged, intense, long day spent with Mona Grace, he looked around his surroundings. In spite of the number of people who frequented the park, it was surprisingly clean and tidy. He wondered who kept it so. He didn't have to wonder for long. He glanced to his left and noticed his new friend, the Whistling Man, wandering around. In his hand, he held a broom. On the top of the broom handle, a large nail protruded. As Lloyd watched, the man swept up the litter from around a trash barrel, placed it in a neat pile. He then flipped his broom upside down and used the nail to pick up the trash and deposit it into the barrel. He saw Lloyd watching him, smiled, shrugged, and said, "Can't afford no rubber gloves, no rubber gloves. Hey, my young friend, how was your day, how was your day?"

Lloyd replied, "It was a good day, thank you. Yours?"

The Whistling Man stretched his cheeks into an impossibly wide grin, displaying both very white teeth and very dark gaps where teeth were missing. "Better than middling, my young friend, better than middling. I had better be on my way – lots of cleaning up to do, lots of cleaning up to do. You have a good night now, have a good night."

Curious, Lloyd asked, "Where will you sleep tonight if you are going to tidy up all the garbage bins around the park? Won't all the sleeping spots be gone?"

The Whistling Man grinned even wider if that was possible. "Aww, everybody knows that they need to leave my sleeping spot alone, leave my sleeping spot alone. If someone tries to take my place, take my place, he or she is gently reminded that if they steal my spot, then they will have to do the clean-up, have to do the clean-up." He chuckled, waved, and carried on his way. Lloyd recognised the tune he was whistling. It was 'You Are My Sunshine'. He wondered how listening to a song that his mother had sung to him and to Lacey when they were small children could be so bittersweet. As the notes whistling through the park faded, Lloyd realised that he would need many more counselling sessions before he would be able to figure out the sorry events in his life. Until then, there certainly wasn't much point in trying to analyse the circumstances of the homeless.

With a lump the size of the opening to his throat, Lloyd swallowed with difficulty, checked his watch and then stood up. Turning back towards the shelter, his stomach protested his neglect at filling it sooner. Before Lloyd returned to the shelter; however, he stood quietly in Oppenheimer Park, listening, smelling the air, all of his senses tuned specifically to the park and its occupants.

Around him, Lloyd detected non-visual signs of poverty. He detected an odour. It wasn't a noxious smell, not really. It didn't burn his nostrils, it was just a faint, intangible something that made Lloyd sniff the air. It reminded him of so many things – salty tears, anxiety, hunger, perspiration, helplessness, emptiness, weariness, but most of all, loneliness! Oh sure, there were definitely homeless people who weren't lonely. Take the Whistling Man, for instance. He wasn't lonely. He loved everyone and it showed. There was no shortage of people willing to talk to the Whistling Man, homeless or otherwise. Then, there were homeless people who were lonely, but by choice. Something in their makeup, whether from birth or by their own volition, directed these types of people to lives of solitude. A great example of this was BeeBee ('Belligerent Bessie'), who ensured her solitary lifestyle by snarling and chasing people away. Lloyd smiled, remembering the firecracker of a woman. He decided he should add "smoky" to his list of homeless odours. The odours of poverty were very complex.

Lloyd was another kind of lonely. Alone, with only the shadows of the missing; alone with his driving need to find not only the three missing girls but also his parents. Only his mission to keep him company. Lloyd felt himself in danger of falling into a pit of depression so deep that he would never accomplish what he came to British Columbia to find.

Sniffing the air once again, he detected a taste of poverty. Having watched a man digging through the garbage for his breakfast, Lloyd vividly imagined eating the garbage that other people threw away. With the exception of the charities that provided free meals for the homeless, the taste of homelessness was very bitter indeed.

Listening intently while standing at the edge of the park, Lloyd heard a lonely, solitary bird singing sleepily on a tree branch high above Lloyd's head. He heard voices softly muttering, coughing, spitting, crying. The voices of poverty sounded desolate and forlorn.

Sighing despondently, he realised fully that he had both the need and the drive, but he didn't have a clear plan. He made a note to himself that he should speak with Mona Grace. He was sure she would be able to help him come up with a game plan, set him on a definitive course of action to find five people and then get back to Alberta and his sister.

A few minutes later, running at full speed, Lloyd barely made it to the cafeteria before it shut down for the night. He stood in an extremely short line-up in the cafeteria – only one other person. There wasn't much choice of food left but Lloyd was nonetheless very thankful for the meal he was about to receive and for the warm, clean bed he had to sleep in after supper. *All in all,* Lloyd thought, *I have had a pretty good life compared to others I have seen in the past two days.*

His last thought before plunging into the nothingness of a deep, dreamless sleep, was that tomorrow he had to come up with a plan.

Chapter 11
The Plan

The next morning Lloyd woke up very early. When he arrived at the showers there was no one in line ahead of him. Feeling only slightly guilty, he took a longer shower than he was allotted time for by moving on to the next shower stall when the hot water ran out of the one he was in, using up that time also.

Once dressed, he made his bed and tidied up the space around it. It was still too early for the cafeteria to be open. He went to the front desk. No one was there, but a notepad and a pen were sitting on the desk. He quickly scribbled a note, requesting an appointment with Mona Grace as soon as she had time. He ended his note with:

"7:00 a.m. I am heading to the cafeteria for breakfast and will check at the desk before I leave for the morning."

Feeling both optimistic and hungry, Lloyd arrived at the cafeteria at 7:05. Already, there was a line-up ahead of him. Controlling his impatience, he reminded himself that he needed to see Mrs Ford before he could even begin a real start to his search. There was no hurry, so he loaded his tray with a big breakfast and two cups of coffee, then went to a corner of the room and sat down to eat.

"May I sit here?" a female voice asked. Lloyd looked up, his mouth full of pancakes. He motioned to the chair across from him.

"Is that second cup of coffee for me?" Mona Grace asked, her voice betraying barely suppressed laughter.

Red-faced, he finally chewed and swallowed the large amount of food he had stuffed into his mouth just before Mona Grace had appeared. "Good morning, Mrs Ford. Yes, of course, that second cup is for you."

"I saw your note, Lloyd," she said. "Okay if we meet right here? Someone is using my office for the next half hour."

"Sure, here is as good a place as any," Lloyd replied. Realising how busy Mrs Ford must be, he got right to the point. "I'm really stuck trying to figure out the best way to begin my search. I was hoping you would be able to help me with a game plan?" He looked at her expectantly, his eyes full of hope.

"I thought it might be something like this," Mona Grace said. "I do have a few ideas to get you started, but you do realise, do you not, that this is going to be a slow process?"

“I sure hope not,” he breathed. “Too much time has passed already. Nobody can afford much more time!”

“I understand that, Lloyd,” Mona Grace said. “Remember, I have a vested interest in your search. My daughter is one of the missing.”

Ashamed, Lloyd nodded his head, a deep blush indicating his embarrassment. Looking up after a minute, he said, “I’m sorry, Mrs Ford. I know Charley is your daughter. She’s my friend as well as my foster sister. So are Amelia and Annie my friends and foster sisters. I guess that I’m just so anxious to find them that I am not thinking with any speck of clarity when it comes to figuring out just how to do that!” He was nearly in tears. He sat there, too choked up to say anything more.

Mona Grace looked at Lloyd, her own eyes welling with sympathy for the young man. Rather than keep him staring at her with those puppy-dog eyes, she began to outline her plan. Firstly, she handed him a notepad and a pen. “Make a list,” she said. “It’ll help you stay on track and hopefully, help you not to get too badly side-tracked or perhaps miss an important clue.

“Number one: You need to get a job. This search is not going to be completed before you spend your $50.00, so you need to find work to tide you through your search. It won’t be anything that pays well, after all, you are not finished with school. Oh yes, as an aside, you do need to finish school, Lloyd!” Mona Grace stared at him sternly, trying to impress upon him through her facial expression how important that was.

“I know that, Mrs Ford,” Lloyd said impatiently. “But first things first. First, I find my parents and the three girls, then I worry about completing school.

“So, first I find a job.” Lloyd wrote down on the notepad, *#1 – Find a Job.* “What’s the next step?”

“Your next step could be more difficult, Lloyd. The second step is to find a place to stay. You can only stay at the shelter for a maximum of thirty days. I know you think that you will have solved the mystery before then, but trust me, it won’t be that easy.”

Lloyd wrote down, *#2 – Place to stay.*

“Luckily for you, Mr Lloyd, I can help you with step #2. As you know from our session yesterday, I live alone in the small two-bedroom house that my parents rented while I was growing up. I have been thinking about renting out the second bedroom to someone. If you would like to rent it, we can work something out – perhaps very inexpensive rent in exchange for some help with the house and the yard work. What do you think?”

“I don’t know what to say, Mrs Ford,” Lloyd said cautiously. “I think it is a great idea, but have you thought this through? I mean, you are used to living alone, won’t you find a tenant distracting?”

Mona Grace smiled. “You forget, Lloyd, I grew up in that house with seven kids and two adults living there. One tenant will hardly distract me!”

She looked directly at Lloyd and said, “I have thought long and hard about it, Lloyd. If I wasn’t sure, I wouldn’t have made you the offer.

"Oh, and by the way, just call me Mona Grace. I'm not married, never have been, probably never will be. I just use the 'Mrs' to avoid being hit on every time I turn around. I just flash my 'wedding ring' and most guys head for the hills." She chuckled and then pointedly asked, "Well, are you game?"

"Yes, Mrs – I mean, Mona Grace – yes, yes, yes! When can I move in?"

Laughing kindly at his enthusiasm, Mona Grace said, "Today if you want to, but take note, I will only give you two weeks to find yourself a job. From your first paycheque, you will have to pay me rent. We will determine the amount of rent when you get a job and know how much money you will earn. Fair?" Without waiting for Lloyd's reply, she continued, "Now, step #3. Any idea what step #3 might be?"

"I do, actually," Lloyd answered. "I think step #3 should involve me speaking to someone at the police station. I'll show them the posters I have of the missing girls, and maybe they will have some ideas about how I can find my parents. I think it is best if the police know I'm here and actively searching."

Mona Grace simply said, "Great! Write it down."

Lloyd added to his list, *#3 – Meet with police.*

"The next step," Lloyd informed Mona Grace, "will be to watch the corner where I was dropped off when I hitch-hiked from Alberta. I suspect that Zo's Hauling truck arrives on that corner pretty much the same time every week. Not necessarily to drop off a hitch-hiker, but to deliver a parcel of some sort. I would really like to speak more with the driver of that pumpkin-orange coloured truck. Maybe he can give me a hint or two. I am nearly positive that he knows something."

"Write it down, step #4," Mona Grace said.

He added, *#4 – Watch for, and meet with, driver of the delivery truck.*

Lloyd opened his mouth to continue, but Mona Grace interrupted him. "That's enough for now, Lloyd. If you have too many things on your list, you will become overwhelmed again and not get anything done. May I suggest that you start at the top, complete the existing list. Then, if need be, you can add more."

Lloyd looked very relieved. "Sounds good to me Mrs – I mean, Mona Grace. Now, if you don't mind, you can get back to work and I will go outside and see what I can see. If you tell me what time you get off work, I will be sure to be packed and waiting."

Once again, Mona Grace found herself grinning. "I have a supper meeting in my office at 5:30. It should be over by 7:00. Why don't you have supper in the cafeteria at 6:30 and then wait for me in the reception area? We'll then head on home and get you settled in."

"Aye, aye, Captain!" Lloyd saluted her sharply. Laughing, he headed up to the dormitory to pack his belongings into his backpack, noted in the register that he would NOT require lodging, and headed out the door.

Glancing quickly at his map, he had a pretty good idea of where he was heading. Setting off with long, purposeful steps, Lloyd headed in the direction of Stanley Park.

He once again approached the food wagon that was situated not far from the entrance to the park. The same woman who had so kindly expanded his lunch order was working today. Lloyd waited until no one was in line and then he approached the lady.

"Is the manager around, ma'am?" Lloyd inquired.

The woman chortled. "That's me, son, I'm the owner, manager, waitress, dishwasher and janitor. Anything needs doing, you're looking at the one and only. What can I do for you, young man?"

"It sounds to me as if you need an employee, ma'am," Lloyd said. "It just so happens I'm looking for a job. I'm a hard worker, I'm honest, and to tell you the truth, I really need a job!"

"How old are you, boy?" the woman asked. "Shouldn't you be in school? Hang on a minute okay? I'll be right out. Just have a seat over at that table there and wait for me." That said, she pulled down the metal awning, effectively closing off the food wagon from the public. She stuck a 'SORRY, WE ARE CLOSED' sign on the outside, locked the side door and went over to the table, handing Lloyd a coffee before she sat down across from him.

Scrutinising Lloyd with eagle sharp eyes, she said, "What's your name, young man? I remember you from a couple of days ago. You interest me."

"I'm Braden Lloyd Jordan, ma'am, but I go by Lloyd. I'm seventeen years old. I fully intend to finish school, but..."

Once Lloyd started talking, he couldn't stop. He explained to the woman what he was doing in East Vancouver, told her about the missing girls; told her about his parents. When he finally finished telling her his plan to find both his parents and his missing foster siblings he paused for breath. Staring intently at the woman, he quietly said, "So, now you know why I need a job."

"I can't pay you any more than minimum wage. I'm a widow and this is my only means of support. That's why I have been trying to handle everything on my own. What I can do is give you a minimum of forty hours per week, plus all of the extra hours you can handle; plus, give you a reasonable amount of time off to pursue your search for your family." She stood up, held out her hand for Lloyd to shake. "My name is Shelby Sidor. The name of my food wagon here is 'Burgers 'N Dawgs'. Welcome to the family! When can you start?"

"Well," Lloyd said. "I can start right now, but I have to be back at the shelter at 5:30 because I am moving this evening." He went on to explain where he was moving to and told her that Mona Grace was the mother of one of the missing girls.

"Then we'd better get your training started, hadn't we? You and I will spend the next hour in the kitchen; then we'll open up the food wagon and you can get your feet wet serving our public. At four o'clock, you can head on back to the shelter. Can you work all day tomorrow?"

"Yes, ma'am!"

"You can call me Shelby; 'ma'am' is too stuffy for me. Come on, young Lloyd Jordan, let's get the training started!"

Precisely at 5:30, Lloyd was waiting in the reception area for Mona Grace to finish her meeting. When she came out of her office at seven o'clock, Lloyd was fast asleep in his chair. She touched him gently on the shoulder. He came awake with a startle, looked up at Mona Grace's face and yelled, "I've got a job! I start tomorrow!"

Delighted, Mona Grace patted Lloyd on his shoulder. "Way to go, Lloyd, way to go! Let's head on home now and get you settled."

"Okay with me," Lloyd said. "We have one other job before today is over."

"Oh? What's that?"

"We need to add two more items to the plan because I already completed #1 – Find a job and also #2 – Find a place to live."

Mona Grace let out a huge belly laugh. "So, we will, Lloyd, so we will."

Chapter 12
East Vancouver Police

It took no time at all for Lloyd to remove the clothing and other personal items from his backpack.

His bedroom, although tiny, was very well organised. The single bed had three plastic containers underneath, each with its own lid, substituting for a chest of drawers. The headboard on the bed was a bookcase headboard. With a twang of nostalgia, Lloyd remembered his parents' bed having a bookcase headboard. It was always stuffed full with books of all kinds. A small nightstand filled the corner to the left of the bed. The nightstand contained one drawer and two shelves, and it was tall enough to double as a writing table. A clothes closet filled the wall to the right of the foot of the bed. The door opened towards the hallway, leaving more space inside the bedroom. A large window on the outside wall was big enough for an adult to escape in case of fire. An overhead light/fan combination completed the efficient bedroom. It was spotlessly clean.

By the time Lloyd filled Mona Grace in on his day, he was yawning. "I have to be at work tomorrow morning at nine," he said. "If I jog, it still takes me a half-hour, so I better 'hit the pit' as my grandfather used to say."

Lloyd stood up. "Thanks again, Mona Grace. I don't know how I will ever repay you, but I'm sure going to try!"

Mona Grace looked at Lloyd, a big lump in her throat and unshed tears sparkling in her eyes. "Just find my daughter, Lloyd, and then I will be indebted to you. Have a really good night's sleep; tomorrow is your first day at work and you will need to be rested."

Just as Lloyd reached the door to his room, Mona Grace called out. "Oh, I almost forgot, Lloyd! I called the East Van police precinct and made an appointment for you to meet with the Sergeant there on Thursday morning at ten o'clock. If your new boss won't give you Thursday for your day off, please call me as soon as possible so I can change it."

"Thanks!" Lloyd said. "I appreciate your help. If I don't call you tomorrow morning, you will know that everything is okay and I can meet with the police on Thursday."

The next morning, he was so eager to train for the new job that he arrived at 'Burgers 'N Dawgs' before his boss! Shelby Sidor arrived shortly after. She was not surprised but was extremely delighted to see Lloyd appear so conscientious and eager.

The two of them spent the morning in the food wagon, doing prep work for the afternoon, and training Lloyd so that he could hopefully man the wagon by himself and give Shelby a much-needed break. The morning flew by. At lunchtime, they each made a hamburger and went to sit at the table outside to eat their lunch.

During a rare lull in customers, his boss told him that he could have any day off he wanted during the week, so long as it was not on Friday, Saturday or Sunday. These were the busiest days of the week and therefore the most profitable for 'Burgers 'N Dawgs'. Lloyd had no problem with that because he wanted to have Thursdays off, at least until he had a chance to speak with the driver of the pumpkin orange truck with 'ZO'S HAULING' emblazoned on the side.

They also agreed that Lloyd would work from 8:30 to 4:30. He would first do the preparation work, and then open up the food wagon for sales to the public at 11:00 am.

"Wow! You weren't kidding, Shelby," Lloyd said. "This is Sunday and we were run off our feet. I can't even imagine Fridays and Saturdays. I really enjoyed the day, though. I seem to be catching on, don't you think?"

"Fishing for a compliment already, are we?" Shelby joked. Seeing the crestfallen look on Lloyd's face, she hurriedly continued, "Just kidding, just kidding, Lloyd. You are doing just fine. A couple more days and I should be able to take some time off. Good job today and excellent clean-up. Looking forward to seeing you tomorrow. Have a good night!"

"Aren't you leaving now too?" Lloyd queried.

"As soon as I get the books up to date. You just run along. See you tomorrow."

Although he knew he should head home, Lloyd felt a magnetic pull emanating from the entrance to Stanley Park. *What the heck,* he thought, *I'll just take a short stroll in the park to unwind a bit and then I'll jog home.* That is what he did.

He arrived at his new-to-him residence just as Mona Grace was unlocking the front door. Hearing Lloyd, she turned and smiled at him. Before she could ask, he was already recounting the events of his day.

A few minutes later, the two of them were in the kitchen, jointly preparing dinner.

Lloyd felt a sense of calm, having Mona Grace to talk with at the end of the day. He was pretty sure that being calm would help him with his mission much more than the despondent feelings he had experienced since his arrival.

Later, in his room, he surreptitiously added two more numbers to his list. He wrote:

#5 – Meet with a representative of the East Van Devils.

Next, he added:

#6 – Interview residents of Oppenheimer Park.

Lying in his bed, still awake at midnight, Lloyd felt slightly guilty about the additions to his list; however, he was pretty sure Mona Grace would veto him meeting with a gang member! Come to think of it, she might not think that interviewing the derelicts in the park would uncover anything useful either. Lloyd couldn't help but think that someone in the gang would know something he needed to know. The big question was; would they tell him anything? He finally fell into a dream-filled sleep. He awoke early Monday morning. He felt exhausted but was looking forward to another day working with Shelby Sidor.

Lloyd slipped quietly out the door, trying not to awaken Mona Grace, whose alarm rang a full hour later than Lloyd's.

Jogging down the street, he was amazed at the number of people and vehicles that were already filling the streets and sidewalks of East Van. A quick glance at his watch told him that it was only six o'clock, but yet the city was bustling, fully and noisily engaged in 'big city mode'.

A sudden pang of homesickness caused him to abruptly stop moving. He missed the slower pace of rural Alberta. He missed his sister and he missed his friends. Mentally giving his head a shake, Lloyd once again promised himself, as well as the persistent but faint shadows of the missing who had taken up permanent residence in his brain, that he would never give up his search. His breathing slowed down, he picked up the pace, headed towards his new place of employment, and very much looked forward to continuing to learn and to grow.

Thursday finally arrived. Lloyd had suffered through yet another night of wicked dreams and restless sleep. Nonetheless, he woke up early but forced himself to stay in bed until Mona Grace was through with the bathroom. He then got up, had a shower and got ready to face the day.

When he entered the kitchen a half-hour later, he was surprised to see his breakfast laid out on the table and a note sitting beside his plate. Sitting down, he quickly read Mona Grace's note. He read:

'Lloyd, I just want to wish you good luck for your meeting with the police this morning. I'm looking forward to hearing all about it tonight when I get home.'

Lloyd smiled as he ate his breakfast of cereal, fruit, muffins and yoghurt. He decided that he really liked his new living arrangements.

After breakfast, he still had two hours until his meeting at the precinct. He used the time to vacuum and dust, wash the dishes and wet mop the floors in the little house.

The precinct was only a short, ten-minute walk from the house. Approaching the building with fifteen minutes to spare, Lloyd gazed thoughtfully at the old, red brick, two-storey building. To the right of the building, a small, poorly paved parking lot exhibited very few empty spaces despite the early hour. The door to the building was scratched and worn, graffiti etched into the door. Blocking his entry, a tough-looking youth was sanding the offensive words from the door. Beside him, a paint can and roller waited for the youth. As Lloyd approached, the boy squinted near-sightedly at him, saying nothing, not moving out of the way. Lloyd simply reached around the fellow and opened the door. "Excuse me," Lloyd said as he gently but firmly shoved the youth out of his way.

The inside of the precinct was as run-down as the outside; however, it was very clean. It smelled of bleach and human desolation, of sweat and anger. Not just anger, rage.

Lloyd approached the desk. The extremely overweight officer sitting behind the desk certainly gave credence to the myth that policemen lived and breathed Tim Horton's coffee and doughnuts! An empty box full of crumbs and icing further accentuated the myth. Lloyd wondered irreverently whether this particular officer had eaten the entire box by himself.

When it became clear to Lloyd that he would have to speak first in order to get the officer's attention, Lloyd cleared his throat and said, "Excuse me?"

The policeman looked up. "Yeah, what can I do for you?"

"I have a ten o'clock appointment," Lloyd said.

"Who with?" asked the officer disinterestedly.

"I'm not sure. I'm here about my missing parents and three of my foster siblings."

"Hmm," snorted the policeman, at the same time as he was picking a piece of doughnut out of his teeth with a grimy fingernail. Lloyd looked away, feeling disgusted.

The officer picked up the phone, dialled an extension and spoke into it. Hanging up, he looked at Lloyd with much more interest. "You're with Sergeant Gablehaus. He'll be right out."

'Right out' meant twenty minutes. A LONG twenty minutes. During the time he was waiting, Lloyd fidgeted, trying to get comfortable in the worn-out chair. The officer at the desk simply sat and did nothing, as far as Lloyd could determine. However, when the door beside his desk opened, he jumped up, pretending to be extremely busy with papers piled high on the credenza beside him.

A tall, grey-haired man approached Lloyd, holding out his hand, shaking Lloyd's vigorously. "So sorry to have kept you waiting, young fella. I'm Sergeant Gablehaus. Come with me."

Sergeant Gablehaus lead Lloyd upstairs to a somewhat larger office than Lloyd expected. Indicating that Lloyd should sit, the Sergeant leaned back in his chair. "What can I do for you, young man?"

Lloyd really liked this policeman; he felt comfortable in his presence. Sergeant Gablehaus inspired confidence and Lloyd felt it.

Pulling out a file folder from his backpack, Lloyd placed five photos on the Sergeant's desk. Pointing firstly at the picture of his father, Lloyd explained that his father had spent time in prison for embezzlement. As far as Lloyd knew, Paul Martin Jordan was no longer in prison, but Lloyd was unable to locate him.

Next, he pointed at a photo of his mother. Embarrassed to have to tell this officer that his mother abandoned both him and his sister, he nonetheless related the entire sordid story. Once again, Lloyd had to admit that he was unable to locate his missing mother.

In turn, he pointed to the pictures of Charlotte (Charley) Ford (age 14 when she disappeared three years prior); Amelia Anderson (age 16 at the time of her disappearance, also three years ago, but at a separate time from the disappearance of Charley); and, finally, Annie Barcley (age 16 when she disappeared the previous year).

Lloyd explained that the girls had all hitch-hiked at separate times, but all three girls had been picked up by the same vehicle, a pumpkin-orange pickup with a matching orange shell on the back, and the words 'ZO'S HAULING' embossed on the door of the pickup.

As Lloyd was speaking, Sergeant Gablehaus flipped open his laptop, typed something, read it and then looked up. "It says on here that a boy went missing not long after the third girl disappeared. What did you say your name was again, young man?"

Lloyd suddenly felt the hairs on the back of his neck stand at attention. "My name is Larry Simpson," he lied.

"Aah, I see," mused the Sergeant. "Just hang on a minute, will you please? I have to go to the back and get some information on these missing persons." He got up from his chair and left the room.

Panic-stricken, unable to breathe, Lloyd quickly grabbed all of the pictures and ran out of the room, exiting the precinct at full speed, nearly knocking the surly graffiti artist on his keester as he raced by.

Lloyd didn't stop running until he reached home. Locking the door behind him, he quickly closed all the blinds and curtains in the house and went to his room.

"What was I thinking?" he asked himself aloud. "Not enough, that's for sure. I should have figured out that someone would have reported me missing by now. Boy, I sure messed this up. I'll just have to go on with #4 – watch for the orange truck and speak with the driver. Other than going to work, I better lay low for a while. The police will lose interest quickly. The disappearances are too old for them to worry about cold files. Besides which, both Amelia and Annie are now legally adults and have every right to go anywhere they want to go; and do whatever they want to do."

So much for police assistance!

As Lloyd was fleeing the detachment, Sergeant Gablehaus was picking up the telephone in another office, making a call to an R.C.M.P detachment in north-western Alberta.

"Hello," he said when an officer on the other end of the line answered. "May I speak with Sergeant Fred Gablehaus, please?" There was a pause as he listened to the person on the other end. "Certainly. Please tell him it's his brother, Sergeant Greg Gablehaus calling from the East Vancouver City Police detachment."

Chapter 13
Belligerent Bessie

Checking his watch, Lloyd realised that he had enough time to get back to the entrance of Oppenheimer Park before the pumpkin orange pickup stopped on its delivery route. Although he had slept away most of the trip, he remembered Adam Draper saying that he had a parcel to deliver most Thursdays at the east entrance to that park.

Lloyd found an empty bench within sight of the '15-minutes only' loading zone. He sat down, prepared to wait. *Man, I'm tired,* he thought. *I seem to be taking three steps forward and two steps back. When will something break? I'll close my eyes for a minute, just to give them a rest. I've got time.*

He woke himself up with a loud snort, with an accompanying neck-wrenching jerk. He looked at his watch. He had been asleep for a full half an hour! Panicked, he stood up, looking wildly around for any sign that he had, or had not, missed the delivery.

The only person he saw was BeeBee. The rag-tag old lady was pushing her fully-loaded cart away from the loading zone, muttering to herself as she shuffled along. With a sinking feeling, he was pretty sure that the taillights he saw turning a corner in the distance belonged to the delivery truck.

"BeeBee! Wait, it's me, it's Lloyd!" He ran over to her, placed his hand on her cart.

"Leggo the cart, boy!" she growled at him. "It's not your cart, it's mine! Just leggo, right now or I'll scream bloody murder."

Lloyd snapped back his hand as if he had immersed it in boiling water. "Sorry, BeeBee," he apologised. "I just want to visit with you, that's all. I wasn't taking your cart, I just wanted you to stop and talk to me."

"Don't like talkin' much, you know that, young Lloyd," she said, her intelligent, expressive eyes belying her grouchy demeanour. "I'm much too busy to spend my valuable time gossiping on a street corner. So, if you want to visit, be quick about it. I'm a busy, busy gal."

"Maybe I can just walk along beside you as you go on your busy way? We can visit at the same time as you finish your busy-ness?"

BeeBee stared at Lloyd. "You trying to get me in trouble, boy? You're lucky I'm here now. Only ones here, or I wouldn't stay here neither. I just got a delivery and I need to deliver it on to the next place, so say what you need to say and then our visit is done!"

Trying to be discreet, Lloyd glanced into her cart. Sure enough, there was a small package stuffed between some clothing in the cart. All he could see was a part of a return address – 'ZO'

"What you lookin' at, boy?" Belligerence personified, BeeBee glared at Lloyd.

Deciding he needed to be brutally honest with the bag lady, Lloyd replied truthfully, "I can't help but think that you just accepted a delivery from a man named Adam Draper. He was driving a pumpkin orange pickup truck, Alberta plates. Said 'Zo's Hauling' on the side of the doors? I was waiting to speak with Mr Draper, but I fell asleep on that park bench over there."

Disgusted with himself, Lloyd kicked at a pebble in front of his right foot, sending it flying all the way to the main street curb, but stubbing his toe painfully in the process. The pain was welcome; it highlighted his poor opinion of himself and his unfortunate nap.

"Yup, you missed him alright. But not to worry, he will be back next Thursday at this time. He will have another package for me to deliver. He pays me $20 for every package I hand over to—"

BeeBee slapped her hands over her lips, horrified that she had nearly let slip where she was about to go on her delivery.

"Well, I see you aren't much in the mood for a visit today, BeeBee," Lloyd said regretfully. "Maybe another day, huh?" He started to walk, ostensibly towards the shelter, waved his hand diffidently in BeeBee's direction. "Have a good one, okay? I'm just going to sit here in the park and relax. I got a job now and I have to work tomorrow."

Clearly not listening to him, Lloyd watched BeeBee take off down the street, not once looking back at Lloyd as she headed out on her very important delivery for which she would be paid a measly twenty bucks. Realising that BeeBee was already suspicious of his intentions, Lloyd decided not to follow her today. Between her distrust and the police, who must surely be looking for him by now, he needed to go home, lay low.

Back at home, Lloyd puttered around in the yard, glanced nervously over his shoulder every time he heard a vehicle slow down. He fixed the lawnmower blade which had fallen off, but fortunately, the screw had not. He mowed the tiny yard and weeded the flower beds.

The day passed slowly. When Mona Grace got home, supper was ready. She gratefully kicked off her shoes and settled down happily to a delicious meal. "Where'd you learn to cook, Lloyd?" she asked him, her mouth too full to speak clearly.

"My mother. She was a firm believer in training both her daughter and her son to be self-sufficient – looking back, I think she was preparing us for what she was going to do – abandon her own children."

Despite Lloyd's power nap at the park, he was still exhausted. After talking about their respective days, they went to bed early.

The rest of the week passed quickly. Lloyd poured all his attention and energy into learning everything there was to learn about the food truck business.

He learned so fast, and so well, that Shelby was already considering turning the books over to him to enter his transactions at the end of each shift. He loved math and looked forward to being taught bookkeeping by his employer.

He got in the habit of taking a relaxing hour in the park at the end of his shifts. He loved Stanley Park. He even convinced Shelby to take the occasional walk in the park with him before they opened the food wagon for the lunch clientele. Soon, she declared that she also loved Stanley Park, and she couldn't figure out why, after living in Vancouver all these years, she hadn't discovered that fact much sooner.

Bound and determined that he would not repeat his disastrous actions from the last Thursday, on Wednesday night, Lloyd went to bed early.

Thursday, Mona Grace called out to Lloyd as she left for work. "Good luck today, Lloyd! I'm looking forward to a full report when I get home later this evening. I have a meeting at seven, so I probably won't get home until 9:30 or 10. Don't worry about supper. I'll pick something up at the shelter cafeteria before my meeting."

Unable to just hang around the house until it was time to go to the park, Lloyd arrived well before he needed to. He wasn't at all sure how he was going to approach the subject, but he was convinced that Adam would know something about the missing girls.

To avoid falling asleep, Lloyd jogged around the perimeter of the park, stopping now and then to pick up pieces of trash on the ground and throw them into a garbage bin. *What the heck,* he thought, *if the Whistling Man takes such good care of the park, I can do my part.*

Looking over towards the shelter, Lloyd spotted BeeBee lumbering towards the loading zone, her worldly possessions piled precariously high in her cart.

He quickly stepped behind an ancient arbutus tree and stood completely motionless. He could see BeeBee and the loading zone, but she couldn't see him (he hoped!) He was very grateful for the giant trees that grew in British Columbia. If he was back in northern Alberta, he would be lucky to find some tall grass to lie down in while he tried to hide. The giant arbutus behind which he hid had several thick trunks branching out in several directions. Lloyd was perfectly camouflaged. There was even a smaller trunk growing out of the larger one, at a perfect height for him to perch one hip on. This made it easier for Lloyd to remain perfectly still.

His nose itched. He didn't dare scratch it. BeeBee might detect the motion and flee before the truck arrived. He needed to sneeze. He held his breath until he saw spots in front of his eyes, but the need to sneeze evaporated. His right eye was watering. He blinked rapidly but did not reach up to wipe the moisture off of his cheek.

Every time he heard a vehicle in the distance, Lloyd was sure it would be the orange truck. Finally, after about a dozen vehicles had stopped at the loading zone to unload passengers, the pumpkin truck arrived. BeeBee was so intent on approaching the truck, she did not see or hear Lloyd walking slowly and softly behind her. Adam Draper glanced over at Lloyd but did not seem to recognise him. He handed BeeBee a small package wrapped in a twenty-dollar bill, tipped his hat and said, “See you next week, ma’am. Sounds like there will be several packages next week for you to deliver.”

Lloyd retreated quickly and quietly, once again stepped behind the huge arbutus tree.

BeeBee cackled at Adam. “So long as the price is twenty bucks per package, keep ‘em coming, man, keep ‘em coming.”

Lloyd made an instantaneous decision. He knew Adam would be back the following Thursday, so, rather than try to speak with Adam today, he opted to follow BeeBee as she rattled away to deliver the package.

Pulling a woollen cap from his jacket pocket, Lloyd pulled it on his head, down low on his forehead, hoping BeeBee would not turn around. He took his sunglasses out of his shirt pocket and put them on his face.

Giving BeeBee a half-a-block head- start, Lloyd slowly walked behind her, shuffling his feet, kicking small pebbles off of the sidewalk and into the gutter. He kept his hands in his pockets, his shoulders hunched and his head down. He was pretty sure that BeeBee would not recognise him, at least from this distance.

After tailing her for about four blocks, BeeBee turned right, entering an alley. Lloyd had to shorten the space between them in order not to lose her. There were garbage dumpsters outside every exit door. He figured if it looked like she was going to stop and turn around, he would have time to dive behind a dumpster and hide.

They must have walked the equivalent of two or three blocks when BeeBee suddenly stopped. Lloyd did his ‘dumpster dive’, making a crashing sound as he landed painfully on one knee! BeeBee looked up, startled. She didn’t see him! After half-heartedly looking around, she shrugged, speaking aloud, “It’s nothin’, you silly old fool, probably just a rat or a cat trying to get into a dumpster and knockin’ somethin’ over. It’s nothin’.” With one last look behind her, BeeBee continued down the alley.

Ignoring the searing pain in his knee, Lloyd tried even harder not to make the slightest noise as he followed the bag lady down the alley. This time when she stopped, Lloyd was more prepared. He slipped quietly behind a dumpster and waited.

To BeeBee’s left, a freshly painted bright red door gleamed in the semi-darkness of the long alley. A peephole was drilled into the centre of the door. Directly below the peephole was a heavy brass knocker. Reaching into her cart, BeeBee withdrew her delivery parcel. She put the twenty-dollar bill down the front of her shirt and approached the door. Lifting the knocker with a grimy hand, she knocked. Lloyd supposed it was a coded knock, but easy to recognise. ‘Shave and a haircut, six bits’ – six knocks in total. She then backed away from the door, standing far enough away that whoever was inside could see her through the peephole.

A short time later, the red door opened. A bruiser of a man wearing a Red Devils sweatshirt stood, arms crossed, completely blocking the doorway. Lloyd whistled silently as he looked at the giant. Shaved bald head, so covered with tattoos that it didn't seem as if he was bald; thick and bushy black beard. At least one hundred ninety-eight centimetres (six feet, six inches) and probably one hundred thirty-six kilograms (three hundred pounds). Obviously a weight lifter – biceps made of steel! Even from this distance, Lloyd felt a shiver of fear. The brute oozed intimidation.

BeeBee, however, didn't appear fazed in the least. Looking way up at the fellow in the doorway, she said, "Usual delivery for the Red Devils." The man held out his meaty hand, saying nothing. "Oh no," said BeeBee, "usual delivery, usual delivery fee."

The doorman snickered. "Okay, BeeBee. Usual delivery fee, $50.00 per item. Here's your money, you greedy cow."

"Just tryin' to survive is all, Brutus, just tryin' to survive!" She handed over the package and tucked the money into the front of her shirt. With a wave of her middle finger, BeeBee turned around and headed back the way she had come. Brutus stared after her, laughing at the old woman's audacity and lack of fear. He respected that. Not many people who saw Brutus were unafraid. He pulled a pack of smokes out of his pocket, looked at it, and without taking a cigarette out of the pack, put it back in his shirt pocket. He turned and re-entered through the shiny red door.

Lloyd stayed frozen in place until he was absolutely certain that the 'Pit Bull man' would not return. By the time he crawled out from behind the dumpster, BeeBee was out of sight. Trying to catch sight of her, he ran at top speed despite the pain in his knee. He did somehow take the time to note some landmarks along the way in case he needed to come back to the Devils' clubhouse.

Even though Lloyd had switched his plan in mid-stream, it was still a pretty good day. The most important thing? He could find the Devils' red clubhouse door if and when the time came that he needed to, although to be honest, he fervently hoped he would not have to.

Chapter 14
Amending the Plan

Another week went by; another trip made to Oppenheimer Park in a futile attempt to speak with Adam Draper.

BeeBee, who prided herself on being a non-conversationalist, had lingered beside Adam and practically talked his ear off! By the time BeeBee had finished her yip-yapping, picked up her parcels and left, Lloyd was unable to get to the drop-off zone before Adam had jumped into the pumpkin orange delivery truck and high-tailed it out of the area at excessive speed.

Lloyd was left standing all alone at the curb. Feeling suddenly like a child's helium balloon, pricked by a needle, he deflated instantly. Disappointment prickled the back of his eyes. He determinedly blinked the moisture away. Slouched despondently, Lloyd slowly headed for home.

He had a long day ahead of him with nothing to look forward to. Almost in the depths of despair, he slept away the day.

When Mona Grace came home after work, the house was dark. No supper was sitting on the stove and there was no sign of Lloyd. Noticing that his bedroom door was closed, she tapped on the door, softly at first and then louder. No response. Alarmed, she pounded on the door, shouting Lloyd's name.

"I'm sleeping!" he finally hollered back. "Leave me alone, Mona Grace, I don't want to talk."

"Well," she answered, "we are going to talk, whether you like it or not! So, get your butt out of that bedroom and come into the kitchen while I make us a bite to eat."

A distinctly disrespectful muttering erupted from behind the closed door. Mona Grace ignored it and headed to the kitchen, where she began to prepare her favourite comfort food – tomato soup and grilled cheese and onion sandwiches. Just as she placed them on the table, Lloyd appeared and sat down, looking childishly surly and unkempt.

Choosing to ignore the state he was in, she simply waited. This was very unlike Lloyd. Mona Grace was confident that his silence wouldn't last beyond suppertime. She had patience. In her occupation, it came with the territory. She would have no problem waiting him out.

When she finished eating, she silently cleared the table and washed the breakfast and supper dishes, said not a word, just waited.

When she was nearly finished cleaning up, Lloyd cleared his throat. "I'm sorry, Mona Grace, I shouldn't have been so rude to you. It's just, well, I've had a really crappy day and I don't know what I am going to do about it."

"Why not just tell me about it, Lloyd?" Mona Grace asked softly. "You already know I'm a good listener. You don't tell someone; it'll just fester inside you until it makes you sick."

A giant sigh eased its way out of the tightness that hovered within Lloyd's chest, somewhat easing his discomfort. Mona Grace put two cups of tea on the table and sat down, prepared to hear about Lloyd's day.

Lloyd couldn't help himself. As he recanted the events of the day, he cried. The more he cried the more upset he got. In between sobs, he managed to convey to Mona Grace that he was seriously agitated, sad and disillusioned.

By the time he finished relating the unfortunate events, he was feeling somewhat better although his breath hitched relentlessly. "The thing is, Mona Grace, I am stumped. I just don't know what to do or where to turn. I can't go back to the police station. They'll probably arrest me. At the very least, I'll feel like a complete and utter imbecile after running away as I did."

Mona Grace was not without sympathy for her young tenant, but she didn't like the juvenile way he was handling himself, and she told him so.

"They haven't anything to arrest you for, Lloyd," she said. "You haven't got a record, and I'm pretty sure your foster parents didn't report you missing."

"You're right about that," Lloyd responded. "They probably just thought, oh well, there goes a source of income! If anybody reported me missing, it would be Lacey, and I know she would give me a fair bit of time to find our missing foster siblings before that would happen. I just feel really bad that I haven't tried harder to contact her. But the thing is, I'm embarrassed. I was so sure that I would come out to Vancouver, waltz right into the City and bang! Enter the conquering hero and there they would be, sitting pretty maids all in a row, just waiting to be found."

"Well, if you had been able to do that, Mr Jordan," Mona Grace said wryly, "you would be a miracle worker. Life doesn't work that way. Heck, even fairy tale characters have their problems!

"Now that you have settled down some, may I suggest something? I have been thinking about it for some time and would like to run an idea by you." She looked steadily at Lloyd, waiting for a response.

"Sure," he said, "what's your idea?"

"I did some checking around on your behalf and found out something interesting. There is a high school only a couple of blocks from here. The school runs night classes three nights a week, as well as every day. What would you think about going back to school part-time; getting your High School Diploma or your Matric? It would acceptably pass the time. You would still be able to follow up any leads you come up with for finding the girls, and at the same time, you would be ready for further education if you so decided that was what you wanted to do. It might take you a bit longer than if you went back to school full time. I know you need to keep working in order to pay rent, but I'm pretty darn sure that your boss would be proud of you for doing it."

Lloyd looked like he had been struck by lightning. "That never entered my pea brain, Mona Grace," he said. "Would it cost much?"

"Well, it likely would cost you to buy some textbooks, but I know that second-hand books are available. If you like, I can loan you the money and you can pay me back when you can. As you already know, I got my education the hard way, but oh, Lloyd! It was so worth it. Want to sleep on it for a day or two?"

"No need, Mona Grace. I love your idea. I'm going back to school, the sooner the better!"

Mona Grace laughed. "Well, it will definitely be sooner, buddy, because the new semester starts next Monday!" She reached down beneath her chair and handed Lloyd a brand-new backpack. Inside were school supplies, an application form, and a calculator, together with a list of textbooks required for Grades X, XI and XII.

"Did I guess right? You were taking Grade XI when you left your foster home to find the girls?"

"You guessed right, Mona Grace." He stood up and awkwardly reached over and gave her a huge hug. "Thanks so much. I'll make you proud, just wait and see! Now, can I use the phone for a minute? I want to call Shelby and make sure it is okay with her."

"You don't need to ask to use the phone, silly." Mona Grace said. "You pay rent and a share of the utilities. It's your phone as much as it's mine." She yawned tiredly. "Well, if you'll excuse me, I have a busy day tomorrow and I'm bushed. Good night, Lloyd, see you tomorrow."

Lloyd went to his room and dug Shelby's phone number out of his old backpack. She answered on the first ring. "Hey Lloyd, what's up?"

When Lloyd finished telling her about his plan to go back to school part-time, Shelby squealed like a teenager. "Lloyd, that's awesome! I'm so proud of you. In fact, I'm so proud that I am going to pay for your schooling. Just bring the invoices to me and I'll see they are covered. Good for you, Lloyd! I knew I was right in trusting my instincts. You are a wonderful young man with a lot of character and drive. You just made my night! Have a good sleep and I'll see you in the morning."

For several minutes, Lloyd just sat in his chair, grinning from ear to ear. *What a change, what a wonderful change,* he thought. Life can change in an instant and it sure has. Still grinning, he headed for bed.

Chapter 15
The Long Wait

It took no time at all for Lloyd to settle into classes. He had always liked school and the truth be told, he missed it. By signing up for three evening classes and two half-day classes, he would be able to complete his Grade XI by the end of a second semester. He could then go on and take Grade XII classes. He figured that if all went according to plan, he would graduate in a year and a half, or two years at the outside. He didn't want only a High School Diploma, he wanted his Matriculation and that became his goal. He realised that in British Columbia, there was a Grade XIII. If he stayed in B.C., he would be required to take the extra grade. He was willing to do that, but he really hoped that he would be able to be back in Alberta and graduate with his friends at his last school. Regardless, one way or the other, he was going to finish high school, no matter how long it took.

The week following his disappointment at not being able to speak with Adam, Lloyd once again headed for the park, hid behind what was becoming his favourite tree, the giant arbutus, and waited for the orange delivery truck.

BeeBee arrived at the loading zone before the truck. When it arrived, she accepted several parcels and then turned to leave. Suddenly, she spotted Lloyd. She immediately turned around and said something to the driver.

"He's waiting for you," she said to Lloyd as she passed him.

"Thanks, BeeBee," Lloyd said, and he hurried over to the driver's side of the truck. Just as he reached the vehicle, the driver's door opened and a stranger climbed out of the cab! Lloyd stood there, staring dumbly at the man.

"Where's Adam Draper?" he blurted out in a choked voice.

"Adam's only a temporary driver," the man responded. "He's not on this run for probably another three months. Can I help you with something, or can I pass on a message to him for you?"

"Not much point if he isn't going to be back this way for three months," Lloyd said glumly. "Do you have a schedule? I can write down when he will be here next, and try and catch him at that time."

"Sure do!" the driver said cheerfully. "The boss does up the schedule six months in advance. We all appreciate it; not many companies do that." He rummaged through the glove box in the truck, finally emerging from the cab with a paper in his hand. "Yup; as I said, Adam should be the driver in exactly three months from today." He wrote down the date on a slip of paper and handed it to

Lloyd. "There you go, young fellow. Sorry you missed him. Better luck in three months."

"Thanks, sir, I appreciate your help," Lloyd said glumly. "Have a safe trip back to Alberta."

As Lloyd turned to leave the park, he thought to himself that at least he could keep more than busy during the next three months! And who knows, maybe he'd get a break in the meantime. Disappointed but handling it better than before, he headed for the house.

Lloyd was certainly right. Between working at the food wagon, learning how to keep the books for the 'BURGERS 'N DAWGS' small business, and going to school, the days flew by. Days blended into weeks, which ultimately blended into the third month.

Almost before he knew it, it was time to visit the old arbutus. He arrived early, went behind 'his' tree, patting it like the old friend it was starting to become. Sheepishly, Lloyd glanced around to see if anyone observed him talking to a tree. *Really, though,* he thought, *what's the difference between talking to a giant arbutus tree in British Columbia and talking to an old tree stump in northern Alberta, the interior of which served as a mailbox? Shoot,* he thought to himself. *All this contemplation is doing is making me feel guilty again for not trying to contact Lacey!*

Lloyd waited until well past the time when the delivery truck should have arrived. He ultimately realised that not only did the truck not arrive, but there was no sign of BeeBee either. He concluded that there must have been no deliveries scheduled. With a sigh, he wrote the date for the following Thursday down in his student schedule. He would try again the following week.

One rare evening a few nights later, Lloyd and Mona Grace had some time to sit and visit. Mona Grace bluntly asked Lloyd what was bothering him. "Does it show that much?" he asked. She just looked at him, and then she actually rolled her eyes.

"Well," Lloyd began, knowing full well that Mona Grace would not quit hounding him until he told her, said, "I'm struggling with the idea of going back to the police station and trying to speak with Sergeant Gablehaus one more time. I don't feel good about the way I left our last encounter and besides, he may very well have a lead on the missing girls. Now women, I suppose," he added as an aside.

"I'm proud of you, kiddo," Mona Grace said. "Tell you what!" she jokingly offered, "If he arrests you, I'll post your bail." She started to laugh, saw the horrified look on Lloyd's face, and stopped joking. "It'll be okay, Lloyd," she said. "He's not going to arrest you. I can almost guarantee it."

Lloyd looked far from convinced. "Anyhow, it's just something I'm struggling with. I have a lot of studying to do for semester finals, so I won't have time to do anything about it for a while. It's just – you asked – and I told, ya know?"

He stood up, yawned and said, "I've got to hit the books a bit before I go to sleep and it will be another busy day at the old 'BURGERS 'N DAWGS', so I better get at it. 'Night, Mona Grace."

"Good night, Lloyd," she replied as she thoughtfully watched his retreating back. "Keep me posted."

"Yup, of course I will."

The following Thursday, it turned out that Lloyd had an unexpected exam. It was worth a percentage of the final mark for that specific subject and Lloyd didn't want to miss it. At least the teacher gave us a day's notice, he grumbled to himself.

As much as he hated to miss showing up to meet with Adam, he didn't go. He really hoped that he could get there the following Thursday. However, he told himself, not for the first time, the school had to come first.

Always prepared, Lloyd found the exam not difficult in the least. He finished very early, handed it into the teacher and went back to his desk to start writing an outline for a term paper. His momentary sharp disappointment at not being able to see Adam faded completely when his teacher stopped him on his way out of the classroom and told him that he had aced the exam – 100%. Lloyd couldn't stop grinning as he headed for the library to do some research for the term paper for which he had prepared the outline.

The following week he went to Oppenheimer Park, but neither the delivery truck nor BeeBee materialised. Mentally shrugging his shoulders, Lloyd simply carried on with his routine. *There's just nothing I can do about it until next Thursday anyhow,* he thought. *I think Lacey would be proud of me and how I am growing. I'm proud of me too,* he thought immodestly, *and I'm going to keep on doing well until I see my sister again.*

Between one thing and another, three more Thursdays evaporated before Lloyd was able to return to the park again.

On the fourth Thursday, when he arrived, BeeBee was there waiting once again. Remembering that she had stopped the other driver from leaving so that Lloyd could meet with him, he didn't bother hiding behind the tree. He walked over to BeeBee, asked her if she minded if he waited with her. She shrugged her shoulders and said, "Do what you want, I ain't gonna stop you. Just leave me do my business with the driver first."

"Sure, BeeBee, not a problem. I can do that."

Hands on her hips she glared at him. "And I don't wanna talk all the time while we're waiting, so just shut the yap, okay?"

With a smile and a wink, Lloyd affirmatively nodded his head, saying not another word.

Fifteen minutes elapsed before the pumpkin truck came. True to his word, Lloyd stayed back while BeeBee conducted her business. It was difficult for Lloyd to stand aside. He had experienced a very long wait to see Adam Draper once again, but he forced himself to wait a bit longer for his turn, albeit not patiently. Patently would probably be a better description.

At last! BeeBee lumbered extremely slowly towards Lloyd. He swore she was doing it on purpose. Sure enough, when she got right up to Lloyd she winked and walked even slower!

Before he could react, though, the driver got out of the truck. He wore a toque pulled down low on his forehead so at first Lloyd could not tell if it was Adam. The man seemed too short to be Adam.

The driver approached Lloyd, stopped and stared. "Lloyd? Lloyd Jordan? Really? How nice to run into you again! What are you doing in Vancouver?"

Lloyd couldn't speak. He just stared dumbly at Zach Olivier. His temper threatened to explode despite the fact that Lloyd knew that if he wanted to obtain any information out of Zach as to the whereabouts of his parents, he had to keep his emotions reined in tightly.

Lloyd's eyes drifted between Zach and the side panel of the pumpkin truck. Slapping the heel of his hand against his forehead, Lloyd moaned aloud. "I'm such a dope! 'ZO'S HAULING'! Of course! Zach Olivier, Z O – you're ZO'S HAULING! It never entered my head, not for one second."

"No reason it should have, Lloyd. Been a long time since we saw each other, man. How are you doing? You look great." Zach truly seemed perplexed when Lloyd reacted so bitterly to his question.

Lloyd said flatly, "As if you give a rat's butt how I am doing. But, since you ask, Lacey and I have had probably the ugliest of lives since you snitched on us. Do you know that Lacey and I were in five, count 'em, FIVE foster homes? Of those five placements, there was one that was just okay and one that was really great. The other three were so bad that the foster parents should be criminally charged. And do you know that in three of those five so-called 'homes', three teenage girls ran away because of abuse?"

Zach had the grace to look embarrassed. "I didn't know that, Lloyd. I never heard anything more about you kids after that day in the prison. I was just helping out a friend, your dad. Your father asked me as a favour to contact the Child Welfare people. When he told me that your mother had taken off and left you two little kids all alone, I really thought we were doing the best thing for you both." Zach looked stricken and sick as Lloyd's summary of the foster homes belatedly sunk in.

After an uncomfortable silence, Zach spoke again. "Believe me when I tell you, Lloyd, that if I had known how it would turn out for you and your sister, I would have tracked you down. My intention was to make your life better until Paul got out of prison, to keep you warm, fed and safe. How was I to know it wouldn't be safe? The Child Welfare system is supposed to protect kids like you, not abuse them. I'm so sorry, man, I am truly sorry."

The unshed moisture in Zach's eyes, as well as the pleading tone of his voice, failed to move Lloyd. He didn't like the bitter taste in his mouth as he stared at the grovelling man, but he was helpless to change how he felt.

"What can I do, man?" Zach asked. "You name it. I'll do anything to make this right."

Lloyd stared scornfully at Zach. "Nothing can make what you did right, Zach, but there are two things that you can do for me."

"Anything, man, anything!" Zach said.

"First, you can tell me where my father is. I don't mean a vague answer either, I want an address. Next, I want to know what happened to my mother. Again, I want an address. If you don't have either address, then I want you to find out where my parents are, one way or another. That won't make up for you being a rat, but it will go part of the way to righting a terrible mess."

Zach turned his back to Lloyd and started to walk away. Lloyd reached forward and yanked Zach's arm.

So furious that his face had turned such a dark red it looked purple, Lloyd screamed at Zach. "What the heck do you think you're doing, Zach? You asked me what I needed, I told you, and now you are walking away?"

Zach threw both his hands up in the air. "Cool it, Lloyd, I'm just going to the truck to get my address book. Hold on to your horses, I'll be right back."

Not trusting Zach for a second, Lloyd walked with him to the cab of the truck. He reached in and grabbed the keys from the ignition, locking them tightly within his fist. He was taking no chances with this weasel. Still holding on to the truck keys, Lloyd walked over to a park bench and sat, prepared to wait for as long as it took for Zach to sift through all the junk he had strewn throughout the cab of the truck. Lloyd couldn't help but wonder how the owner of a company could let his property turn into such a disastrous mess.

After an uncomfortable wait, Zach finally emerged from the cab, a small leather book in his hand.

Leafing through the pages, Zach said to Lloyd, "I'll give you the latest address I have for your dad. I haven't seen him for a while, but as far as I know, you can find him at this address." Zach wrote it down on a blank piece of paper at the back of the address book, tearing out the page and handing it to Lloyd. "I swear, I don't know where your mother is. Your dad might know, but I don't have a clue."

Lloyd made sure the address was legible before he handed the truck keys back to Zach. Then he turned and walked away from Zach Olivier, not acknowledging him in any way. He held the note tightly in his hand, his life preserver, he hoped!

Suddenly, Lloyd gasped, turned around and ran towards Zach. Zach looked momentarily startled, thinking perhaps that the kid had lost his mind and was going to attack him. He backed up several steps before Lloyd reached him.

Puffing heavily, Lloyd asked Zach, "Those three girls that went missing from foster homes in northern Alberta were in the same foster homes as Lacey and I. They ran away at three different times but every one of them was picked up by your 'ZO'S HAULING' truck. If you really want to make things up with me, tell me this – were you the driver who picked up the hitchhikers?"

"No, Lloyd, I swear to you, I wasn't the driver."

"Well," Lloyd continued, "if you weren't the driver, you must have talked about the missing girls with your drivers. Northern Alberta had three missing teenagers in a very short time. That's big news. Did any of your drivers tell you where they dropped them off?"

Zach looked at Lloyd for a long moment before he answered. "I guess I owe you this, Lloyd. It's not much, but I can tell you that Adam Draper told me that he dropped the girls off in Hope, B.C. What happened to them after that, I have no clue. None of us heard from them. Heck, we didn't even know their last names until we heard about those girls on the news." He sighed heavily, shrugging his shoulders. "If I knew anything more, I'd tell ya, kid, honest I would."

Lloyd glared at Zach, disbelief radiating from him like an electrical charge. He turned on his heel and headed away from the loading zone.

Lloyd didn't consider himself religious in any way since all the foster home fiascos, but as he walked towards home, he prayed. *Dear Lord, please let this address be my dad's. Please let him tell me where my mother is, and maybe he'll even be able to give me some guidance as to how to find the missing girls. Please let my long wait be over. Thank you, Lord. Amen.*

Feeling slightly guilty about praying *only* when he needed something, Lloyd nonetheless felt better by the time he reached the house. Approaching the door, he was surprised to see lights on inside. Glancing at his watch, it read 6:32. Really, he thought, that took up a lot more time than I envisioned.

Mona Grace was in the kitchen fixing supper. Looking up, she smiled at Lloyd, asking, "How did it go? Did you speak with Adam Draper?"

"Hang on for a couple of minutes and I'll tell you all about it," Lloyd said.

Coming out of the bathroom, he asked what he could do to help with supper. She told him everything was under control, would he please just sit down and fill her in. Her curiosity was killing her!

While they ate, Lloyd told Mona Grace all about his day, ending with the news that the girls had each apparently been dropped off somewhere in the town of Hope, B.C.

"Where?" Mona Grace asked. "Where in Hope did they get dropped off? Why there? All three of them at the same place, although at different times?"

Giving a nonchalant shrug of his shoulders, Lloyd said, "Your guess is as good as mine. Zach could have just been filling me full of bull-crap. He wanted to get on the road. He could have made that up on the spur of the moment just so I would leave him alone." Quiet for a minute, he looked over at Mona Grace. "But you know, somehow I believed him. When I hitched a ride with Adam Draper, he made a delivery stop in Hope. I couldn't begin to tell you where it was, but I seem to remember it was a really old and crappy mobile home. It was parked a block away from some other mobile homes. Like I say, though, I don't know if Zach was telling the truth or not. His record of truth-telling is pretty skinny as far as I'm concerned."

They had just finished cleaning up the kitchen when Lloyd stopped. "Hang on, Mona Grace, I forgot to look at the address that Zach gave me. He said that as far as he knows, it's my dad's last-known address." He went into his room and got the slip of paper out of his jacket pocket.

Returning to the living room, he handed it to Mona Grace. "Do you know where this address is?"

"Hmm," she mused. "I'm not sure, but I think that it's not that far from here. If I remember correctly, you have to go down an alley to get to the building entrances for quite a few addresses like this one, but I can't tell you for sure. There are a lot of strange addresses in this part of Vancouver, difficult to find." Sorry that she couldn't be of more help, she handed the piece of paper back to Lloyd. "Maybe tomorrow someone else may be able to tell you where it is."

"Yeah," Lloyd said, thinking that perhaps BeeBee might know. "Thanks anyway, Mona Grace. I'll check around tomorrow after work. I have a city map in my backpack. I'll check further tomorrow."

Just before his bedroom door closed, he called out, "By the way, I have an appointment to see that policeman, Sergeant Gablehaus, again next Thursday. I hope that meeting goes better than the last time I was there! And I really hope he doesn't arrest me for something, even though the only thing I did wrong was take off before we had a chance to talk. I guess I'm worried that he will send me back to Alberta before I can accomplish the things here that I came to do."

Thinking of something else, he called out yet again, "Hey, Mona Grace, I had my eighteenth birthday last Friday. That makes me legal age in Alberta. I know British Columbia's legal age is nineteen – do you think that makes me a minor here, or, as an Albertan temporarily in B.C., does it make me the age of majority?"

Mona Grace stuck her head out of the bathroom door, speaking around a mouthful of toothpaste. "Does it matter? You have to be a resident of British Columbia for at least three months and be nineteen before you can vote. There's no election pending so you don't need to worry about that. You have to be nineteen to get into the bars in B.C. but you don't drink, so you don't have to worry about that either. Why do you ask?"

"I guess I am just wondering if they can ship me back to Alberta because I'm not nineteen."

"Ask the Sergeant. He'll tell you. But you know, I really don't think he will do that. You are eighteen years old, you have a local address, you have a job, you're going to school, and making excellent grades, I might add. You have never been in any legal trouble. When you explain that you are looking for your parents, I'm sure he can give you some tips about finding them. And, don't forget to show him that address. He'll know where it is."

As Mona Grace exited the bathroom, Lloyd opened his mouth to ask something else. "Good night, Lloyd," she said and closed her bedroom door firmly. "See you tomorrow!"

"Yeah, tomorrow," Lloyd whispered as he crawled into his bed. He placed the piece of paper containing the address where his father supposedly would be carefully on the dresser beside his school backpack, He would hang onto that piece of paper just in case, he thought, but he had already memorised it.

Just as his eyes were closing, Mona Grace hollered at the top of her voice, "WHAT? YOU TURNED 18 AND YOU DIDN'T SAY ANYTHING? HAPPY LATE BIRTHDAY DOUGH-HEAD."

Lloyd gave a soft chuckle and closed his eyes.

At last, silence!

***

3:30 a.m.

Exhausted, he reached the rocky beach. He swore as he slipped while trying to throw himself up on to the jetty. He caught himself but not before his knee banged painfully against the side of the ancient wooden structure.

He attempted clumsily to untie the equally ancient wooden canoe but his bleeding fingers were stiff with cold. Finally, the knot broke free. He lunged into the craft, picked up an oar, prayed that the canoe would float. He began to paddle hard. Rounding the end of the island he spied the other canoe in the distance, already nearing the far end of the lake. He called out, but the wind direction and the exhaustion in his entire being made it impossible for his voice to carry that far. Tears of frustration, heart pounding with anxiety and disappointment, he turned the canoe around and headed slowly back to the jetty. He collapsed on the shore and, chest on fire, he breathed raggedly until his breathing evened out

***

Lloyd awoke screaming, in a cold sweat, shivering violently. His sheets and his pillowcase were damp. They clung to his body, felt like a straight-jacket as he struggled to untangle himself from the cluster of bedding.

He gradually became dimly aware that Mona Grace was banging on his door. "Lloyd! Are you okay? Answer me please or I'll have to open this door and come in!"

"I'm okay, really, Mona Grace. It was just a nightmare, the same old one. Guess I'm more worked up about meeting with the police and the possibility of seeing my father than I thought. I'm so sorry I woke you. Go on back to sleep."

It took a long time, however, for Lloyd to fall asleep again. Twice he got up and had a drink of water, trying to unsuccessfully shake off the remnants of the nightmare. Finally, he managed to doze off just as the sun was starting to rise.

Mona Grace must have an early meeting, Lloyd thought. *Her alarm rang before mine today.* He lay there quietly, waiting for Mona Grace to finish in the bathroom before he got up to shower and get ready for work.

He heard her leave even though she tried to be very quiet.

When he walked into the kitchen he started to laugh. Stuck into a piece of cold and soggy toast Mona Grace had put a happy face drawn out of peanut butter, and two candles, a '1' and an '8', together with a little note:

"Happy 'LATE' 18th Birthday, Lloyd! Let's celebrate when you turn 19 – I won't forget the date so don't bother trying to be sneaky. Have a good day! MG"

The morning air was crisp. The fluffy, slow-moving clouds looked too lazy to release any rain. Birds were chirping happily and there was the easily-identifiable salty smell of the Pacific Ocean wafting through the slight breeze.

Lloyd was still chuckling as he came up behind a group of runners. He sped up and passed them. He ran the entire distance to the food wagon.

You know, he thought, as 'BURGERS 'N DAWGS' came into his peripheral view, *if I ignore the bad things, my life at this moment is actually pretty good. I have a job, a nice place to live, a great boss, a great landlady, and I'm going to school and loving it. So, Braden Lloyd Jordan,* he admonished himself, *why don't you just smarten' up? What's your problem anyhow?*

Arriving at the food wagon, Lloyd set his backpack down beside the steps so he could unlock the door, which tended to stick if you didn't pull on it with one hand while you inserted and turned the key with the other.

That's odd, he thought, *the door isn't locked. I wasn't working yesterday, but I know I definitely locked it on Wednesday when I left. Shelby was working yesterday, but she would never leave the door unlocked in a million years.* He pushed gingerly on the door, his feeling of unease growing by the second. When the door was about one-third of the way open, it bumped against something and would move no further. Thoroughly alarmed now, Lloyd pressed his shoulder against the door and shoved as hard as he could. An unknown object crashed loudly as the door was freed. Lloyd fell forward into the trailer.

The interior was completely trashed. All the condiment bottles were emptied out onto the floor; the grill had been tipped over. It was lying upside down, dripping grease from the grease-catcher. All the contents of the refrigerator, the large freezer and the coolers were dumped out, melting in sticky puddles on the floor. The taps at the sink had been opened up and left running. They had overflowed, joining the mess on the floor before the water tank had emptied and the flow of water had ceased.

A tiny groan sounded from behind the door. Holding his breath, Lloyd carefully pushed the door, trembling, ardently praying that whoever did this was not still in the food wagon.

Shelby Sidor leaned against the wall of cupboards, a large lump on her forehead. Blood trickled from the top of her head, down her left cheek and onto her shirt. By the size of the pool of blood, she had whacked her head hard, had been bleeding for some time.

Glancing wildly around, Lloyd spied a clean dish towel hanging on the rack. He wet the cloth from the cold water in the sink, folded it into quarters and placed it on Shelby's bleeding head wound. "Hold this tight, Shelby," he said more calmly than he felt. "I need to call for help." Her teeth chattered but Shelby managed to nod her head slightly. The small movement had her wincing, grinding her teeth from the pain and the effort to keep the pressure on the towel. Her hand moved off her head.

"Please! Don't let go, we need to stop the bleeding," Lloyd said.

The telephone was not sitting in its usual spot. He found it lying underwater in the sink. He turned to Shelby and said, again very calmly, "Shelby, I'm just going outside for a minute to call for help. I won't be long. You just keep pressing that cloth tight. I'll be right back." Ashen-faced and shaking from cold and shock, Shelby tried to nod. It was too painful. With a deep sigh, she leaned back and waved at Lloyd to go, go, go. Lloyd practically flew out of the building, missing the bottom step and landing painfully on the side of his foot.

Luck was with him. A patrol car slowly rolled by the food wagon, on its way to the Stanley Park entrance. Lloyd ran over to the car, banged on the passenger side window. The officer stopped abruptly, got out of his vehicle. "What the—?" he exclaimed. "Why the heck did you hammer on my car?"

Lloyd couldn't speak. He simply pointed at the officer and then over at 'BURGERS 'N DAWGS'.

He finally found his voice. In a rapid staccato, he rattled, "My boss, she's injured. Someone broke in. I just got to work and found her. Please, call an ambulance! I've tried to stop the bleeding. The food wagon is trashed. Please, help! She's hurt!"

Before he finished his almost incoherent babbling, the policeman was on his radio, giving instructions. "Let's go, son," he said, "show me."

Clearly taken aback, the constable knelt down beside Shelby as they waited for the ambulance to arrive. From her shadowy, incoherent responses to his questions, he was pretty sure she had a concussion, among other injuries. He didn't press her for answers. There would be time enough for further questioning after she was examined at the hospital.

It took about twenty-five minutes for an ambulance to arrive, even though St. Paul's Hospital was only seven minutes from Stanley Park. Lloyd squeezed Shelby's hand, assured her that he would answer all the questions the police might have, told her that he would come to the hospital once things settled down and see how she was doing. The officer told Shelby that they would come to the hospital later in the day, once doctors had a chance to examine her. The constable was so pleasant, told her not to worry about anything, just concentrate on resting, told her that they wouldn't question her until she felt up to it. Grateful, she patted the officer's hand. She then squeezed Lloyd's, whispered "thank you" then closed her eyes as the paramedics lifted her out of the cold water and onto a stretcher, covering her with a heated blanket. She was so cold. She had lain in that damp wetness since eleven o'clock the night before. "Thank heavens for Lloyd," she whispered to the constable. "I don't know what I did before that tremendous young man entered my life."

Once the ambulance drove away, lights flashing, the officer guided a shell-shocked Lloyd over to a picnic bench and made him sit down. Picking up his radio the officer spoke to someone on the other end. "Can you stop at Tim Horton's on your way? Bring a box of coffee and a box of muffins. There's a young fellow here needs something to warm him up, get the blood flowing again. Thanks."

He looked at Lloyd. "Hope you drink coffee, young fellow." The constable gave a weak, bashful laugh. "Don't know why, but I always feel slightly foolish when I order from Tim Horton's. All about being stereo-typed, you know?"

Under ordinary circumstances, Lloyd would have laughed. Today, though, he barely managed a sickly smile and a brief nod of his head.

Suddenly noticing that Lloyd was wet and shaking, the policeman opened the trunk of his cruiser and withdrew a large woollen blanket. He wrapped it securely around Lloyd, before taking out his notebook and pen. "Are you up to answering some questions?" he asked.

Lloyd nodded, "Ye-ye-yes, I, I am u-u-up, up to it," he stammered. So cold that his jaw would barely move, he pulled the blanket tighter and tried to stop vibrating. "But, b-b-but I d-d-don't know much."

Just then a second police vehicle pulled up. A female officer got out, carrying a large box of coffee and a carton of half muffins/half doughnuts. Returning to her car briefly, she came back holding paper cups and napkins and Styrofoam plates. She poured three cups of the hot coffee, handed one to Lloyd. He nodded his thanks as she passed him packets of whitener and sugar. "Add lots of sugar," she instructed kindly. "It should help with the shock. I imagine your blood sugar is pretty low, what with all the excitement." Lloyd nodded again and shakily dumped four packs of sugar into the hot beverage. Taking his first sip, he closed his eyes, sighing. After several sips, he felt somewhat stronger.

The two officers waited considerately for Lloyd to finish his first cup of coffee; the female poured him a second one.

"Okay," Lloyd said. "I'm okay now. Ask away. I have to tell you though, that you likely know as much or more than I do. My boss, Shelby Sidor was working yesterday. It was my day off. I arrived only a few minutes before I stopped you, sir." Lloyd nodded towards the male constable.

Answering what he presumed were routine questions, Lloyd tried to be as complete as possible.

"What's your name, officer?" Lloyd asked the male policeman. "I don't think I caught your name."

"I'm sorry! I don't think I gave it to you. I'm Constable Brian Barker and my partner here is Constable Betty Evans. Now, let's get on with the questioning." The constable opened his notebook, prepared to begin.

"No, sir, Constable Barker," Lloyd said in response to the officer's first question, "Shelby – Mrs Sidor – keeps the books at her home. She brings them with her every day that she is working, and does the day's entries before she leaves here, but she always takes the books and the cash home with her when she leaves."

"What about the days when you are working? What happens with the bookwork then?"

"I keep all the receipts and the cash in a lockbox," Lloyd said. "Shelby has a small safe installed behind the medicine cabinet in the bathroom. To get to the safe you have to push what looks like a small screw, holding it pushed in while you slide the mirror to the right. The safe fits into the structure of the wall behind the mirror. I secure the lockbox and then put it in the safe before I leave. I always make sure the safe is locked and the mirror securely slid back into place before I leave."

"Can you open the safe for me now, Lloyd?" Constable Betty Evans questioned.

"Of course." Lloyd rose and shakily walked back to the trailer, followed by both police officers.

The medicine cabinet was undisturbed; the mirror looked just like any other mirror on a bathroom cabinet. Lloyd slid back the mirror. He opened the safe. Just as he had said, the safe was empty. Shelby had worked the day before; she took everything from the safe home with her.

When the officers were through examining the safe, they motioned for Lloyd to lock it up once again.

"Good system," Constable Barker murmured to Lloyd. "Not one I've seen before."

"Shelby's – Mrs Sidor's husband made it," Lloyd offered.

"Talented man. Does he work here also?"

"No," Lloyd answered. "He passed away. Mrs Sidor is all alone."

"What about insurance?" interrupted Constable Evans. "I sure hope your boss has insurance!"

"She does," Lloyd said. He named the insurance company. "But you will have to ask my boss about the details. I've never seen the policy myself."

Lloyd eyed the mess, feeling overwhelmed. "Should I start cleaning up? I have to open to the public for lunch at eleven, and it's going to take some time to get this in shape."

Constable Barker looked grim. "Sorry, Lloyd, but the insurance company is going to have to do their thing before this business can be repaired and ready. We'll get the details from your boss. If she is able to speak with her insurance agent when we see her later, we can let you know what's up. Have you got a telephone number where we can reach you?"

Lloyd gave him Mona Grace's home telephone number. "I'll be home most of the day, but I go to night school. My landlady does have an answering machine though, so if you can't reach me, please leave a message."

"I can do that," Constable Barker said. "Here's my card. I'll keep in touch."

"Any more questions for me?" asked Lloyd.

"No, I don't. Oh yes, I do! How are you going to get home?"

"Walk," Lloyd said. "Sometimes I ride my bike, but today I felt like running, so I did."

Officer Evans smiled at Lloyd. "Where do you live?" Lloyd gave her the address. "That's right on my way back to the detachment," she said. "Want a ride?"

Thankful, Lloyd nodded.

Dropping him off at the small house, the constable smiled at Lloyd. "You've had a tough day and you look frozen nearly to death. If you don't mind a suggestion, take a hot bath!"

"Thanks for the ride, ma'am," Lloyd said. "I am going to take your advice. Here's the blanket back that Officer Barker wrapped around me."

By the time Lloyd had a long soak in the tub, during which he had a long nap, it was well into the afternoon.

He looked up the phone number for St. Paul's Hospital and dialled. He obtained Shelby's room number from the receptionist, then asked to speak with someone at the Nurses' Station on the ward where Shelby Sidor was a patient. Lloyd waited impatiently on the line for his call to be put through.

"Nurses' Station, Leona speaking," a bored-sounding voice announced.

"Yes, Leona, my name is Braden Lloyd Jordan. My boss, Shelby Sidor, was admitted this morning, injured in a break-in? Can you please let me know how she is doing?"

"Are you family?" She obviously hadn't picked up on Lloyd's mention that Shelby Sidor was his boss.

Time for a little white lie. "Yes, ma'am!" This was said with Lloyd's hands behind his back, fingers superstitiously crossed.

"She's a very lucky woman," said Nurse Leona. "Mrs Sidor sustained a concussion from a blow to the head. Doctor Black stitched up the laceration – it took twenty stitches. Let me see, what else. Oh yes, several broken ribs, left side. Her left wrist is fractured, there is a severe crack in the radius, again left arm, and the ulna is badly broken. Her left shoulder is dislocated. They have her scheduled for surgery to repair her arm and pin her shoulder at five o'clock this afternoon. Doctor Black says it looks as if someone very heavy literally stomped up and down on her entire left side. She is so bruised, there isn't a centimetre of normal-coloured skin showing on that arm.

"One last thing, she's going to need to see her dentist once her jaw heals. She must have been kicked in the teeth. She is missing two, and a couple more are loose. Her lower left jaw is cracked, but it should heal on its own."

Lloyd felt sick. "That's awful. How long do you think she'll be in the hospital? I know you can't say for sure, but can you please give me your best estimate?"

Nurse Leona sighed. "Well, honey," she said, "it won't be for several days, that much I can tell you. And even when she does go home, she is going to need some help until she heals more."

"Thank you, Nurse Leona," Lloyd said. "One final thing. Would you be so kind as to tell Shelby that Lloyd will be up to see her tomorrow? I have night school tonight, but I'll be there tomorrow for sure." Empathy for his boss was choking him. Lloyd sounded devastated even to his own ears. Nurse Leona certainly heard the desolation in his voice.

"Not a problem, Lloyd," she said kindly. "I will be sure to tell her."

After he hung up, Lloyd suddenly couldn't fathom spending the rest of the day in an empty house. Hastily throwing on a jacket, he headed to the shelter, needing to talk with Mona Grace.

For the second time in one day, Lloyd was lucky. The first time was when the police cruiser was right outside the food wagon. The second time was when he arrived at the shelter and found that Mona Grace had time to see him. He followed her down the hall to her office and sunk into one of the leather chairs.

For the next three-quarters of an hour, Lloyd recounted the day. Mona Grace just sat and listened, instinctively realising that Lloyd really needed to vent.

At the end of his narration, he began a diatribe, vowing earnestly to find out who had committed this crime against his boss; to make whomever had committed the vandalism pay for their actions. From the amount of damage inflicted, Lloyd was almost certain that more than one person was involved.

Feeling much steadier, Lloyd stood up to leave. "Thanks, Mona Grace, for your ear. I have night school this evening. Having temporarily released some of my frustration, I can at least now go and concentrate on my schoolwork. Tomorrow I need to go and see Shelby. It's Saturday, but my job will be on hold for a while, at least until the insurance company gives us the go-ahead to clean up the mess. See you later."

The following afternoon, Lloyd set out for St. Paul's Hospital. He had decided to walk and save himself the trouble of figuring out what to do with his bike if he rode it.

After getting directions from the receptionist, Lloyd stopped at the Nurses' Station on the third floor to make sure it was okay for him to visit. The Unit Clerk checked her records and told him it was okay. Just as he turned to go to her room, an older nurse stopped him. "Are you Lloyd?"

"Yes, ma'am. Do I know you?"

She smiled at him. "Only indirectly, young man. I'm Nurse Leona. We spoke on the telephone yesterday."

"Yes, I remember," Lloyd said. "Thank you very much for your help. I appreciated it very much."

"Just a quick comment, Lloyd, and then you can go in and see Mrs Sidor. She looks pretty scary. There is extensive swelling and bruising. Don't be alarmed; she looks much worse than her injuries actually are. She has nothing wrong with her that won't heal completely over time.

"She's in a great deal of pain, but she is heavily sedated. She's looking forward to seeing you, but please, when you notice that she is fading, then leave. Don't stay too long this time. By tomorrow she will be in more of a position to talk. I told the policeman and policewoman this morning that they should come back tomorrow."

She pointed towards a private room fairly close to the Nurses' Station. With a nod of thanks, Lloyd walked towards Shelby's room.

He noticed a uniformed policeman dozing on a chair outside of Shelby's room. *That's odd!* Lloyd fleetingly thought, but the image rapidly sifted through his brain like grains of sand in a windstorm. He thought no more about it as he walked into the room.

He couldn't help himself. Lloyd cried out with alarm at his first glimpse of Shelby. His boss lay on the bed, deathly still. A large bandage covered a good-sized portion of the left side of her skull. Her entire face was a mass of lacerations and bruising. Lloyd would be hard-pressed to see any undamaged skin. Her eyelids were two swollen globes, only a skinny slit in each eyelid permitted Shelby to see dimly out. Her left arm was cast from the heel of her left hand all the way up to several inches above her elbow. Her shoulder was heavily bandaged and the entire arm and shoulder were immobilised against the side of her body, secured by long ribbons of gauze wrapped around her arm and shoulder, all the way around her entire body. Each gauze strip was tied against her right side.

She spoke weakly, her gravelly voice barely above a whisper. "Hey, Lloyd, come closer so I can see you. As you can see for yourself, a zombie has nothing on me! It looks worse than I feel." With her loose and missing teeth and a cracked jawbone, Lloyd had to listen hard to understand her at first. However, as she continued to talk, his comprehension improved.

"Take a load off, my boy. Pull up a chair where I can see you and so I don't have to strain my voice."

Lloyd's knees were wobbling. He happily fell into a chair and sat to Shelby's left, her injured side, being very careful not to touch the bed.

"No point in asking you how you feel," Lloyd said wryly, "but, do you want to go dancing?"

Shelby tried to smile, groaned and gave up. "Please, Lloyd," she said, gasping painfully, "no jokes. I have enough trouble breathing with broken ribs, let alone laughing!"

"I'm sorry," Lloyd said contritely. He sat quietly for several minutes while Shelby concentrated on getting her breathing under control.

Finally, Lloyd asked, "Do you know an armed policeman is sitting outside your door?"

"I do," she said simply.

"Why?" Lloyd asked, staring down at his hands. No answer. Looking over he saw that Shelby was asleep. He got up and left the room. Stopping at the desk, he asked the clerk to let Mrs Sidor know that he, Lloyd, would be back to see her tomorrow at two o'clock when visiting hours began.

The following day, Lloyd was at the hospital right at two. He had ridden his bike, locked it securely to a bicycle rack he had spotted the day before.

Arriving at her room, he noticed Constables Barker and Evans standing at the doorway, speaking to the officer keeping watch outside Shelby's room. Spotting Lloyd, they both smiled, then gestured for him to follow them into the room.

If possible, Shelby looked more battered and bruised today than she had the day before. She reached for Lloyd's hand with her uninjured one, whispered, "Hello Lloyd, please sit." She continued to hold on to his hand tightly as she focused her attention on the officers.

"Are you perhaps up to a few questions today?" asked Constable Evans.

Shelby nodded in the affirmative.

"At your request, Mrs Sidor, we have posted an officer outside your door for your protection, just as a precaution. Do you remember asking us for this service yesterday?"

Shelby looked apologetic. “I’m sorry, I don’t remember much.”

“That’s okay, ma’am,” Constable Barker said. “If you don’t mind, we will just start over again. Please answer as clearly as you can. If you get too tired, just say so and we will stop so you can rest.”

“Thanks.” Shelby had to speak through her stiff, cracked jaw. Between the pain meds and her hoarse voice, she hoped to be able to answer all of their questions so that they wouldn’t have to return.

Constable Barker took out his notebook and a recording device. Constable Evans, the female officer (FO) began the questioning:

FO:	“Do you know who could have done this to you, ma’am?”
SHELBY:	Nods in the affirmative
FO:	“I’m sorry, Mrs Sidor, you’ll have to answer aloud. This is being recorded. I realise that your voice is very weak. Is it okay if this officer sits beside you so you don’t have to speak so loudly?”
SHELBY:	Points to a vacant chair to her left.
FO:	“Now, again, Mrs Sidor. Do you know who could have done this to you?”
SHELBY:	(Weakly) “Yes.”
FO:	(Surprised) “Really? Who?”
SHELBY:	“Gang members.”
FO:	“Which gang?”
SHELBY:	“East Van Devils”
FO:	“East Van Devils? Are you certain? How do you know?”
SHELBY:	“One wore the Club’s signet ring.”
FO:	“You recognised it?”
SHELBY:	(Points to her left cheek. Emblazoned on her cheek was a clear outline of the EVD insignia, standing for East Van Devils. It appeared as if tattooed into Shelby’s flesh.) “Heated it on the stove. Pressed it into my cheek. Hurt.”
FO:	(Pale, visibly shaken.) “And what about the second man, Mrs Sidor? Was he wearing a signet ring as well?”
SHELBY:	(Shakes her head.) “Sorry, no. He wore gang’s colours. The jacket looked new.”
FO:	“Are you okay, Mrs Sidor? Would you like to take a break?”
SHELBY:	(Emphatically.) “No, I’m okay.” (Takes another sip of water from the glass that Lloyd is holding for her)
FO:	“Okay. Now, Mrs Sidor, why do you think they attacked you and trashed your food wagon?”
SHELBY:	(Authoritatively.) “I don’t think, I KNOW why.”
FO:	(Waits for Shelby’s coughing spasms to stop.) “Please, tell us why?”
SHELBY:	“I won’t pay their protection money.”
FO:	“Uh, huh! Did they ask for money?”

SHELBY:	"Several times." (Points to water glass and straw – Lloyd assists her.)
FO:	"Can you be more specific? I know, it hurts you to talk but if we are going to catch these thugs, we need as much info as you can give us. First of all, though, can you describe these two men for us?"
SHELBY:	(Closes the slits in her eyelids, as her eyes are already nearly closed.) "Two men. Young guy a big bruiser, like, a bouncer? One maybe early twenties. The other maybe late thirties, early forties. Older man about my height, the younger man maybe his. (Points to male officer.) Young one, black hair, maybe native. Older one appeared to be observing."
FO:	"Would you recognise them if you saw them again?"
SHELBY:	"Older man, maybe. Younger one for sure. Had a tattoo on his leg, above his boot."
FO:	"Can you describe the tattoo?" (Waits for Shelby to drink more water, and for the nurse, who has entered the room to inject more pain meds into her intravenous line.)
FO:	"Now, again Mrs Sidor, can you describe the tattoo?"
SHELBY:	"Yes, saw it clearly when he kicked my face. Pantleg came up. Right leg, on calf, just above the ankle bone. Large; skull and crossbones. Said 'DEVILS' under it. Black and white."
FO:	"Are there any other identifiable features about the Tattoo man that you can recall?" (Notes Shelby's utter exhaustion.) "Mrs Sidor, do you want to stop for now? We can return later after you've had a chance to rest."
SHELBY:	(Weary but emphatic.) "No, please, I'm okay. Meds are starting to help. I want to finish. Important. Ask me again?"
FO:	(Waits for nurse to place ice pack on Shelby's cheek.) "I asked you if there are any other identifiable features about the Tattoo man that you can recall?"
SHELBY:	"Yes, more tattoos. Full sleeves on both arms, including hands. Face, head and neck completely covered with full-colour tattoos. Couldn't see any bare skin."
FO:	"What about the other man? Do you recall what he looked like?"
SHELBY:	"Not really. He was – older. Thinning grey hair, much shorter. Smaller than Tattoo man. He just watched, he didn't touch me. Cold expression, no emotion."
FO:	"That's helpful, Mrs Sidor. Did you hear either one of them refer to the other by name?"
SHELBY:	"No."
FO:	"If we bring you some photos, do you think you might be able to recognise the two men who attacked you?"
SHELBY:	(Nods her head.) "Sorry. Yes."

FO: "Just a couple more questions, Mrs Sidor. Think hard. Can you recall how many times someone approached you, offering you protection in return for a monthly sum? And, was it the same person or persons every time?"

SHELBY: "I think, four times. Calendar at home. Can give dates when I'm back home. Same man, every time. Tattoo man, kicked me."

FO: "Yes, when you are better and can go home, we would like those dates, but don't worry about them for now. So, you say the man who kicked you in the face, the 'tattoo man' as you referred to him, is the same man who approached you asking for money for the East Van Devils to provide your business with 'protection', is that correct?"

SHELBY: "Yes."

FO: "Was he alone? Each time he asked you for money?"

SHELBY: "No, older man was with him. Older man just stood back, watched. He didn't ask for money."

FO: "How much money are we talking about here?"

SHELBY: "Lots. More than I could pay."

FO: "Can you give me an amount?"

SHELBY: "$5,000.00 a month. Price went up by $1,000.00 each time he came and demanded the money. That's more than I usually clear in some months."

FO: "What did you tell the tattoo man when he asked you for $5,000.00, $6,000.00, $7,000.00 and finally $8,000.00 per month?"

SHELBY: "What I said. More than I can pay, sorry. Leave me alone, I told him."

FO: "And what did he say?"

SHELBY: "Said if I didn't pay, he'd kill me."

FO: "Did you believe him?"

SHELBY: (Calmly) "Yes."

FO: "And that's why you asked for police protection outside of your hospital room, is that correct?"

SHELBY: (Nods her head painfully.) "Sorry. Yes."

FO: "Despite the tattoo man saying he would kill you if you didn't pay up, you still kept telling him no, correct?"

SHELBY: "Correct."

FO: "Would you be willing to testify against him in Court?"

SHELBY: "Yes."

FO: "Aren't you afraid he will kill you if you do?"

SHELBY: (Calmly, clearly) "I don't care if he does."

FO: "Mrs Sidor, that's a strange comment. Why do you say you don't care if the tattoo man kills you?"

SHELBY: "My husband is dead. I will testify. If Tattoo man gets convicted, good for me. If he gets off, then, well, I get to join my husband."

FO: (Horrified) "Mrs Sidor, if it comes to that, and I pray to God it does not, then the R.C.M.P. can offer you witness protection. Would you be willing, if necessary, to change your identity and move away, start again, somewhere safe?"

SHELBY: "I would think about it. Either way, I will testify. Tired, now. Need sleep. Bring pictures, I'll pick them out for you – tomorrow."

Lloyd stood up to leave with the officers. Patting his boss gently on her good shoulder he said, "You need to rest now. I will come back tomorrow. Hopefully, you will feel well enough by then to contact your insurance agent. I want to clean up the food wagon, but I cannot until your insurance agent gives the okay. Please, try not to worry. Just rest and get better."

Turning away from the bed, Lloyd left the room, nodded once again to the police officer sitting in the hallway, left the hospital, and rode home on his bike.

At supper that evening, Lloyd told Mona Grace all about his day. He rarely, if ever, swore but he couldn't help himself. "Dammit, Mona Grace, Shelby is such a wonderful, kind-hearted woman. How could that thug actually stomp on her face, kick out her teeth, crack her jaw? How could he be so ruthless, or live with himself after he did that? And even more perplexing, how could that second man just stand there and watch without trying to stop the attack?" Mona Grace simply shook her head; after all, what was there to say that could even begin to justify such evil?

"Strictly a rhetorical question, Mona Grace." After all, nothing anyone could say would make it right.

"So, Lloyd," Mona Grace asked, "Any word from the insurance adjusters yet?"

"No, Shelby isn't up to dealing with that yet. Hopefully tomorrow or the next day. Like I told you, she is continuing to pay me even though I can't do anything. I sure hope the insurance settlement is quick; I just don't feel right accepting her money when I'm not actually doing anything."

Lloyd put his head in his hands, visibly miserable.

"You don't feel like you are doing anything, Lloyd," Mona Grace said gently, "but you are. You're easing Shelby's mind so she can heal faster. She knows she can count on you. You are a great comfort to her. I suspect she was a very lonely, ageing woman before you came into her life."

"I assume you are going to the hospital again tomorrow?"

"Yes. I want to be there to see the photos the police are bringing. If she can identify those two animals, it will save the other business people in that area a lot of headaches."

Lloyd stood up, stretched. "Well, I better get to my night class. See you tomorrow sometime."

After Lloyd left, Mona Grace simply sat at the table, shaking her head. *That kid has had more than his share of troubles,* she thought, *Please Lord, can you cut him a break? He doesn't ask for anything for himself, and his heart is made of pure compassion. Please, just cut him a small break.*

The next day dawned cloudy, threatening rain. Rather than walk, Lloyd chose to ride his bike. He rode firstly to the food wagon. It was surrounded by yellow police tape which read *'Crime Scene, Do Not Enter'*. Ignoring the tape, Lloyd bent underneath it and checked the door to be sure it was still locked. It was. He crawled back under the tape, looked at his watch. Too early to go to the hospital.

Despite the fine mist that was leaking like tiny teardrops from the sky, he decided to bike through Stanley Park, not only to kill time until he could go to St. Paul's and visit with his boss (and clearly, good friend), but to clear his head.

The park was nearly deserted on this drizzly early afternoon. Only die-hard runners braved the chilly dampness.

Lloyd pedalled through the park at a moderate speed, taking time to notice various trees and plants as he rode along; taking the time to sniff the slightly musty but pleasant odours of the rain forest. Finally, exiting the park, he rode back to the food wagon once more, this time stopping outside the police tape.

He sat down at a picnic table and simply stared forlornly at the empty trailer. A couple of people who also had businesses in the area stopped and inquired about Shelby, clearly worried and concerned. He replied that she was doing pretty well, all things considered but was still in a lot of pain. When a third businessman appeared to be approaching, Lloyd couldn't face more conversation. He quickly stood up, grabbed his bike and headed towards the hospital.

Arriving outside Shelby's room, he nodded politely towards the policeman stationed in the hallway, and then he entered the room.

Shelby was sleeping, a deep scowl creasing her forehead, even in slumber. Lloyd sat down beside her bed, removed a textbook from his backpack, and studied while waiting for her to wake up.

"Well, what a pleasant surprise!" Shelby broke the silence an hour later, her raucous voice sounding like a very old automobile trying to start but not quite succeeding.

Lloyd put his textbook back in his pack and smiled as he turned towards Shelby. "Nice to see you almost smiling," he said. "Do you feel any better today?"

A deep croak, masquerading as a dry laugh, eased its way cautiously out of her throat. "Yeah," she said wryly, "I now only feel like a single car of a freight train hit me, as opposed to the entire line of freight cars."

Lloyd winced visibly. "Ouch! Want me to call the nurse?"

"No thanks, Lloyd, I want to try and lengthen the time between pain meds if I can."

"Have the police been here yet today?" Lloyd queried.

"Yes, sir! Here we are," chirped the pleasant voice of Officer Evans from the doorway. "Are you ready to look at some pictures, Mrs Sidor?"

“The sooner the better,” Shelby said. “Let’s do this thing.”

For the next half hour, with Lloyd assisting by holding the book and turning the pages, Shelby examined many different mug shots. From time to time, she would indicate that she would like a certain photo removed and placed in a separate pile. After that, she had Lloyd go back to the beginning of the album and she looked through it a second time. The longer she looked at the pictures, the more agitated she became.

Finally, she leaned back and rang for the nurse, who promptly arrived and gave her some medications. The nurse smiled. “I see you have graduated from pain killers by injection to pills. That’s a good sign, Mrs Sidor. However, please don’t wait until the pain is almost unbearable to ask for more medication. If you wait too long, they won’t work as well.”

“Thank you, nurse. I won’t wait so long again,” Shelby said regretfully. “I definitely waited too long just now.”

After the nurse had left the room, Shelby looked up at the police officers. She pointed to the small pile of pictures that she had had Lloyd remove from the album. Flipping them right side up on her bedside table, she merely said, “These are all photos of the two men that attacked me.”

Constable Barker looked at the pictures. Six in all, they definitely depicted the two men from several different angles, their photos portraying the two men that Shelby had described verbally the day of the attack.

“You’re sure?” he asked Shelby. “I have to ask, even though I believe you.”

“I’m sure, officer,” Shelby replied resolutely. “I am willing to swear in a Court of Law that these are the men.”

“Get someone to pick ‘em up,” Constable Evans said tersely to her partner. “But tell them not to approach alone. They’ll need a team to overpower those two. And have them get a search warrant. There could easily be some identifiable items that they took with them from the trailer. Once you make those arrangements, I’ll meet you at the detachment.”

She turned to Shelby. “Thank you so much, Mrs Sidor. You are very brave and you will be doing the City of Vancouver a tremendous service by helping us put those men behind bars.”

As the constable turned to leave, Lloyd called after her, loudly. “Ma’am, can you please wait just a minute? It’s important!”

He scrambled wildly through his backpack and came up with the crumpled piece of paper that Zach had written the address on. “Ma’am, I have a hunch. Do you recognise this address, or can you find out for me where it is?”

She looked at the address, looked up at Lloyd and said, “Why do you have this address?”

Lloyd explained that he had been told that his father, Paul Martin Jordan, resided at that address.

“Please, can you come with me? I’m going back to the detachment and there are some things we need to clear up. I’ll explain things to you when we are there.”

Alarmed, Lloyd said of course he would come to the detachment. He turned to Shelby and said that he would talk with her later. Then he quickly turned and followed the officers to their patrol car.

"Wait! My bike," Lloyd said.

"Someone will bring you back to the hospital when you're done at the detachment," said Constable Barker. "You can pick it up then."

"Okay," Lloyd said. He climbed into the back seat of the patrol car and sat silently during the ride. He had never before been in a police car. It felt very strange. Even more strange were the guilt feelings he was experiencing. He had never been in trouble with the police, so what was with the feelings? He felt a sudden chill; he shuddered. *Must be the spirits of the criminals that still resided within the vehicle*, Lloyd laughed to himself. *Or not!*

Once at the station, Constable Barker dropped his partner and Lloyd off before he went to make the arrangements to have the two thugs picked up. Constable Evans and Lloyd entered the detachment. The officer took Lloyd to an interview room. They stopped at a pop machine on the way. Lloyd got a coke; Constable Evans got a coke for herself, and a cup of coffee for her sergeant. She then went to find him, telling Lloyd she would be right back.

When she returned to the interview room, they sat, waiting. Neither Lloyd nor Constable Evans said a word. After about fifteen minutes, the door opened and Constable Barker and his sergeant entered.

"Well, well, well," exclaimed Sergeant Gablehaus, "if it isn't my young friend, Lloyd!"

Beet-red with embarrassment, Lloyd mumbled something.

"Sorry?" Sergeant Gablehaus said, "I didn't hear you."

Lloyd spoke up. "I said, sir, that I apologise for running out on you before."

"Aah!" breathed the Sergeant. "And can you tell me what that was all about?"

Lloyd sat up straighter in the uncomfortable chair. Swallowing several times, he began telling everyone in the room his story. Why he was in British Columbia, how he had arrived in East Van, what his mission was. He also explained that he was working for Shelby Sidor at the 'BURGERS 'N DAWGS' food wagon, paying rent for accommodation at Mona Grace's house, as well as going to school to get his matriculation.

He concluded his recitation with, "Sergeant Gablehaus, sir, I am so sorry I ran out on you. I panicked. I thought that when you found out that I had hitchhiked from northern Alberta to Vancouver, you would send me back to that terrible foster home without giving me a chance to find my missing foster sisters, my father or my mother." He stopped speaking, clasped his hands together on the top of the table, and waited miserably for the Sergeant to speak.

"That's quite the story, young fella," Sergeant Gablehaus began. "How old are you now?"

"I'm eighteen, sir," Lloyd said.

The Sergeant thought briefly, then summarised all that Lloyd had told him, referring to notes that he had made while Lloyd was telling his story.

"You've accomplished a lot in your life so far. Good for you, Lloyd." The Sergeant stared across the table at Lloyd for what seemed like forever but was probably a minute at the most. Gazing intently at Lloyd, he continued. "You realise, though, do you not, that we have detectives and policemen and women trained to find missing persons; that it is very dangerous for you or any other untrained person, to barge ahead on their own?"

"Yes, sir, but—"

"No buts, young fellow," Sergeant Gablehaus said. Again, he stared across the table at the visibly squirming, visibly wretched Lloyd.

"Tell me about this address that you asked my officers about."

"Zach Olivier, the owner of ZO'S HAULING, a delivery company that travels between northern Alberta and East Van, gave it to me. I had asked him if he knew where my father is. They are good friends. In fact, my father had Zach call Child Services and they picked me and my sister, Lacey, up at the prison when we were there to ask my dad for help. I figured, and still do, that Zach owed me at least that much for ratting on us to the Child Services workers, for putting Lacey and me in such dangerous living situations."

Sergeant Gablehaus sat, deep in thought. Obviously arriving at a conclusion, he sat up even straighter. He was a very intimidating figure; however, when he spoke next, his voice was gentle and compassionate.

"Lloyd, do you know where that address is, what that location is?"

"No sir, I do not, just, that is the address where Zach said I could find my father."

"That, my young friend, is the address of the clubhouse for the East Van Devils. You're sure that is the address Zach Olivier gave you? There can be no mistake?"

"No, Sergeant," Lloyd said sickly. "I double-checked it."

"You haven't been there yet, have you, Lloyd?"

"No, sir. Oh! Wait a second!" He then told them about following BeeBee as she made a parcel delivery to that address, but how Lloyd had hidden himself behind a dumpster. He was positive that the bouncer at the door had not seen him.

Sergeant Gablehaus was obviously a deep thinker. Lloyd waited impatiently. He felt as if the Sergeant spent more time thinking and staring into space than talking.

Finally, he looked over at Lloyd. "Tell you what, Lloyd. I simply cannot have you going to the East Van Devils' headquarters alone. On the other hand, I don't want a uniformed officer showing up at their door without just cause."

Officer Barker said something indistinct.

"Sorry?" Sergeant Gablehaus asked. "I didn't get that."

"I said, sir," the young officer repeated, "what about BeeBee?"

The Sergeant broke out in a grin. He said, "Heck of an idea, Barker, heck of an idea!"

Turning towards Lloyd, he said, "How about this, Lloyd. We'll arrange for you to accompany BeeBee to the East Van Devils' clubhouse. She makes regular deliveries there and seems to be the only person that has any type of friendly relationship with their doorman. You should be safe with her. Use your discretion. Let BeeBee talk first. Then, if it seems timely, you can ask the doorman if you can speak with Paul Martin Jordan.

"If your father comes out, don't say anything. Let him speak first. Wait for his lead. In exchange for allowing you to approach the gang like this, you have to promise me that you will be extremely cautious; don't say anything to create suspicion; in particular, say absolutely nothing with regards to the assault on Shelby Sidor, or the break-in of the food wagon. Stick strictly to your reunion with your dad. Don't talk about anything except your parents, your foster parents and siblings, you and your sister. Got it?"

His stomach in knots of combined tension and excitement, Lloyd could barely contain himself. "Yes, sir, Sergeant Gablehaus. I get it."

"Good. One other thing. After you meet, you need to come back here and report. If I'm not here, speak to either of these two officers." (He waved his hand in the general direction of the officers standing behind him.)

"Now, hang on while I contact BeeBee and make some arrangements." Sergeant Gablehaus rose and left the room.

Lloyd looked at the constables. "How does he know BeeBee?" Lloyd asked.

No response, so he asked again, "How does Sergeant Gablehaus know BeeBee? No, let me rephrase that, how do all three of you know BeeBee?"

Before either constable could speak, Lloyd slapped his hand against his forehead. "Ah, I got it! She's one of you, only she's an undercover cop! I should have guessed when I saw her delivering a package to the Devils' clubhouse!"

Sergeant Gablehaus heard Lloyd as he came back into the interview room. "Well, Lloyd, you are extremely smart to figure that out. Do me a favour. No matter what, make no mention of the police to your father or anyone else, not your landlady, not your friends, your boss; absolutely no one. Don't talk about BeeBee. I include in that, no mention about BeeBee's connection to this case. You would put her in extreme danger by doing so.

"Now, that being said, BeeBee says for you to meet her in Oppenheimer Park Thursday when she picks up her packages from the ZO'S HAULING driver. Sorry, I know how hard it will be for you to wait, but you'll just have to hold your horses until then.

"Any questions?"

"No, sir, I don't think so," said Lloyd.

"Okay, then. Summarise for me what you are *not* to do. I'm a big believer in summarisation as you may have noticed," Sergeant Gablehaus said earnestly.

Lloyd spoke up. "No mention of police to my dad or anyone else; not my landlady, my boss, my friends, absolutely no one other than you, BeeBee herself, Constable Barker and Constable Evans. Don't talk about this assault case, the break-in, BeeBee; absolutely no mention of BeeBee's connection to this case to anyone.

"I am to meet BeeBee on Thursday and accompany her to the East Van Devils' clubhouse.

"When I see my father, don't say anything. Let him speak first. Wait for his lead.

"The only things I can speak with my father about are my parents, my foster parents and siblings, me and my sister.

"I absolutely cannot speak with anyone with regards to the assault on Shelby Sidor, or the break-in of the food wagon.

"I have to be extremely cautious.

"Finally, I have to report back to either you or Constables Barker or Evans once I have had contact with my father.

"It also goes without saying, sir, that I must make no mention to anyone about BeeBee being an undercover cop."

Lloyd leaned back in his chair, catching his breath.

"Great! We completely understand one another, Lloyd," Sergeant Gablehaus said grimly. "Now, carry on with your schooling until Thursday. I'll talk with you after that."

"Whoops! One more thing, sir?"

"Yes, what is it?" the Sergeant asked.

"Well, the thing is, Shelby Sidor is continuing to pay my wages while the food wagon is out of commission. I'll have to talk with her about repairs to the structure once the insurance company gives us the okay to fix things up."

"Yes, I guess you will. However, make sure that you ONLY discuss things that are pertinent to getting that business repaired and in operation again. No mention of anything else, right?"

Lloyd agreed wholeheartedly. "Talk to you sometime next Thursday," he said. "Thanks for being so understanding about my chickening out on our first meeting, sir." He turned and left the room.

"Hang on a minute, Lloyd," Constable Evans called after him. "I said someone would drive you back to the hospital to pick up your bike. I'm on my way out. I'll drop you off."

"Thanks, ma'am, that would be great," Lloyd said.

As he exited the police cruiser at the hospital, Constable Evans said, "Good luck on Thursday, Lloyd. I hope you find your father and everything goes well."

Lloyd looked very sceptical but thanked the officer. He unlocked his bike, adjusted the straps on his backpack, and headed for home. His already long wait to see his father again would seem much longer as he waited for Thursday.

Chapter 16
Reunion of the Wrong Kind

When he arrived at the house, Lloyd found a note on the kitchen table from Mona Grace, saying she had an unexpected opportunity to take a week's holiday with a good friend. They were going tenting near Long Beach on Vancouver Island. *Hmm,* Lloyd thought to himself, *I hope it's a VERY GOOD friend, and of the male persuasion!* He grinned. Mona Grace was older than him. He was pretty sure she knew what she was doing, and didn't need Lloyd to look after her or her love life. He just hoped she had a wonderful week off. She deserved and really needed the time.

Lloyd was thankful that he was all by himself for a week. It would make it easier to do what he had to do with BeeBee. It would, as well, make it easier not to talk with Mona Grace about what he was doing.

Lloyd knew that the only way he could stand the wait until Thursday arrived, would be to throw himself into his studies. For once, he was grateful for the many pop quizzes that his instructors were so fond of springing on their students.

It seemed as if it was more than a month-long wait instead of just a few days, but Thursday finally arrived. He was already sitting on the closest bench to the drop-off area when BeeBee arrived. Lloyd smiled at her and opened his mouth to say something.

BeeBee held up her hand and mimed zipping her mouth closed.

"Stop right there, young Lloyd. The safest thing for you to do is not to speak at all until the time comes for you to speak with your father. I won't have you screw up this investigation. Get it?"

Lloyd understood completely and although he wanted to tell her so with words, he simply nodded his understanding. Thus, they sat on the bench, side by side, totally silent, one waiting patiently for the arrival of the pumpkin truck, the other squirming with nervous anticipation. A few times Lloyd looked kind of like a fish out of the water as his mouth repeatedly gaped open and closed wordlessly. Not wanting BeeBee to be sorry he had to tag along, he finally got used to the silence and sat more calmly.

The truck arrived, right at its usual time. Lloyd realised he had been hoping that the driver would be Adam, but it was not. It was the same driver who had filled in for Adam once before. Lloyd was disappointed. Not that Lloyd needed to speak with Adam; he had the information he needed regarding the whereabouts of his father, (at least he hoped he was still at that address), but he genuinely liked Adam and would have enjoyed even a brief visit. Once the driver had gone on his way, BeeBee came back to the bench and sat down beside Lloyd.

"Just listen, don't speak unless I tell you to," BeeBee told Lloyd in a very quiet voice. Her tone left no doubt that she meant what she said. "If you speak before it's time, or do anything else to jeopardise this operation, I'll throw you to the wolves. Understand me?"

Lloyd caught on quickly. He simply nodded his assent.

"Well, if you are ready to go, I am also. Come on, young Lloyd, let's hit the trail." With that, BeeBee stuffed several packages into her cart and started pushing her worldly possessions and delivery packages up the road. Lloyd struggled to catch up with the woman. *Wow,* he thought to himself, *this gal can really hustle!*

In a relatively short time, they approached the alleyway that lead to the shiny red door. BeeBee motioned for Lloyd to stand back beside her cart. She climbed the steps and gave the 'secret code' knock – shave and a haircut, six bits – six taps in all, then backed down a couple of steps and waited for Brutus to answer the door.

Oh Lord, Lloyd thought nervously, *help me show no fear!* He hung on tightly to the handle of BeeBee's shopping cart to hide his shaking hands.

The door opened and Brutus ('Tattoo Man' as Lloyd thought of him) came outside.

"What'cha want, woman?" he growled at BeeBee. She lifted her middle finger. Her rude gesture caused Tattoo Man to laugh heartily. "Usual deliveries, I suppose?"

Up went the middle finger again. BeeBee certainly showed no fear and she also said not a word, just waited for the giant to finish having his fun.

The two of them completed their business dealings. Brutus turned towards the door. Finally, BeeBee spoke. "Hang on there, big man," she said. "Got another delivery here, but this one is for Paul Jordan."

"Well, then," Brutus said. "Hand it over."

"No, siree," BeeBee said. "Have to deliver this parcel personally."

"Says who?" sneered the doorman.

"Says me," BeeBee responded firmly. "Ain't going nowhere until Paul Jordan comes out to accept delivery. If you ain't gonna go get him, I'll just set me down here on your steps and wait until you do."

Brutus watched her in amazement as she gathered up all her skirts and proceeded to sit down, effectively blocking the entire steps.

"Good God woman, are you wearing every piece of clothing that you own?" Brutus asked.

BeeBee gave a twisted smile. "Pretty much," she said simply.

"How's anybody supposed to get by you?" Brutus whined, by now totally frustrated with BeeBee.

"That's their problem," BeeBee said with an impish chuckle. "I'll just tell them that you wouldn't help a poor old woman in a crisis and they'll blame you, not me."

Tattoo Man rolled his eyes and growled at her. "Well, now that you are all comfy, I'll just go and see if Mr Jordan is here. Excuse me, madam!" Brutus bowed deeply from his middle, revealing a naked woman tattooed on the very top of his bald head.)

Oh Lord, Lloyd thought again, *some people's kids!* His nervousness was reaching the point where, if Paul Jordan didn't soon appear, Lloyd thought he might well just walk away and never come back.

While Brutus was gone to find Paul, BeeBee gathered up her numerous skirts and tried with great difficulty to arise from the step. Just as Lloyd was preparing to go to her aid she managed to stand up.

The door opened.

"What's this all about, BeeBee?" The voice wafted through the doorway before the speaker showed himself.

Paul Martin Jordan stood on the top landing, peering over the top of his reading glasses at BeeBee. With a deep breath, Lloyd stepped out from the handle end of the shopping cart and approached the steps. He stood below his father, looking up at him. It made Lloyd very uncomfortable, not being on even ground, so to speak.

"Hello," Lloyd simply said. "Long time no see. Out of prison, huh?"

Paul gasped, clutched his chest in a dramatic gesture. The colour drained out of his face as he said, "Lloyd? Oh, it is so wonderful to see you, son! Why are you here? How did you find me? How's your sister? You're really here?" The questions shot out in rapid succession, faster than Lloyd could process them in his own mind, let alone answer any of them.

Lloyd turned to BeeBee and quietly said, "It's okay, BeeBee, if you want to leave, I'll be fine."

"I'm not going anywhere," she whispered to Lloyd, "so don't even think that I will. I will wait for you for as long as it takes. See that old chair over there, by the dumpster? You probably recognise that dumpster, right?" (She grinned as she said it.) "I'll just sit me down on that chair and wait for you. Don't worry, I brought a lunch and a book to read." She turned and pushed her cart over to the dumpster, gathered her many skirts around her pudgy thighs and sat down.

Lloyd shrugged, resigned to the fact that when he finished with his father, BeeBee would still be waiting. Actually, if the truth be known, he was very relieved to know it.

He turned back to his father. "I'm not going to be answering your questions in any particular order," Lloyd said sarcastically. "I came to find you. How I found you is not any of your concern, really. Lucky for you that I did the finding, though, because it saved you the trouble or bother of YOU finding ME. I heard through the grapevine that you were out of prison. I came to B.C. for a number of reasons. The main ones were to see if I could find my parents. I guess, mainly, I'm hoping that you can tell me where my mother is."

Paul Jordan stood quietly. He at least had the grace to look embarrassed as his son bitterly spit out his reasons.

"Son, it certainly wasn't that I cared if it would be a lot of trouble or bother to search for you. But, you see, I got out of prison and had to find myself before I was in any shape to find my two children, let alone care for two kids by myself.

"It's not easy to find a job when you are an ex-con, but I have found a new home and a great career. I've been so busy learning the ropes that I haven't had time for anything else. I probably, no, strike that, I would have looked for you eventually."

Lloyd felt like he had been sucker-punched. He let out a heart-wrenching sigh that extended from his toes and up through the top of his head. He hadn't realised just how terribly angry he was with Paul Jordan; just how much he had dismissed Paul in his mind, as a father.

"Well, take a load off and let's talk awhile." Lloyd patted the cement step, two below the one he was sitting on. He had no intention of giving his biological sperm donor any power over Lloyd. Thus, he wanted to be sitting looking down on Paul Jordan, (both physically and psychologically) as they talked.

Paul looked painfully uncomfortable, but he did as his son asked. For several minutes, the two men sat, saying not a word.

Finally, breaking the uneasy silence, Lloyd spoke first. "So, tell me about this new, important job, a job that is so important you would forget about reuniting with your wife and children. It intrigues me, this job that is so wonderful. What is the title of this glorious position?"

The acid-dripping sarcasm was not lost on Paul. He recoiled visibly from Lloyd's tone of voice, but then suddenly Paul stood up, pointed an accusatory finger at Lloyd and authoritatively uttered through his clenched teeth, "That is enough, young man! That's no way to speak with your father, or for any other adult, for that matter."

Lloyd said, calmly, quietly, but perfectly audibly, "I don't consider you my father any more, Paul. In fact, I won't bother you again after this meeting. I do want to know, though, if you know where my mother is."

Lloyd was not, nor had he ever been, the sort of person to be deliberately rude or cruel to any other person. However, today, his anger had viciously sparked inside of him like a downed live wire in a lightning storm. He could not seem to control his anger, his words or his tone of voice.

Lloyd covertly glanced over at BeeBee. She ignored him. Lloyd was almost positive that she was taping the conversation between the two Jordan males. Somehow this made him feel more raw and exposed; however, he pushed his feelings to the back of his brain and turned his full attention back to Paul Jordan.

Paul appeared to be mulling over exactly what and how much he would tell his son about his life in and out of prison. Finally, he decided that there was nothing to be gained by lies or omissions and he began to talk.

"Well, son," (Paul failed to notice Lloyd wincing painfully as he called him 'son'.) "I got very lucky. While in the Mountain Institution at Agassiz, my fellow inhabitants learned that I was an accountant. They started coming to me for assistance with their money management problems. I developed quite a practice while there. Helped me immensely to keep my skills up to date. I had use of the library at the prison and so was able to keep myself updated on any tax changes, loopholes, things like that. The Warden was very accepting of any requests that the inmates had for additions to the library. Consequently, I had updated tax volumes every tax season.

"Anyhow, to make a long story shorter, just before my release, I had a visitor. A fellow named Domingo Sanchez. He was, and still is, the head of the East Van Devils, a local group of – businessmen, you might say. Said he was looking for a guy just like me, a smart accountant who could head up the entire financial affairs of the Devils. The starting salary was far more than I ever made at the firm where I worked before I was sent to prison. It was a salary that I could not pass up. I shook Domingo's hand immediately, sealing the deal.

"The day I was released, Mr Sanchez was at the prison to pick me up and bring me here, to the head office. His job offer included a small apartment in this building here." Paul waved his hand behind him, towards the shiny red door.

"And the title accompanying your fantastic accounting job?" Lloyd questioned.

Without thinking, Paul opened his mouth and said, "Money Man."

"Fancy title," Lloyd said sardonically. "What duties go with this weighty title?"

Paul chose to ignore the scorn in Lloyd's voice as he posed his questions. "I'm the main – hell, I'm the only – person who handles all the money that ebbs and flows out of the Devils' activities. It's a powerful position, one I am very grateful for every day. I've even progressed to going along with Brutus as he makes collections and hands them over to me for safekeeping. I tell you, Lloyd, it is a position of high responsibility."

"Good for you," Lloyd deadpanned. "I'm happy for you."

Paul observed his son. He guessed he couldn't really blame him for feeling so bitter towards him. "Look at me, son," he directed. Lloyd did.

"Lloyd, what are you doing here?"

"I told you, I'm looking for you, my mother, and three missing foster sisters who disappeared from three of the five foster homes I lived in while you were first in prison and then working for the Devils, too busy and too important to search for your children."

Paul quietly asked, "And Lacey? Where is she?"

Lloyd felt the tears clogging his throat, threatening to overflow and embarrass him in front of Paul and especially, BeeBee. "I don't know. Our last foster home was so bad, I am pretty sure she will have been moved to a sixth place. I haven't spoken with her since I left Alberta."

"Why not?" Paul asked in a subdued voice.

"I didn't have anything to tell her," Lloyd said gloomily. "I promised myself that I wouldn't go back without news of our parents and our foster sisters. So far, the only thing I have discovered is you."

"What else are you doing, Lloyd?"

Lloyd perked up, but only a little. "I'm finishing my high schooling, part-time, and working in a food wagon, part-time. Once I get my Matric, I'll think about what else I want to do."

"Where do you live?"

"Here, in East Van. I have room and board in a house close to where I take my classes."

Suddenly Lloyd became painfully aware that Paul had completely switched things around. He was now doing all of the questioning, learning all kinds of things about Lloyd, and Lloyd was learning nothing! *I'm such an idiot,* he thought to himself.

Paul was part-way into another question when Lloyd stood up. "Uh, uh, not on your life!" Lloyd said emphatically. "I told you what I need to know. Please, quit evading the issue and tell me about my mother."

Once again Paul debated with himself as to how much to tell Lloyd. Cautiously he said, "Lloyd, I don't know where your mother is. I haven't seen her since I got out of prison."

"What do you mean, you haven't seen her since you got out of prison? Does that mean you saw her while you were in prison?"

Silence.

"Did you see her?"

Paul struggled to remain silent. It would do no good to tell Lloyd what really happened the last time Paul saw Anna.

"I know you have something to tell me! Why can't you just spit it out?" Lloyd sounded desperate, heartbroken and hopeful, all at one time. "Please, Dad, I need to know," he begged, forgetting for the moment that he was angry enough to disown his father.

"What do I need to do in order for you to tell me about my mother? I'm begging you! You have no idea what being deserted feels like. Lacey and I are both pretty screwed up, damaged. We feel like we are worth nothing if our parents cannot even stand to be around us. I think you owe me at least that much. Where is your wife, my mother, Lacey's mother?"

Lloyd's voice trembled as he teetered on the brink of complete hysteria. His teeth started to chatter and he began to shake uncontrollably, so much so that Paul became extremely concerned.

"Okay, okay, kid. Calm down and I'll tell you. Just, for Heaven's sake, calm down!

"I honestly do not know where your mother is now. She came to see me several times while I was in Agassiz. Each time she came, all she could talk about was you and Lacey. She wasn't even the least little bit interested in me. She just wanted to use me to find out if I knew where you kids were. Not once did she ask me how I was doing, when I would get out. She never even asked if we were going to stay married, still live together as man and wife!"

Lloyd thought he would choke. The pity-party role his father was revelling in at the moment sickened him. He forced himself to ask, "Well, what were your plans for when you got out?"

Paul said, "I already told you. I had to find myself before I could find and help anyone else in the family."

"So, what did Mom think of that idea, or did you even bother to talk with her about it?"

Without even the slightest glimmer of remorse, Paul Martin Jordan continued his lament. "Anna didn't understand. I *could not* continue with my life the way it was before. You kids were better off in foster care than living with me or with your pathetic mother! She couldn't look after herself; she couldn't look after you kids, and she sure couldn't look after me."

With growing anxiety, Lloyd managed to ask, "What happened?"

Paul shivered with apprehension. What he was about to tell Lloyd would either make or break any relationship that could possibly happen between the two of them. Despite his misgivings, he continued:

"The last time Anna came to see me in prison, she was still whining about how we should do this; how we should do that; should she find us an apartment or a house; blah, blah, blah. I had to tell her, finally, to just shut the fuck up! I told her that there was no more Anna and Paul, no more Lloyd and Lacey. Everyone would just have to look out for themselves from now on. Our family was totally fucked up, a dysfunctional non-entity. I told her that I was going to look out for me, myself and I. I will be the number one person in my own life, I told her. I said she should just forget about me, forget about you and Lacey. Just look after yourself, I told her. You'll forget about us all being a family. I told her she should get on with her own life. She had only herself to look after now. I said she should enjoy it instead of wallowing in self-pity."

Lloyd felt his gorge rise. How could that man, that evil ex-convict, live with himself?

Lloyd could not even begin to believe that this was the same man, his unselfish father, the mentor that he had worshipped as a young boy; the father who would give anything, do anything for his family.

"Anything else?" Lloyd asked, swallowing hard, trying to avoid vomiting all over the Devils' clubhouse steps.

"Yeah, Lloyd, there is. I told her that she had abandoned her kids once; it wouldn't be so difficult this next time. I left that crazy, selfish bitch blubbering in her visitor's chair. I walked away and haven't seen or heard from her since."

Paul stood up, stretched and headed up the steps.

At the door, he turned and said, "Oh yeah, kid. I'm looking for an apprentice, a trainee. My accounting duties are getting too heavy for one person. If you want to give it a try, the money is awesome. Think about it and let me know. Nice talking to you. If I don't hear that you want to work for me, then have a good life!" He opened the shiny red door with a key and disappeared.

Lloyd simply stood motionless, staring at the door. He stood on the bottom step in complete and utter shock. He suddenly shook so badly that he couldn't stand up. He collapsed onto the ground. His entire body seemed to sink into itself as if it had no bone structure whatsoever. Tears threatened to blind him and chafe his skin as the salty liquid poured copiously, like spring runoff from a mountain stream, down his face. He cried so hard that he couldn't catch his breath. Finally, he sensed BeeBee sitting next to him, her hand on his shoulder.

"Come on, kid, let's get you back to the detachment," she said, her own voice trembling with empathy. "Forget about that asshole; you're a million times better man than that gangster will ever be." She helped Lloyd get to his feet. She placed Lloyd's hands on the shopping cart handle. "I'm kind of tired," she said, "so can you please hang on to my cart and push it for me?"

"Sure," said Lloyd dully, totally drained from the encounter with Paul. "I'm kind of unsteady on my feet. Your cart will help me."

Slowly, they began walking in the general direction of the police station.

When they arrived at the detachment, Lloyd was relieved when he was told that Sergeant Gablehaus was out of the office for the balance of the day. When he asked about Constables Brian Barker or Betty Evans, he was informed that they also were gone for the day. The soonest that Lloyd would be able to see the Sergeant would be Monday.

Lloyd thought for a moment, then made an appointment to meet with Sergeant Gablehaus on Monday morning. He left the building, stopped briefly to thank BeeBee again for her support, then stumbled on home. He wanted nothing more than to sink into his pillow and collapse for twelve hours. Maybe by then, he would be ready to dissect what had happened today. Lloyd felt more dejected than a young child who had just been told there was no Santa Claus. In the time it took to utter Paul's last sentence, *'If I don't hear that you want to work for me, then have a good life!'* Lloyd was shattered. The sentence reverberated in Lloyd's brain and echoed itself in his aching heart.

He closed the blinds and when they didn't darken the room sufficiently, he draped a dark blanket over the valence rod at the top of the window. Then, fully clothed, he crawled under the covers and slept around the clock.

He awoke groggy, disoriented, but most of all he woke up devastated. He crawled out from under his quilt, surprised to see that he was fully dressed. He even had his shoes on.

Stumbling to the bathroom Lloyd turned on the shower. While he waited briefly for the water to heat, he stared at his reflection in the mirror. He barely recognised himself. Although Lloyd was fully aware that the reflection was just that, a reflection of Lloyd, the face that stared at him out of the mirror appeared to have aged twenty years since the day before. The eyes were sunken, with large black circles underneath. The skin was mottled, puffy and raw. The hair stood out in every direction. It looked as if he had just removed a woollen toque on a dry winter's day in northern Alberta, or perhaps had even stuck his finger in a light socket. He stepped into the shower and let the hot water soothe both his aching body and wounded spirit. He stood there until the hot water ran out and the showerhead only spit out cold water.

Shivering, he quickly dried himself and then got dressed in a pair of jeans and a T-shirt, no socks, no shoes.

Naturally neat, Lloyd tidied the bathroom and made his bed before going into the kitchen. He wasn't hungry, but he knew he had to eat. Looking at the clock on the stove he could not believe that he had slept for twenty-four hours straight!

He cooked himself breakfast entirely on autopilot. He didn't even remember fixing the meal, but when he sat down at the kitchen table, a plate of three poached eggs on toast sat gawking up at him. When Lloyd finally started to eat, he discovered he was ravenous. He ate all of his eggs, made himself two more pieces of toast and a hot chocolate.

The shock of the disastrous reunion with Paul was easing but only very slightly. He foggily remembered making an appointment with the constable on the front desk at the police station to see Sergeant Gablehaus on Monday morning. In the meantime, Lloyd had a lot of hours to fill before then.

Feeling a sudden need for fresh air, Lloyd hurriedly cleaned up his breakfast things, grabbed his runners from beside the back door. Once his laces were tied, he grabbed his backpack and house key, left the house and locked the door behind himself.

It was a beautiful day. Already late morning, the sun beamed down a comfortable temperature, neither too hot nor too chilly. Lloyd did some stretches in the back yard before he set off jogging at a medium pace, heading for where he had no clue. He just let his body take him to an unknown destination as he concentrated solely on putting one foot in front of the other. When his muscles were sufficiently warm, he found himself racing at full speed down a running trail through Oppenheimer Park. He glanced around but saw no sign of BeeBee.

He ran without thinking; he ran blindly, narrowly missing various obstacles and pedestrians along the way.

When next he became consciously aware of his surroundings, Lloyd found himself standing outside BURGERS 'N DAWGS. The police tape was gone, but a large sign proclaimed that this was private property and trespassers would be prosecuted to the fullest extent of the law. He made a mental note to himself to visit Shelby and ask her whether the insurance people had released the property back to her yet. He turned away from the desolate sight and continued running.

He raced through the entrance to Stanley Park, ran along the seawall. Not stopping to admire any view, he continually ran until he finally ran out of steam. Dropping down to the grass he fought to catch his breath. When his breathing finally eased, he went from a sitting position to lying flat on his back, staring up at the lazy white clouds hovering nearly motionless overhead.

After some time, during which he wrestled with himself to push yesterday's events to the back of his brain, he decided to go to St. Paul's, try and wash off the dried, salty sweat from his body in a washroom and then have a bite of lunch in the cafeteria before going to have a visit with Shelby.

Chapter 17
Shelby Sidor

The vigilant policeman was still stationed at the entrance to Shelby's room. Lloyd nodded and smiled, but he was silently asking himself, *what did that cop do to aggravate his commanding officer badly enough to assign him to isolation duty in St. Paul's?*

Lloyd walked into Shelby's room and was delighted to see that, not only was she awake, she was actually sitting in a chair beside her bed.

"Well, well!" Lloyd exclaimed, "What a lovely sight! And just look at you, sporting so many rainbow colours today!"

Shelby frowned at him, although her eyes were sparkling. "Don't make me laugh. Jaw still hurts like crazy."

"Sorry! I'm just so happy to see you out of bed, Shelby. You are looking much better than you were. You must be a very fast healer."

Lloyd pulled up a second chair and sat down beside his boss.

Shelby looked very serious. "Lloyd," she whispered. She nodded towards the door and put her pointer finger against her lips, making a shushing noise. "Cop can hear us. Shut the door, please."

Looking perplexed, Lloyd nonetheless went and closed the door tightly. He then returned and sat down in the chair next to Shelby.

"What's up, Shelby?" he asked. "What's with all the secrecy?"

Shelby pointed to the drawer in the nightstand next to her bed. Lloyd opened it and then looked over at Shelby.

"Envelope," she said, "read it. From insurance company."

Lloyd opened the envelope and placed it on the nightstand while he read the letter from the insurance company. When he finished reading, he stared dumbly at Shelby, "What the heck? This letter states that they can't cover any of the vandalised damages to the food wagon! That's bizarre. What gives anyway?"

Tears trickled down Shelby's cheeks. "I know what – going on, Lloyd."

Lloyd reached over and gently placed his large hand over Shelby's delicate one. "Tell me," he simply said. He then leaned back in his chair and waited.

"I had – visitor last night. Cop guarding me – dirty."

Lloyd sat up straighter, opened his mouth to say something, but Shelby just held up her hands. "Lloyd, please hear me. I'm tired. Speaking hurts my jaw, so let me tell you – first."

"Sorry," Lloyd said sombrely.

“Okay,” Shelby looked worn down and defeated. After taking a sip of water from a glass on her bedside table, she said, “My visitor – from gang, East Van Devils. He spoke to – door cop. When finished he reached – his pocket, handed cop money. Door cop left – went somewhere.

“Gangster came – my room. Said he was – money man?”

Shelby was so intent on her narrative that she didn’t notice Lloyd turn white and grip the arms of his chair so tightly that the veins in his hands popped up and turned a darker blue. Nor did she hear him moan heartbrokenly.

She kept talking, pausing for a sip of water whenever her voice gave out, which was often.

“Told me boss is – Domingo Sanchez. Gang boss forced insurance company not to cover my –”

At this point, Shelby choked and had to stop for a moment. Lloyd handed her the water glass and took it back from her when she was finished.

She completed her sentence – “not to cover my claim.”

She continued in a quiet, calm monotone. Unheeded tears coursed down her cheeks, belied her outwardly calm appearance. “Money man said – give me one week to pay protection money – I didn’t pay before. Not paying now, I said. He said gang keeping food wagon – but I still have to pay! Then he left my room. Little while – dirty cop –- back my door.”

Lloyd could scarcely believe his ears. His brain ached, his mind spun as he tried to list everything in his head. Money man and the dirty cop? No insurance coverage? Domingo head boss of the East Van Devils? Protection money for her now-defunct business? He leaned down, put his head between his knees so he wouldn’t faint. Alarmed, Shelby reached for her call bell.

Lloyd reached for her hand. “No, Shelby, don’t! I’ll be fine in a second. Just give me a minute, please. This is nuts! I believe everything you just told me. I just can’t figure out what the gang has to gain by all of this. If you can’t get your rightful insurance coverage, what makes Domingo think he can get it?”

Shelby looked at her young trainee sadly. “Only thing – make any sense,” she said, “is if insurance company is owned by The Warlords. They are – most notorious gang on the west coast – have power, control – every other local gang.” Exhausted, Shelby closed her eyes. “Shall I leave so you can have a sleep?” Lloyd asked. Shelby just shook her head slowly from side to side. “Okay – a minute,” she said. “Wait please.”

Lloyd stood up. “Tell you what, I’ll just run down to the cafeteria and get myself a drink. Would you like something?” Shelby whispered, “No thanks. Come back?”

“Of course, I’ll come back. You just rest until I get back here. I won’t be long.” Lloyd went to the door, noticed that the so-called police guard outside the door was asleep! Counting his blessings, Lloyd managed to tiptoe quietly past the dirty cop undetected. He disgustedly thought to himself, *Now that’s a useless guard dog if I ever saw one.*

As soon as he was in the cafeteria, he bought himself a Coke and went outside, walked over to an unoccupied area of the hospital’s postage-stamp-sized front lawn. The rest of the grounds were all concrete sidewalks and parking garages. Glancing around to make sure no one was within hearing distance, Lloyd thought, not for the first time, how fortunate he was that Mona Grace had convinced him to buy a cell phone. After the trashing of the food wagon and the attack on Shelby, Mona Grace had been most insistent. *I didn't think I would need one,* Lloyd thought, *but turns out it could be the best purchase ever!*

He reached into his backpack and found Sergeant Gablehaus's business card. The policeman had hand-written his cell phone number on the back of that card, and it was this number that Lloyd called.

The Sergeant answered on the second ring. "Greg Gablehaus."

Lloyd spoke as quietly as he could, enunciating every word hoping to make up for the lack of volume.

"Sir, it's Lloyd, Lloyd Jordan. I'm sorry to bother you on your private phone, but..." Lloyd told the Sergeant about the happenings since they had last met. It took more than ten minutes before Lloyd finished his discourse and paused for breath.

Sergeant Gablehaus was silent for a minute. "When are you and I supposed to meet next? What's today? I don't have my schedule on me."

Lloyd told him, "Monday, sir. Today's Saturday"

"Well, I think we need to jump those cables and meet sooner. Can you meet me at the detachment in, say, a half hour?"

Lloyd said that as soon as he went back and said goodbye to Shelby he would head straight over.

"Okay. In the meantime, I am going to have the 'unscrupulous constable' at Shelby's hospital door removed and replaced by one of my own men. After you and I meet, I will go to the hospital and talk with Shelby.

"I'll see you in a half hour or so, Lloyd. I'll pick us up some sandwiches at Tim Horton's on my way back to the office and we can eat lunch while we speak."

In spite of the seriousness of the situation, Lloyd couldn't hold back a chuckle.

"I know, I know, the old 'Tim Horton's and the Cops' witticism. I don't care, laugh if you want, but I'm hungry and I like the soup and sandwiches at Tim Horton's. Bye for now!" As the Sergeant ended the call, Lloyd was pretty certain that he heard the officer laughing heartily as he turned off his cell phone.

Lloyd hurried back up to Shelby's room, forcing an incipient smile towards the dirty cop who was now awake. Entering the room, he firmly shut the door behind him.

Shelby was back in bed, looking exceedingly wan and exhausted, and suffering a tremendous amount of pain in her jaw from speaking too much.

Lloyd drew his chair nearer to the bed so he could speak softly enough that the crooked cop allegedly guarding the door could not hear anything.

"I have to leave, Shelby, I have a meeting in half an hour. Oh, and by the way, I ran into Sergeant Gablehaus earlier and he is coming to visit you this afternoon. In the meantime, though, he is replacing the dirty cop with one of his own members, so you will be safe.

"The new police presence will have firm instructions not to allow anyone in to see you except for me, Sergeant Gablehaus and anyone else who has been approved by you. If the constable does not know the person, he will stand in the doorway with him or her and ask you if it is okay. If you don't know the visitor, or even if you do but don't want to see that person, all you need to do is shake your head 'no' and the constable will get rid of them. Sound good?"

Shelby patted Lloyd's hand. "You – doing – fine job – looking after me. Can't thank you enough – all you – done for me. What did I do without you?" She cleared her throat and turned away hoping to diminish the threat of tears.

"One more thing – before you leave. Night table drawer – envelope – for you. Please take it now."

Lloyd gave Shelby a quizzical look but did as she asked. He withdrew a large envelope from the drawer and tried to give it to his boss. She shook her head, saying only, "Take it – put – safe place. Now go to your meeting. Nurse – coming –- help me shower – wash my hair! Feel – Heaven – after bed baths. Then – nice nap before Sergeant comes. See you tomorrow?"

"If not before," Lloyd said, and then impulsively he leaned over and kissed the elderly woman on her cheek. She reached up and patted Lloyd's face gently. "Thank you, dear," she said. "You –- strongest medicine for me. Now, away with you!"

As Lloyd reached the door, he heard Shelby whisper something. He turned around.

"Envelope – you forgot – take it!" She appeared frantic and so Lloyd went back and hurriedly picked up the envelope which he had set on the floor earlier.

"Got it, boss! I'll be putting it in a safe place, boss! Leaving again now, boss! Have a good shower and a good rest, boss! See you tomorrow, boss!" He walked backwards towards the door, the envelope clutched carefully against his chest. Shelby was holding her jaw as she tried not to laugh but failed.

Just outside the main doors to the hospital, Lloyd stopped walking and looked at the front of the large brown envelope. On it, written in shaky but legible letters, Shelby had printed:

BRADEN "LLOYD" JORDAN
TO BE OPENED ONLY IN THE EVENT OF
MY DEATH

What the heck? Lloyd thought. *Her pain meds must be stronger than I thought. They're causing her to overreact. I will humour her, though, and keep this envelope in a safe place, hopefully for many years.* He took the time to place the envelope carefully in his backpack so it wouldn't bend and set off at a medium jog for the detachment and his meeting with Sergeant Gablehaus.

He arrived at the police station only slightly out of breath, and with ten minutes to spare before the time of his meeting.

Right on time, the Sergeant entered the reception area and waved at Lloyd to follow him back to his office. He stopped at a vending machine and got two bottles of Coke before continuing on down a long hallway and then climbing a set of stairs to the right.

Compared to the other offices that Lloyd had seen along the hallway, it was luxurious. Not with respect to furnishings, which, other than the desk and matching credenza, were standard government issue, but because it was at least three times the size of any of the others. Also, the large desk was twice as full of files. Lloyd was impressed by the neatness of the entire office. There must be a hundred files sitting on that credenza alone, Lloyd thought, but there were no sloppy piles in danger of spilling over onto the floor. *Wow,* he thought, *I wish I was half that neat!*

"Have a seat, Lloyd, and grab a Coke. I'm just going to pull a file here and then we need to talk."

Sergeant Gablehaus found the very thick file he was looking for, extracted it carefully from the bottom of a pile on the right-hand side of his desk. Lloyd thought he could read "BeeBee" on the file label but he only got a quick glance; he didn't want the Sergeant to think he was snooping, (even though he was).

"Okay, Mr Lloyd Jordan, tell me about your trip with BeeBee to the home of the East Van Devils. I've spoken with BeeBee, of course; now, it's your turn."

Sergeant Gablehaus sat quietly in his chair, ramrod straight, a very imposing figure indeed. He noticed Lloyd's hesitancy, smiled gently to put him more at ease. Then, he leaned back and patiently waited.

"What do you want to know, sir?" Lloyd asked.

"Just tell me in your own words how your trip to the clubhouse went. I'm taping our conversation, but just ignore the machine and look at me; just talk to me."

After a couple of stutters, Lloyd began to speak. Once he started, he didn't stop until he was sure he had told the Sergeant everything. He had been afraid that he wouldn't remember, that he would leave something important out, but when he was through, he was satisfied that he had told the policeman everything there was to tell.

"How did you feel when you found out that your father was the money man for the gang?"

Lloyd couldn't stop the bitter words that came out of his mouth. "How do you think I felt, sir? I was hoping to find my father again, yes, but I certainly didn't want to find out he was still a criminal. Not only a criminal but the right-hand man to the leader of a gang! I was horrified to find that my selfish, egotistical, criminal 'father' had blown my mother off in such an evil, uncaring way. I expected to find out where she is, but that piece of dog poop just walked away as if she never existed! And then he had the audacity to ask me if I would come and work with him for the East Van Devils!"

By this point in his recall, Lloyd was sweating profusely, starting to hyperventilate. Alarmed, Sergeant Gablehaus rose from his chair. "Stand up,

Lloyd and take some deep breaths. You did fine; I have heard everything that happened. Your story coincides with BeeBee's.

"Tell you what, let's take a break and eat our Tim Horton's lunch. After that, I have a proposal for you. What do you say?"

Drained, all Lloyd could say was, "Fine, sir."

Although he wasn't the least bit hungry, he forced himself to eat. After all, Sergeant Gablehaus had gone out of his way to ensure they had lunch. As Lloyd ate, he was totally cognisant of the fact that tears were showering down his cheeks, plopping on to his already salty sandwich, but he couldn't control them.

Greg Gablehaus chatted away, ignoring Lloyd's distress, acting as if this were just a normal lunch hour and they were simply discussing the weather. Lloyd greatly appreciated that. He could feel himself becoming calmer as his stomach filled and his blood sugar resumed normal levels.

When he finished eating and his tears had finally ceased, Lloyd asked the Sergeant where the nearest washroom was. Gablehaus pointed at his own private washroom. "I can use a staff one," he said awkwardly. The Sergeant simply pointed again. Lloyd got up and went.

When he returned, he sat in his chair and waited more or less calmly for Sergeant Gablehaus.

"Lloyd," he said when he returned from his washroom, "how would you feel about working with your father?"

Lloyd stared at the man in total disbelief. He had endured such a terrible week that it was several minutes before he realised that he was being asked to work undercover, in the East Van Devils' clubhouse, with his biological sperm donor, the money man for Domingo Sanchez! (Lloyd was pretty darn certain he could never again think of that arrogant ex-con as his father.)

"I don't know if I could, sir," Lloyd said. "Although I would dearly love to bring down both Domingo and Paul, what if I can't control my disdain for both those crooks? What if they figure out that I'm actually working for the police because of something I inadvertently say or do?"

Sergeant Gablehaus both listened and carefully watched Lloyd as he rambled on. He fully understood the boy's panic at the thought of infiltrating a criminal organisation, particularly one where his own father was the money man for the leader of the gang. Every police informant felt the same way at the beginning, but rarely, if ever, did an informant have such a close relative involved.

When Lloyd finally quit panicking out loud, the Sergeant spoke, "Listen carefully, Lloyd. There is no way that I am going to send you into that place without proper training. By the time you spend a week here with us, you will be totally prepared and even eager to commence your undercover duties. If you need to think about it, you can let me know tomorrow."

With a lot of resolve and not much introspection, Lloyd straightened up in his chair in an unconscious imitation of Sergeant Gablehaus' posture.

"No need, sir," Lloyd said. "I'm ready to be trained. Who will be training me?"

Sergeant Gablehaus grinned. "Who do you think, Lloyd?"

"You, sir?"

"And who else? You can't guess?"

"Well, if I have to guess," Lloyd said, "my guess would be BeeBee?"

"Bingo!" Greg Gablehaus blurted out. "See you tomorrow morning, eight-thirty sharp. Wear comfortable clothes and bring a lunch. You're in for a few long days."

Sergeant Gablehaus suddenly said, "Lloyd, I'm sure you know this already, but out of an abundance of caution I feel compelled to tell you that you cannot utter even a syllable of this discussion with anyone outside of this office, not even Shelby. Not only would the downfall of both Domingo and his money man be compromised, but your life would be at risk if this covert operation were to crumble. Get it?"

"Certainly, I do, sir, my lips are sealed." Ignoring the nervous fluttering in both his stomach and intestines, Lloyd rose and held out his hand to the Sergeant. They shook hands.

"Okay, Lloyd," said the Sergeant, "I have a meeting with Shelby. You go on home and get some rest. You look like the wrath of God. I'll see you tomorrow."

"What will Shelby think when I don't show up to visit her, sir?"

"I'll tell her that you have some heavy-duty exams coming up and you've been neglecting your schoolwork the past several days. I'll tell her you are studying at the library, fewer interruptions. Think she'll understand that?"

"Definitely," Lloyd responded. "In fact, if she thought I wasn't studying, she'd climb out of that hospital bed and kick my butt all the way around an entire city block!"

On his way out, Lloyd paused at the doorway and turned to face the Sergeant. "Sir, is there any way you can try to find out where my mother might be? I sure didn't get any satisfaction when I asked 'the Money Man!" (This last statement was uttered with a very distinguishable combination of profound sarcasm and bitterness). He added one more thing. "And maybe re-open the files regarding my missing foster sisters?

"You successfully complete your part in the covert operation delving into the financial affairs of the West Van Devils, Lloyd, and I guarantee you, my next order of business will be to organise a team to either find your mother and the missing girls or at least find out what might have happened. I and my team will give it our all.

"Now I really have to run. See you tomorrow."

Although Lloyd knew that Sergeant Gablehaus couldn't guarantee that something more urgent wouldn't come up and once again delay a concentrated search for his mother and the missing girls, he nevertheless felt more settled, determined and optimistic than he had in some time, Lloyd left the office and headed for home.

Greg Gablehaus waited until Lloyd had left the detachment before he grabbed his jacket and headed to St. Paul's to meet with Shelby Sidor, and at the same time, ensure that the dirty cop had been relieved of his guard duties.

When he arrived at the hospital, he asked at the front desk for Shelby Sidor's room number.

"Are you family?"

Sergeant Sidor flashed his badge, smiled tightly but said nothing. The receptionist, a striking young blond, obviously new, blushed furiously and gave him the room number, at the same time muttering, "Sorry, sir."

Just outside Shelby's room he encountered a junior member from his shift – a young, squeaky-clean constable who was cheerful and eager, and who was guarding Mrs Sidor more fiercely than any Pitbull, Doberman or German Shepherd guard dog.

Sergeant Gablehaus shook the young man's hand and then turned and tapped on the frame of the open door. Ever since Shelby had witnessed the dirty cop and the money man doing their shifty business just outside her room, she had not allowed her door to be closed any longer than the time it took for the nurses to tend to her. And, of course, when she was speaking with Lloyd and didn't want the so-called protector policeman to hear anything.

Shelby Sidor lay in her bed, very lethargic and ashen-faced. She pointed to a chair beside her bed after Greg Gablehaus had introduced himself. He sat.

"Sorry, not feeling so well today, sir. Better – yesterday. Need to tell you – insurance company." She stopped speaking to rest a moment. Now her face was shiny with perspiration and she was trembling visibly.

Sergeant Gablehaus pulled a small notebook out of his shirt pocket and wrote down the name of the insurance company, the phone number, and the name of the agent that Shelby dealt with. His wife kept bugging him to learn to use all of the features in his cell phone and save himself the hassle of little pieces of paper everywhere by making notes on his phone, but so far, her husband was clinging to the old methods like a dog with a bone.

Shelby haltingly told the Sergeant, with many breaks so she could recover her breath, that she was pretty sure that the East Van Devils had threatened the insurance agency, ordered them not to pay out the policy. She also spoke of her unspoken terror because the Devils' money man wanted protection money all the way back to when she first opened her 'BURGERS 'N DAWGS' food wagon, despite the fact that her business was now defunct. She couldn't do the repairs without the insurance money, and she knew the gang would not let her get away without paying the protection money. Shelby knew that the gang would take the food wagon away from her and either fix it up or replace it. If she couldn't pay them, she would be in terrible danger.

Greg Gablehaus had been a policeman for a very long time and had grown a reputation for having armadillo-thick skin. His wife would tell you, though, "Piffle! Greg is the biggest softie in the entire Force. He just acts tough because it intimidates the crooks.'

Having met with Lloyd and sensing the strong bond between the earnest young man and this weary woman, he wanted to leave the hospital immediately and beat the crap out of both Domingo and his money man. However, he hadn't reached the rank of Sergeant by going off half-cocked. He took a deep breath to allow himself to calm down and to allow Mrs Sidor time to rest her voice.

When next he spoke, his voice was compassionate. “Mrs Sidor, I realise how terrifying this whole experience has been, and continues to be for you. You don’t need me to tell you that you are justified in your fears. The East Van Devils are a wild bunch of thugs. Most of the members of that gang grew up bullying kids of their own age or younger. Now, they are bullying people of all ages. Unfortunately, the bullying has progressed from childhood playground name-calling, shoving and pushing, to intimidation, severe physical assaults, pushes for control, and, sadly, even torture and murder.

“Unfortunately, the Devils are themselves under the control of The Warlords, the major gang that controls all the small gangs on the west coast. The Warlords take a large kickback from all money dealings carried out by every small gang. This kickback comes from innumerable sources. Drugs, prostitution, protection, small businesses such as your BURGERS ‘N DAWGS; anything that brings money into the gang is subject to The Warlords’ control.

“I can suggest a few things.” The Sergeant reached into the briefcase that he carried with him wherever he went and extracted several pages of information on the Witness Protection Program administered by the R.C.M.P. He handed them to Shelby. Sergeant Gablehaus explained that there were three types of protection – one type was a temporary program where she could go into protective custody for ninety days. If, at the end of the ninety-day period, there was still a significant risk, it could be renewed for another ninety days.

The second type was permanent protective custody. This suggestion was much harder for the victim because everything pertaining to their past and present life would be changed. There could never be any contact with relatives, former friends, employers, the list went on and on. In some cases, plastic surgery might even be required in order to complete the transition to the new identity. It could be psychologically very difficult, in Mrs Sidor’s case, for her to completely wipe out seventy years of life and begin again.

Noticing that Shelby had become more stressed, he exited the subject of witness protection for the time being.

Continuing, he said, “We could also provide you with 24/7 surveillance until things settle down; however, the length of time we could provide this service would depend upon budget concerns and the number of officers required. So, this might not be as effective as the protective custody scenarios.”

Shelby held up her hand to stop the Sergeant. Looking directly at him, she said simply but definitively, “Won’t cost police – anything. Not doing any of that. Going home. Be careful. Too old – subterfuge. Thanks anyway, sir. Sorry, wasted – your time.”

Greg Gablehaus sat still, watching Mrs Sidor intently before he said, “I’m sorry to hear you say that, Mrs Sidor, but I have to respect your wishes.

“I would like to ask one thing of you, though, if you please. Take that information I gave you on the Witness Protection Program and study it. You don’t have to do anything, just read it.

“If you change your mind at any time, please call me.” Reaching into his pocket he withdrew a business card. He wrote both his cell phone and home telephone numbers on the back before he handed it to her. “Call me anytime, anywhere, day or night. We will continue from our end doing everything we can possibly do to stop these punks from destroying the lives of all of the good people in East Vancouver, and that definitely includes you, ma’am.”

He stood up and put on his overcoat. Just as he turned away from Shelby to pick up his briefcase, he heard a strange gasp, and then Shelby said, “Pain – so – bad – 20 out of 10.” The policeman instinctively pushed the call button. He then stuck his head out of the door and yelled at the top of his voice, “Help! Emergency! Mrs Sidor has a problem! Help!”

The Sergeant barely got out of the way before a team of medical personnel raced into the room with a crash cart. He stepped into the hallway and waited with the young constable while the medical team worked furiously to revive their patient. After what seemed like forever, everything stopped. In the silence, Sergeant Gablehaus heard a male voice. “Time of death, 15:15.” The curtain surrounding the bed was pulled back. The Sergeant caught a very brief glimpse of Shelby as she lay lifeless, staring blankly at the ceiling before a nurse leaned over the deceased lady and gently closed her eyes.

Greg Gablehaus stopped one nurse as the team left the room. He showed his badge, asked simply, “Do you have any idea what just happened?”

The nurse placed her hand on the Sergeant’s arm and explained, “An autopsy will confirm the cause of death, of course, but we are pretty sure that she threw a blood clot, either to her heart or her lung. She had one yesterday in the groin area of her left side. They put her on meds to dissolve it.” She looked at the policeman sadly. “This just happens sometimes and there is nothing that can be done about it. I’m so sorry. Were you close?”

The Sergeant shook his head. “I barely knew her, but I know her only employee. I will speak with him and get back to you about what happens next.” He then turned and walked away. Telling someone about the death of another person was always difficult, but telling Lloyd about Shelby’s passing was going to be one of the most difficult yet.

Sergeant Gablehaus made a quick call to the detachment and asked for the address of Mona Grace Ford. He scribbled it down on the reverse of the paper he had written the insurance company details on. Noting that the address was only a few blocks away, he elected to walk rather than drive there. He hoped that by the time he completed his short journey to the house, he would have his jumbled thoughts together.

Soon, he was standing at the front door, alternatively ringing the doorbell and knocking on the old wooden door with his fist. Just as he was about to leave, Lloyd cracked open the door just a touch.

Without looking, he irritably called out, “Go away, I’m sleeping!”

Before he could slam the door shut, however, Greg Gablehaus stuck his foot in the opening. “Lloyd, it’s me, Greg Gablehaus. I’m so sorry to wake you, but something’s come up.”

Lloyd flung the door open wide. He must have been sleeping because his hair was standing on end and his eyes were puffy. "I'm so sorry, sir!" he said. "I didn't look. I just assumed it was a salesman of some sort. I was sound asleep. What's come up?"

"May I come in?"

"Oh, of course, sir, pardon my ill manners! Want to sit in the front room or the kitchen?"

"The kitchen's fine, Lloyd. Lead the way."

As they walked the short distance from the front door to the tiny kitchen, the Sergeant couldn't help but admire the tidiness and cleanliness of the small house. He, by force of habit, sat down at the head of the small table and waited for Lloyd to seat himself.

White-faced and anxious, Lloyd sat and waited for Sergeant Gablehaus to fill him in. He wondered what could be so necessary that he would come to Lloyd's home, in person, only an hour or so from the last time they spoke. A thought hammered inside his head and he hesitantly asked, "Is it, my mother? Have you found out what happened to her already? That's mighty fast police work, sir if I do say so."

Greg put his hand over Lloyd's. Lloyd finally stopped rambling, and the Sergeant said, "No, Lloyd, it's not about your mother. It's about Shelby Sidor."

"Shelby! Did the insurance company change their minds and agreed to pay out her claim?"

"No, Lloyd, it's not that. Just listen to me, please. There is no easy way to say this, so I am going to just spurt it out. Shelby Sidor died. I was with her when she suddenly experienced severe pain and then stopped breathing. A specialised trauma team was in her room, literally within seconds. They worked for many minutes trying to revive her. They could not."

Lloyd was dumbstruck. Finally, he croaked out, "Was it a heart attack?"

"They don't think so, Lloyd. They won't know for sure until they perform an autopsy, but they feel it was a blood clot that broke off and travelled either to her lung or to her heart. They could, sadly, do nothing for her. I can tell you though, because I was there, that she suffered for only a couple of minutes at the very most before she died. It was quick, mercifully."

Lloyd stood up so quickly that he knocked his chair over on its side. "Murderers!" He screamed at the top of his voice. "The East Van Devils are murderers. They killed Shelby as surely as if they had shot her cold-bloodedly right through her head.

"I am now even more motivated to help you, sir, get those bastards that killed a kindly old woman. Just point me in the right direction."

It was only then that shock started to wear off. The reality of what Sergeant Gablehaus had told him really began to sink in. He crumpled to the floor, leaned back against the side of the stove and his tears released in a veritable waterfall of salty liquid.

Greg Gablehaus sank to the floor beside the young fellow, put his arm around Lloyd's shoulders and let him weep.

Finally, Lloyd appeared to be devoid of tears. "Thanks for the shoulder to cry on, sir. I'll be okay now. I just feel sick. That bloody gang. They deprived her of a successful business, of her dignity, and now of her life. A kindly old soul who, I would be willing to bet, never hurt another person in her entire life. It's not fair, sir, it's just not."

He turned his head towards Greg and asked in a soulful voice, "Will you charge them with murder, sir?"

"Second degree, Lloyd, yes. Mrs Sidor already identified her attackers from a photo line-up. We know who to charge."

Lloyd said quietly, "I already know that one of the attackers is Brutus something or other. I never heard his last name. Shelby called him the Pitbull Man; I call him the Tattoo Man. But, sir, can you tell me who the second man is? I didn't see his photo when Shelby picked him out, and she changed the subject when I asked her who it was. Can you please tell me? I have a pretty good idea. I can take it." Lloyd stared at the Sergeant, a long, fierce, dark stare.

"Your father. Paul Martin Jordan, also known as the Money Man.

"I'm so sorry, Lloyd, I know this is a terrible shock. If you choose to back out of the upcoming operation, I will understand."

"Are you kidding, sir?" Lloyd sputtered. "Believe me, I have never been so determined in my entire life. Never fear, sir, I can do this. I WILL do this, or die trying."

He stood up, helped Sergeant Gablehaus to his feet. Plaintively, he asked, "Sir, I know how busy you are, but could you stay with me, just for a little while? Mona Grace will be home from work in about an hour. Can you stay just that long? If she isn't here in an hour, I can call her."

"Absolutely. Just give me a minute to call the detachment and let them know where I am."

Lloyd flopped down on a kitchen chair and numbly waited while the Sergeant made his phone call.

Just before Sergeant Gablehaus hung up, Lloyd remembered something. He stood up and went into his room, retrieving from his backpack the brown envelope that Shelby had given him. When he got back to the kitchen, he handed it to Sergeant Gablehaus, who looked at the outside and read:

BRADEN "LLOYD" JORDAN
TO BE OPENED ONLY IN THE EVENT OF
MY DEATH

"What shall I do with this, sir?"

"Open it."

"Isn't it a bit soon, sir? I don't want to appear disrespectful."

"I'm pretty sure Shelby wouldn't think you were disrespectful, Lloyd. Her death has occurred; she wanted you to open it after her death. Maybe she has some instructions for you about what to do after she died. She doesn't have any family, does she?"

"No, sir. There were just her and her husband, and he passed away. They never had any children. She was alone."

"Would you like me to leave so you can open it in private?"

"No, sir, please stay. I may have some questions for you, and I really appreciate your company."

Lloyd knew he had to open it, but for the life of him, he couldn't force himself to rip open the envelope. Finally, he got up and retrieved a knife out of the cutlery drawer. Sitting back down he made a couple of attempts to slice open the envelope, but he was shaking so badly he was sure he would slice off his finger! The Sergeant reached over and took both the knife and the envelope out of Lloyd's trembling hands. He quickly split the seal, put the knife in the sink and gave the now-opened envelope back to Lloyd.

"Thank you, sir," Lloyd said dully.

Noticing a coffee pot on the kitchen counter, the Sergeant stood up and began to make a pot of coffee. Then, waiting for the coffee to brew, he sat back down yet again beside Lloyd at the table and waited.

Coffee finished, he poured himself a cup, raised his eyebrows at Lloyd. "No, thanks, sir, but there is sugar in the jar on the counter and milk in the fridge."

"I take it black. Lloyd, open the envelope before it grows legs and walks away!"

Hands still trembling, Lloyd finally removed the contents which were paper-clipped together.

The top document was a hand-written, two-page letter written by Shelby to Lloyd. He read it aloud in a shaky voice:

"My dear Lloyd:

When you read this letter, I will be gone. Don't mourn for me, as I will be happily reunited with my beloved husband, once again safe in his arms and in the arms of our Lord. I missed my husband so much. I welcome being with him in the hereafter, although you have made my loneliness so much easier to bear.

You were so eager to learn that I looked forward to working with you in the BURGERS 'N DAWGS food wagon every day. How terrible it is that the East Van Devils spoiled that for both of us!

I have only known you for much too short a period of time, but in that time, you have become my son, the son that I would have been so proud to have raised; however, as you already know, my husband and I were never blessed with children. Perhaps that is why I became so attached to you, so quickly.

Anyway, I am digressing from my main purpose of this letter.

Lloyd, I have been to a lawyer and prepared a new Last Will and Testament. Everything in my estate (which is not a fortune, but it will help) I leave to you. Do with it what you will, but I truly hope that you will use some of it to finish your high schooling and more of it to further your education. There is some money in several bank accounts, the details of which are on a separate sheet of paper in this envelope. The balance of the estate consists of my vehicle and my condominium. It is your choice what you do with the vehicle and the condo. Perhaps you might choose to live in the condo; perhaps you might choose to sell it. Whatever you decide, just know that I would support your choice; you can do nothing that would disappoint my faith in you.

I fervently hope that the police can figure out who is behind the insurance company's refusal to pay the settlement on the food wagon damage. If they can, that is some more money for you to add to the estate. The way it stands at the present time, my estate, all-inclusive, is worth approximately two million dollars, give or take.

My dear Lloyd, I wish you much success in your search for your mother and your missing foster sisters.

Use my lawyer. He will assist you whenever you need legal assistance. He has been our lawyer for many years and is very reliable. His name, address and telephone number are included on a separate sheet.

Be strong, young Lloyd and know that you brought much joy and sunshine into the life of a lonely old woman. May God Bless you, and may you continue to be the fine, upstanding man that you have become.

Love, Shelby.

When he finished reading the letter, he was unable to speak for several minutes. Finally, he leafed through the remainder of the contents of the envelope, then carefully reassembled them in their original order.

"Wow, Sergeant Gablehaus, isn't this something?"

"Sure is, Lloyd, but don't ever kid yourself, you deserve it. Shelby said it herself, as far as she was concerned, you were her son."

The front door opened, and Mona Grace stepped inside. Walking into the kitchen, she smiled at Sergeant Gablehaus, whom she had dealt with on more than one file at one time or another.

"Hey, Lloyd! What's new?"

Lloyd once again had leaking eyes. Before he could say anything more, the Sergeant stood up and quietly announced that he had to get back to work. Lloyd walked him to the front door. Sergeant Gablehaus whispered in Lloyd's ear, "See you tomorrow at 8:30, Lloyd – remember, not a word about the upcoming operation!"

"No, sir, not a word. I'll be there. Thank you for staying with me."

The Sergeant left; Lloyd went to the bathroom. One look at Lloyd had convinced Mona Grace that there was something she needed to do before listening to Lloyd. While he was in the bathroom, Mona Grace quickly put a box into the deep freeze and a gaily-wrapped parcel into her dresser drawer. She already somehow knew that this was not the time to celebrate Lloyd's nineteenth birthday.

Lloyd came back into the kitchen, sat down and prepared to tell Mona Grace about Shelby's death and the contents of the envelope.

Chapter 18
East Van Devils

After a mostly dream-filled and restless night, Lloyd finally got up early and reviewed all of the documents that Shelby had prepared and left for him. The Will was straightforward enough, leaving everything to Lloyd once he was nineteen years of age. Before that, the Public Trustee would administer the Estate.

Lloyd got up and looked at the calendar stuck to the side of the refrigerator. Wait! Yesterday was his birthday! His age wouldn't be a problem – he was now nineteen! He had completely forgotten about his birthday. He briefly felt a tiny bit disappointed that Mona Grace hadn't remembered, but when he thought about it, last night definitely wasn't a good time to celebrate anyway.

The balance of the items in the envelope consisted of bank passbooks, bank statements, service records for Shelby's vehicle, a copy of the insurance policy insuring 'BURGERS 'N DAWGS, a Bill of Sale whereby Shelby had purchased the food wagon and a clear title to the condominium. The final paper listed the name, address and phone number of Shelby's lawyer. There was everything he needed to commence completing the Estate except for the Death Certificate. Not being versed in legal requirements, he made a note to himself to set up an appointment with the lawyer as soon as possible.

Lloyd thought to himself, *Today's the day I start training for the undercover operation.* A shiver of apprehension knifed its way throughout his body. "Lloyd resolved, "*I'm going to make Shelby proud. If she were here, she would tell me to do my best, stay strong, and learn from my mistakes. That,* he silently promised her, *I am going to do!*

Somehow, thinking about Shelby comforted him rather than making him inconsolably sad. He knew she was now reunited with her beloved husband in Heaven and there was no need to worry about her. She was completely safe. The gang couldn't hassle or intimidate or hurt her any more.

Lloyd could concentrate fully on helping to bring down the EAST VAN DEVILS or, at the very least, bring down Domingo Sanchez and Paul Martin Jordan (Domingo's main man, the 'Money Man.') He knew that he would be expertly trained before Sergeant Gablehaus would let him anywhere near the clubhouse. This fact alone made Lloyd feel stronger, braver, more determined. BeeBee also would be watching his back. He was in good hands.

By the time he reached the detachment at 8:15, he practically sprang up the steps. His confidence exuded an aura so strong that Lloyd was sure that everyone around him could see it.

Three-quarters of the way through the morning, Lloyd had changed his tune. He was beyond exhausted. If previously he had any misguided notion that this assignment was going to be a piece of cake, he now knew with complete and undeniable certainty that what he was about to undertake was complicated, necessary, and deadly serious. Lloyd had not a smidgeon of doubt that his complete compliance with everything he was being told was truly a matter of life and death.

His brain was gyrating. *A whole week of this?* Lloyd felt that his head would probably spin around and fly off long before that!

Most of the morning had consisted of Sergeant Gablehaus and BeeBee outlining for Lloyd the EAST VAN DEVILS' modus operandi when it came to any and all illicit activities carried out by the gang members.

They explained that some of the youngest recruits were only thirteen years old, and as fledgeling members, they either had to 'shape up or ship out'. Unfortunately, in extreme cases, 'ship out' was permanent. Sadly, to date, the police had been unable to prove that the demise of several young people amounted to murder.

Under the gang leadership of Domingo Sanchez, no crime was too small or too large.

It was also explained to Lloyd that even though Domingo Sanchez was the leader of the East Van Devils, he and his gang were accountable to The Warlords. The leader's name was Pedro Santana. If Domingo was not complicit with the orders from Pedro Santana, too bad for him. He had no choice but to do exactly as Santana directed.

Sensing Lloyd's near panic, the Sergeant looked at BeeBee. "Should we take pity on the young lad and take a lunch break, do you think?"

BeeBee grinned. Lloyd caught the grin and said, in a voice that strained to be civil, "You think this is funny, BeeBee? This is darn hard; I'll never be able to remember all this stuff. I'm sure to screw up this operation. You guys need to find somebody else!" He put his head in his hands, weary to the bone, feeling very sorry for himself.

BeeBee reached over and patted Lloyd's shoulder.

"Kid," she said. "A week from now you'll know everything there is to know about these scumbags. You will also be so well trained that nothing that is thrown at you will be a problem, so long as you don't get cocky. The key to dealing with these guys is not to get overly confident and never, not for one millisecond, let your guard down."

Sergeant Gablehaus stood up. "Grab your lunch out of the fridge, my friend. Too bad we couldn't all go out for lunch, but suffice it to say, the three of us cannot risk being seen together. You never know who is watching or for what purpose. For that matter, we don't recognise most of the gang members. The East Van Devils are growing larger and stronger day by day. So, unfortunately, for the next week or so, you are stuck having lunch alone in my office. I, on the other hand, will continue with my calendar of luncheon dates, and BeeBee will continue her charade of being a street person every lunch hour."

The Sergeant returned to his office a few minutes before one o'clock. BeeBee was nowhere to be seen.

At 1:00 p.m. sharp, there was a knock on the office door. Sergeant Gablehaus was on the phone so he motioned for Lloyd to answer the door.

Standing at the door was a slim, trim, gorgeous young woman, dressed in sweats and a T-shirt. Her casual apparel and lack of makeup did nothing to mask her beauty. She had dark brown eyes and beautiful hair, highlighted in several different rich shades of auburn. Lloyd glanced from the woman back to the Sergeant, who was still on the phone.

"Hey, young Lloyd," said the beauty. "Aren't you going to ask me in?" Sensing his discomfort, she suddenly laughed, a hearty, robust belly laugh. "Don't you know me?" She grinned, struck a seductive pose, then laughed some more, this time louder, heartier.

Sergeant Gablehaus finished his conversation. "Come on in BeeBee, and give the kid a break."

Lloyd's jaw literally dropped. "Pick your chin up off the floor, Lloyd," BeeBee smirked. She then said, with great affectation, "Ain't ya never seen no lady before?"

By this time, even the Sergeant was laughing. "This is what I mean, Lloyd," he said jovially, "about not knowing who is watching.

"Now, enough teasing poor Lloyd, BeeBee. Let's get back to work."

The afternoon was spent on self-defence instructions. By the end of the afternoon, Lloyd was stiff and sore from being thrown onto a very thin mat numerous times by BeeBee, who was a black belt in some sort of martial arts. All Lloyd wanted to do was go home and crawl into a very hot bath to try to iron out some of the kinks and wounds inflicted upon him.

"See you tomorrow, kid," BeeBee grinned.

"Yeah, sure," Lloyd grumbled. "That is if you haven't killed me!" Despite his grumbling, he managed a weak smile as he limped to the door.

Sergeant Gablehaus gave him a piece of good advice. "When you get home, Lloyd, do some exercises to stretch out some of the kinks before you have a hot soak in the tub. Throw three cups of Epsom salts into your bath water. You're young and in great shape. You'll survive. See you tomorrow."

The next day, Lloyd showed up at the detachment right on time, and only slightly sore. The Sergeant's advice had been helpful.

"Morning, Lloyd," said the Sergeant. "Morning, Lloyd," echoed the ravishing BeeBee.

"Good morning to both of you and thanks for giving up your Sunday to train me," responded Lloyd.

Sergeant Gablehaus leaned back in his chair. A chalkboard stand rested to his left, complete with plenty of chalk and an eraser.

"So, Lloyd," the Sergeant began, "Yesterday we pushed you pretty hard, for two reasons. One, to test your mettle, see what you are made of. Despite some grumbling, which only makes you human, you passed our appraisal of you with flying colours.

"Second reason, we have only one week from tomorrow to inculcate a nearly impossible amount of information and skills, to bring you up to speed and condition before this operation begins. You're a very fast learner, my young friend. BeeBee and I both agree sincerely that you are going to be a huge asset in this action.

"So, BeeBee, would you be so kind as to jot down my thoughts as I verbalise them?"

"Not a problem, sir," she said as she walked over to the chalkboard, picked up a long piece of chalk and waited expectantly for her boss to begin.

Time Line – One Week from Monday

Lloyd will approach East Van Devils' clubhouse and ask to speak with his father, Paul Martin Jordan. If Brutus tries to blow him off, Lloyd will tell him it is an emergency; it is regarding Paul's daughter, Lacey.

Lloyd interjected. "Sir, wouldn't it be better to begin on a Thursday? BeeBee has her deliveries on Thursdays. That way we could approach the clubhouse together."

BeeBee herself answered Lloyd's question. "Too dangerous, Lloyd. If, after all this time, I show up with a partner when I am delivering illegal goods to the East Van Devils, a red flag will not only wave right in front of Brutus' eyeballs, it'll probably whack him right between those squinty eyes!"

"Never thought of that," Lloyd said. He turned to the Sergeant. "Sorry to interrupt, sir, please continue."

Day 1 (yesterday, Saturday) – Training regimen:

A.M. – Outline EAST VAN DEVILS' modus operandi respecting any and all illicit activities carried out by the gang's members. / *P.M. – Martial arts training.*

Day 2 (Sunday) Full day

Examine math skills. Teach a couple of the most-used computer bookkeeping methods – debits and credits; possible headings to watch for, code words for activities used by the Money Man when posting transactions, bank accounts (how many, where, balances). *Math Exam* – include Grade XII math and bookkeeping math.

Day 3 (Monday)

A.M. – More martial arts training – BeeBee / P.M. – Poker, if time permits.

At this point, Lloyd couldn't wait; he had to interrupt once again. "Poker, sir?" he asked incredulously. "Poker? As in the card game?"

Sergeant Gablehaus grinned broadly. "Sure is, young Lloyd. Ever played?"

"Well, yes, sir, some. But I don't understand; what's poker got to do with the East Van Devils' stuff?"

The Sergeant queried, "Do you know what a poker face is?"

"I think so, sir."

Greg Gablehaus said, "Lloyd, the most important thing you are going to have to do while you are in the presence of members of that gang, and particularly with your father, is to hide your negative feelings and to project an earnest, likeable demeanour at all times. That is the only way that you are going to hoodwink these characters. I've noticed that you have a hard time masquing your feelings when something is important to you. A poker game will give you the opportunity to practise being poker-faced. If it takes a dozen poker games before a week from Monday, so be it. We'll play poker for twenty-four hours a day if need be. I warn you though; our friend BeeBee here will whip the stuffing out of both of us. She's that good!"

Lloyd looked up at BeeBee. "Is there anything you are NOT great at BeeBee?" he asked wryly. She just smiled and winked at him, then cheerily grinned. "Nope," she said, then winked again.

"Let us continue," the Sergeant said tersely. "Time's wasting."

Day 4 (Tuesday) – full day, if required

Psychological Assessment / Poker, if time permits.

"Let me guess," Lloyd said facetiously, "BeeBee is a Psychologist."

Sergeant Gablehaus chortled. BeeBee shrugged her shoulders. "Master's Degree in Psychology; specialising in Criminal behaviours."

Lloyd looked stricken. "Do you think that I am exhibiting criminal behaviours?"

She smiled gently at him. "Not yet, but I sure hope you do by the time we are done here, training you to work among some of the best criminals in the Vancouver area.

"Basically, I will be speaking with you to try to determine if you have any problems, either pertaining to your preparations for this covert operation or evolving from your earlier life. This will give you an opportunity to release any pressures you may have *before* you encounter any new ones once you infiltrate the gang. I would suggest that you make a list of any questions you may have for me before we meet on Day 4 for your intensive psychological review."

"Oh boy!" was all that Lloyd could manage to say.

Day 5 (Wednesday)

A.M. – Review of Bookkeeping methods and any math problems that may have arisen from the previous exam. *P.M. – Martial arts practice* and, if time permits, another poker game.

Day 6 (Thursday)

A.M. – Review of East Van Devils' operations; *P.M. – Martial arts practice* / Poker game

Day 7 (Friday) – Full day

Review of everything learned in the 7 days to date. Psychological reassessment.

Day 8 (Saturday) – Full day

Video / Audio Spy Pen

"This is probably the most important tool we can give you, Lloyd, other than your own self-control that is," the Sergeant said. "It is the most up to date Video/Audio Spy pen on the market today. It is not available to the public; it is strictly for use among crime investigators. We will be carefully studying the video pertaining to this tool, and then going through its abilities in minute detail. You will be practising using the pen today and tomorrow. The most important use for this device will be for you to photograph the books that your father controls. Don't worry if they make any sense to you or not. That will be a job for our lab technicians to decipher. Rule of thumb? If you are not sure, take the picture. Better too many than not enough.

"The battery lasts for up to six hours. The memory on this little gadget is amazing, as is the resolution of the images. Also, by simply pushing a secret button beneath the clip that attaches the pen to your pocket, the information goes straight to my cell phone. Once the pen has received confirmation that my cell has successfully received the information, both audio and video, it automatically deletes the data in your pen. It is ingenious, and simple to use.

"However, unless I am 100% certain that you know all of the procedures and information you are learning this week inside and out, the entire project will have to be scrapped."

Day 9 (Sunday)

Practise with Audio Spy Pen/code words for emergency assistance once inside the clubhouse. *Last chance for review and questions* before the covert operation begins tomorrow (Monday). *Final exam, both written and oral*, in the afternoon.

"Oh boy!" was all that Lloyd could still manage to say.

The week flew by. Lloyd wavered between despair that he would never learn so many things in so short a time, and feeling self-confident and eager to begin.

On Day 6, BeeBee wasn't present, Thursday being her regular delivery to the Devils' clubhouse. Lloyd spent the day reviewing the copious material and procedures with Sergeant Gablehaus. Lloyd actually threw the Sergeant to the mat four out of six times during his martial arts practice. Lloyd handily won the poker game they played in the afternoon. It earned Lloyd a 'thumbs up' and a cheer from the leader of the operation, although Lloyd did notice that a bit later in the afternoon the Sergeant was gingerly rubbing his hip.

Day 9, Sunday, the final day arrived. For the first hour, Lloyd was encouraged to ask questions of Sergeant Gablehaus and BeeBee. He was assured that no question was too ridiculous, that he should feel comfortable asking anything he needed to.

When the first hour expired, there was a last martial arts practice and a few hands of poker were played.

After lunch came the exam; first, the written portion, followed by the oral testing. When the exam was completed, Lloyd thought he had probably done fairly well, but he nonetheless waited anxiously for Sergeant Gablehaus and BeeBee to return to the office after marking his exam.

With serious, unreadable expressions, Lloyd's two mentors pulled their chairs up in front of Lloyd and sat down, saying nothing for several minutes. Finally, Greg Gablehaus spoke.

"Well, young Lloyd, this has been one intense week, not only for you as a student, but for BeeBee and I as instructors. If we couldn't train you adequately so that the covert operation could proceed, we would have failed as much as you." Here, he stopped, prolonging Lloyd's agony. The Sergeant then turned to BeeBee and said, so quietly that Lloyd couldn't hear him clearly, "You have the honour, BeeBee."

"My great pleasure, sir," she said. "Stand up, Lloyd."

Although his knees were quaking, Lloyd did as he was directed.

"It gives me the utmost pleasure, young Lloyd, to tell you that you have passed your exam with the highest marks of any undercover student that we have trained, and that is a mark of 98.25%. You missed only one question. And, because I know you are going to ask about the other 1.75%, there was an error in the makeup of the exam. There was no question, just a descriptive preliminary. With no question, there could be no answer. If that error had been noted and corrected before the exam, you would have aced it! Congratulations!

"I also feel that I need to tell you that I listened very, very carefully to your life story as you related it to me in great detail. It touched me. Young Lloyd, you and your sister have survived much adversity in your young lives, and yet you are persevering and improving every single day.

"You impress me, Mr Jordan, a great deal. Congratulations, and 'Go Get 'Em' Let's bring the *EAST VAN DEVILS* down!" BeeBee then reached forward and gave Lloyd the biggest hug. He swallowed hard, trying unsuccessfully to dislodge the lump at the back of his throat. "Thanks, BeeBee," he whispered as he hugged her back.

Sergeant Gablehaus cleared his throat. "My turn," he ordered with a smile. "Congratulations, Lloyd, you have made both BeeBee and I very happy. Your ability to learn has made training you an absolute pleasure and joy. Now, get a good rest because tomorrow you start your new employment.

"Oh, before you go, here is your pen, replacement batteries and ink cartridges. I look forward to receiving many photos and oral messages in the coming months. Remember the passwords, especially the SOS one. Someone will always be on duty near the clubhouse, always listening in case you need backup." The Sergeant hugged Lloyd and then shook his hand, saying somewhat brokenly, "Good luck, Lloyd, and as BeeBee said, 'Go Get 'Em!'

Wow! Lloyd said to himself, not for the first time, *just, Wow!*

***

Monday morning dawned gloomily, but at least it wasn't raining. Lloyd made himself a piece of toast and a hot chocolate, but he could neither eat nor drink.

The start time for the covert operation had been set by Sergeant Gablehaus for 10:00 am. Lloyd checked the clock – only 6:15.

Mona Grace would be getting up in fifteen minutes. Lloyd decided not to shower until she was finished in the bathroom and left for work.

He went back into his bedroom to review in his mind everything he had studied. It was no use. He couldn't concentrate. He picked up a Grade XIII textbook. He could always study. His final semester exams weren't very far away. *Yes,* he thought, *I'll study until Mona Grace has gone to work. Hah!* He put his textbook away and put on a tracksuit.

Mona Grace's alarm rang at 6:30.

"Hey, Mona Grace! I'm going for a run before class. Have a good day." He went out the back door, locked it behind him and started off at a slow jog, increasing speed gradually until he was travelling at a full run. Forty-five minutes later he returned to the house, physically tired but mentally wired. Mona Grace had left him a note on the kitchen table. *Good,* he thought once he completed reading the note, she *has a meeting this evening and won't be home until late. I won't have to worry about making up some story about what I did today.* He looked at the clock once again – 7:15 a.m.

Lloyd picked up his cold and soggy toast and dumped it into the garbage. While he reheated his cocoa, he made himself a fresh piece of toast. When his breakfast was once again ready, he choked down the toast, scalded his tongue on the hot chocolate as he tried to drink it too quickly, then headed for the shower. Even though he stayed in the shower until the water turned cold, it was only 8:00 when he finished in the bathroom.

Lloyd dressed carefully in clean blue jeans, a blue plaid shirt, clean runners. Despite having spent at least ten minutes carefully styling his hair, he plopped a Blue Jays ball cap on top of the carefully coiffed hairdo. He very carefully scrutinised his pen, reassuring himself that it was in working order. He clipped the pen on to the pocket of his shirt, looked in the mirror. He could barely see the pen sticking out of the shirt pocket. Pleased with himself and feeling a bit more composed, less anxious, he decided to go hang out in Oppenheimer Park until it was time to head out for the clubhouse.

He chose a bench on the outskirts of the park, closer to the direction he had to walk to get to the clubhouse. No sooner had he sat down, he heard a familiar whistling. In a short time, the Whistling Man came into view.

"Hey, Man!" he greeted Lloyd. "I haven't seen you around for a while. How's things?"

"Good, good, thanks. I have been working part-time down by Stanley Park and going to school part-time. I'm nearly done my Grade XIII. Feels really good."

"Glad to hear it!" The Whistling Man appeared genuinely interested and happy for Lloyd, but Lloyd could tell he was anxious to carry on picking up the trash from the park so Lloyd stood up, said "Sure was good to see you again. You have a good day now," thus releasing the whistler from any anxiety he was already exhibiting.

FINALLY! Lloyd looked at his watch for the hundredth time already today and decided that if he walked at a leisurely pace, he could head out in the direction of the East Van Devils' clubhouse.

As he walked, he reminded himself that he had to keep a poker face, no matter what. Sergeant Gablehaus had assured him that after a day or two, it would become second nature, not to worry, just carry out his duties as assigned to him by his father, and to remember to transmit data whenever it was safe to do so.

The shiny red door of the clubhouse appeared. Lloyd pulled his shoulders back and, calling upon every bit of inner strength he possessed, knocked on the red door. Just an ordinary knock, not BeeBee's 'shave and a haircut' coded knock. Trying to wait patiently, he finally knocked again, louder this time.

"Who is it?"

Lloyd took a very deep breath and released it slowly before saying, "Lloyd Jordan, sir."

The door opened partially and the deep, unfriendly voice said, "Don't know any Lloyd Jordan. You must have the wrong place." The door started to close.

"Wait just a minute" Lloyd quickly called. "I don't have the wrong address, I can assure you. Please, can you open the door?"

The door opened wide and the by-now familiar Tattoo Man showed himself as Lloyd discreetly pressed the video/audio controls on his pen. "Make it quick, kid," he growled, "I ain't got all day."

Right! Lloyd thought to himself, *All you have to do is check the door, destroy businesses and beat up innocent old ladies.* He managed to think this behind his newly-acquired poker face, a face completely devoid of expression despite his latent rage towards this giant of a man. Knowing he had learned well somehow made him feel more comfortable, less afraid.

"As I said, my name is Lloyd Jordan. My father, Paul Martin Jordan, lives and works here. He told me to come and see him."

Brutus glowered at Lloyd. His sour demeanour expressed his opinion that the kid had crawled out from under a sewer somewhere. He was tempted to tell the little turd to take a hike but decided (wisely) to let the Money Man know his kid was here.

"Hang on, I'll see if he's around," Brutus sighed. He turned and re-entered the clubhouse, leaving Lloyd standing alone on the bottom step.

Just as Lloyd was beginning to think that Brutus hadn't passed on the message, the shiny red door opened once again, and Paul Jordan stepped outside. A smile nearly emerged, but Paul stopped it before it could spread across his entire face.

"Well, well, well, if it isn't the prodigal son – returning to the fold, are we?"

Lloyd bit his tongue. Now was not the time to mouth off. He said calmly, "You said to think about whether I wanted to work with you or not. Well, I've thought it over. If your offer still stands, I'd like to give it a whirl."

Paul suddenly turned around and slammed the red door shut with such force that there was a cry of anguish from the other side.

"Serves you right, Brutus," Paul snarled through the now tightly-closed door. "There's times for eavesdropping, but this ain't one of 'em. Bugger off and let me visit with my son."

Lloyd smiled at his father as he secretly pressed the video/audio controls on his pen.

Paul turned to Lloyd. "Sorry about that. Now, where were we?"

"I asked if your job offer still stands," Lloyd said quietly.

"Are you any good at math? This job is all about numbers."

"Math is my best subject. I really enjoy anything related to numbers."

Paul said, "Well, then, I'll give you a try. One thing, though, you are absolutely not to talk about anything that you are working on here in the clubhouse, not a word to anyone other than me, got that?"

"Yes, sir, I am not to speak to anyone about what I am working on. I understand." (Lloyd chuckled silently behind his poker mask and thought, *But you didn't say anything about taking pictures or writing about or recording what happens here. You simply said just don't speak to anyone about it!)* "You're the money man for Domingo and his gang, correct? This is an illicit operation; that's why I can't talk about it. I get it."

"That's right, kid. And let me tell you, if you get caught, the consequences for leaking information from the Devils to anyone else are deadly."

He looked down at Lloyd. "Where's your things?"

"My things?" Lloyd asked.

"Well, you must have some stuff to move here. Why didn't you bring your clothes and other things with you?"

Lloyd said, "I'm not going to be living here with you, Dad. Besides, I wasn't even sure that you were serious when you offered to have me work with you. Why would I have brought all my stuff?"

"Why don't you want to live here with me?" his father inquired. Suspicious by nature, he scrutinised his son's face, carefully looking for anything that might make him uncomfortable.

Lloyd explained, "Well, I am going to night school. I'm just finishing up my final semester and then I will have my Grade XIII. I live very close to school and I can study at the library. I know you want me to live here with you, but I'm pretty sure there are too many distractions and too much commotion in this clubhouse for me to be able to prepare for my final exams. I have made excellent grades up to this point and I'm not going to change my routine now.

"So, I'm saying thanks, but no thanks, Dad. I'll work for you every day, but I'm going back to my home every night."

Outwardly, Paul allowed himself to appear annoyed; inwardly, though, he was rather proud of his son for standing up for what he wanted to do.

Paul asked, "When can you start?"

Lloyd asked, "What's wrong with right now?"

"Not a damn thing, Lloyd. Come on, I'll show you around." Lloyd tried not to cringe as his father put his arm around Lloyd's shoulders possessively and squeezed him conspiratorially, his hand frightfully close to Lloyd's shirt pocket. Paul removed his arm and unlocked the clubhouse door.

Just inside the shiny red door was a meeting room of some sort. There was a podium at the far side of the room. It looked rather like a church because rows of wooden pews were set up in front of the podium. Two closed doors read Men's and Women's respectively. A very large refrigerator sat against the wall to the right of the podium.

"Beer fridge," Paul said in response to his son's quizzical glance in that direction. *So much for a church,* Lloyd thought, laughing on the inside, poker-faced on the outside.

He followed Paul down a short hallway which ended at a staircase. There did not appear to be any other rooms on this main floor.

They climbed the stairs to the next level. Numerous doors lined both sides of the hallway, similar to a hotel. Lloyd looked at Paul and raised his eyebrows. "Members' rooms," Paul said. "Each room has a double bed; each room has its own full bath. Although local members live here, there are a few empty rooms reserved for visiting members of The Warlords. If, for some reason, let's say for the sake of argument, a convention, there are more than a couple visiting gang members here, our local members have to give up their rooms for the visitors.

"Here, at the far end of the hallway, is the kitchen and dining room. It is fully staffed with a chef, a sous chef and some beautiful 'waitresses', who are also available for 'room service' if you get my drift." Paul gave a lewd chuckle. Lloyd felt sick. This wasn't how a father should talk with his son.

Lloyd walked into the dining room. It was beautiful, lavishly appointed with rich wood dining room furniture. A very large, two-sided fireplace regally presided over the centre of the room. Elegant flower arrangements were scattered throughout. An equally elegant private dining room occupied a back portion of the main room.

The kitchen was a hub of activity. Completely furnished with top of the line stainless steel appliances, the chef and the sous chef were busy preparing tonight's dinner. Lloyd turned towards Paul and asked, "Do you eat your meals here also?"

"I eat supper here. Only one meal a day is cooked, supper. Breakfast and lunch, I either cook for myself in my apartment, or I go out to eat."

"Hmm," Lloyd muttered non-committedly.

"One more level," Paul said. "There is an elevator, but I prefer the stairs. Gotta keep the old beer belly under control." To prove his point, he ran up the stairs, two at a time. At the top, he turned and grinned down at Lloyd, unsuccessfully trying to hide from his son the fact that he was out of breath, gasping for air.

Lloyd continued a leisurely ascent, mostly to give his father time to recover from his rather unfortunate attempt to show off in front of his son.

Once Lloyd reached the third floor, Paul led him down a short but very opulent hallway. There was only one double door. It was huge, taking up nearly all of the wall. Expensive and beautiful, made from rich, dark cherry wood, the door produced a certain degree of intimidation, which was exactly what the leader of the East Van Devils had intended when he had the door designed. In front of the colossal doors, on each side of the hallway, two beautiful, oversized, buttery leather chairs beckoned. Despite the fact that they looked to be very comfortable, they were distinctly uncomfortable once you sat down. The design was such that you had to sit extremely upright. Discomfort plus awkwardness equals further intimidation. Domingo Sanchez was all about intimidation.

"Have a seat," Paul said and pointed towards one of the chairs. He approached the right side of the gigantic doors and pressed a doorbell. A melody filled the waiting area with a classical tune that Lloyd thought he should recognise but could not. It wasn't until the whole chorus finished that Paul stood up and waited.

"Who is it?" boomed a very loud voice.

"It's me, Domingo. My son is with me."

"Okay, just give me five minutes and then I'll let you in."

It was closer to fifteen minutes before the doors swung open inwardly. A rather dishevelled young woman appeared. The woman was dressed in a wrinkled black skirt and white blouse. She was awkwardly trying to button up her blouse as she quickly walked out, looking neither left nor right. She was carrying black fishnet stockings in one hand.

"Sorry, Lilly, I didn't know you and Domingo were busy. Kicked you out of bed in a hurry, huh?" Paul gave the unfortunate woman a lewd wink. Lloyd felt sorry for her.

Domingo showed up in the doorway tucking a teal silk shirt into his black leather pants. He waved them in, then turned and inspected Lloyd carefully. "So?" Domingo uttered. "Who are you again?"

Paul started to speak, but Domingo shushed him. "I'm speaking with this young man now, Paul. Just sit down and be quiet unless I speak to you directly." While Domingo was focused on Paul, Lloyd checked his watch. Still lots of time to keep recording before the audio/video pen's battery died.

Domingo turned back to Lloyd who by this time was starting to feel like a pig in a poke.

"Name?" Domingo barked.

Lloyd shuddered slightly, then stood straight and replied, "Braden Lloyd Jordan, Mr Sanchez. I'm Paul Martin Jordan's son."

"Age?" Domingo's voice was raspy from cigarettes and whiskey. Listening to it made Lloyd's throat feel sore.

"Nineteen."

"What are you doing here?"

"Visiting my father."

By this time Lloyd was thinking that his father hadn't talked with Domingo about this job. He looked over at Paul, but Paul didn't seem overly concerned.

"Did your father fill you in on the do's and don'ts of working and living in this clubhouse?" Domingo Sanchez asked in a menacing way. It made Lloyd shudder again.

"He certainly did, Mr Sanchez. I am not to speak with anyone about anything I see or do here, and definitely not about any of the books that I work on. I understand, sir, the importance of discretion with regard to all things involving the East Van Devils. I can guarantee you that I will not speak with anyone outside of my father and yourself regarding any of the duties I have here."

The Grand Master of intimidation asked Lloyd harshly, "Did Paul tell you what would happen if you break your guarantee?"

"He did, sir, but there was no need. I understood what my duties entailed and the need for secrecy."

"That's good then. Welcome aboard."

He reached forward and shook Lloyd's hand. Holding the highest office in the gang, Lloyd would have thought Domingo would have a firmer, more authoritative grip. It was kind of limp and sweaty, in Lloyd's humble opinion.

"Just have a seat over there, next to the bar. If you want something to drink, help yourself. I just need to speak with your father about a couple of things. Make yourself at home."

Lloyd walked through the large living room area and took a seat. Suddenly he stood up. "May I use your washroom, please?" Lloyd asked Domingo, even though he didn't need to go.

"Yeah, sure kid." He waved his arm towards a hallway on Lloyd's left. "It's down the hall."

Lloyd walked towards a doorway and stepped through. The hallway ran the full width of the apartment. He first turned left. At the very end was a large bedroom. From the state of dishabille, the luxurious colours and fabrics, the expensive furnishings, and the massive size of the room, it would appear that this room belonged to Domingo. A walk-through closet was packed full of expensive, colourful clothing. Lloyd backed out of the room and turned around, walking down the hall in the opposite direction.

To his left, directly across from the living room doorway, was the washroom. *Wow!* Lloyd thought, *his bathroom is bigger than Mona Grace's kitchen!* He admired the sunken jacuzzi bathtub, noted the luxuriously thick Turkish bath sheets hanging on heated towel racks. His eyes popped when he saw the large shower that was separate from the tub. Numerous jet massage sprayers at different levels made Lloyd wish he could just hop in and get a shower massage.

Feeling a bit guilty for snooping, he unnecessarily flushed the toilet and turned on the taps, pretending to wash his hands in the marble pedestal sink.

Lloyd came out of the bathroom; turned to his left. The next room was a large but cosy media room. Furnished with theatre seats, a bar along one wall, and even a commercial popcorn maker. One entire wall supported a giant television screen.

The next and last room was a gym, complete with a whirlpool bath, a steam room and a shower, *and* a personal trainer, who asked Lloyd if there was anything he could do for him.

"No, thanks," Lloyd answered. "I'm just waiting for my dad and Mr Sanchez to finish up some business." The trainer said he, also, was just waiting for Mr Sanchez. He had a workout scheduled when he was finished with Paul. He showed Lloyd around the gym; he even showed him how some of the more complicated pieces of exercise equipment functioned. Lloyd then thanked the man, nodded farewell and went back into the living room.

Lloyd couldn't hear what the two men were discussing, but he certainly hoped that the super pen, with its state-of-the-art innards, would be able to.

While he sat, Lloyd discreetly assessed the leader of the gang. Remembering Mona Grace's description of her boyfriend from so many years ago, Lloyd noted that he was still tall and slim, but with definite muscle definition. He suspected though, that without the benefit of the personal trainer and daily workouts, he would not be in great shape.

His face looked the worse for wear. Besides a lot of acne scars, it appeared to Lloyd that Domingo's nose had been broken at least a time or two. Unless he was a much better- looking young man and not so domineering, Lloyd just couldn't figure out Mona Grace's attraction. At this time in his life, Domingo looked like what he was, a hard-core, vicious gang leader.

However, the attraction between Domingo and Mona Grace was probably a good thing, in the long run, Lloyd thought to himself. *Something good came out of that union – Charley!*

With a start, Lloyd realised that he hadn't thought of the missing girls for quite a long time. Feeling guilty, he prayed that they were all right. He was anxious to complete this covert operation for several reasons, but the main one was that Sergeant Gablehaus promised to look into the cases of the missing foster girls when this was all over.

"Hey, Lloyd, earth to Lloyd, come in Lloyd!"

His father's feeble attempt at humour finally broke through Lloyd's cloudy, meandering mind.

"Sorry, I was daydreaming. Did you say something?"

Paul said, "Just asked if you're ready to see the rest of this floor."

"Of course." Lloyd turned to Domingo. "Mr Sanchez, you have a beautiful place here. Nice to meet you. See you again soon."

Domingo waved his hand towards the door, flashing a knuckle-duster of a diamond ring. "Same here, kid. What did you say your name was again?"

"Lloyd, sir."

With great difficulty, Lloyd refrained from rolling his eyes.

Back out in the hallway, Lloyd followed his father to the head of the staircase, where a wing ambled a long way from the landing to the end of the hall. Paul didn't tell him what was down that wing so Lloyd asked, "Anything of interest down that way?" He discreetly flicked the switch to activate the pen. (CLICK ON)

Paul stopped and pointed. "My office is the first door on the right. Beside my office is a library. You'll see both rooms later when we get to work. Beside the library is an empty room, which I think will make a good office for you. Domingo agreed. He said for you to tell me what you want for furnishings and I'm to order it." He continued, "The rest of the wing contains two storage rooms, an unused clothes chute, and another empty room which has never been used for anything."

"Why isn't the clothes chute used anymore? I would think it would save a ton of steps."

"Oh, I forgot about that. The laundry was in the basement, but Domingo wanted it on the same floor as his apartment. So, there is now a laundry room down at the end of this hallway. You can do your laundry there. There are five washers and five dryers, so there is usually a machine or two not in use."

Paul continued walking towards the opposite end of the hall from Domingo's palatial residence. He stopped in front of a double door that was very nice but not, of course, as impressive as Domingo's. Paul unlocked the door and said in a stupid falsetto (stupid in Lloyd's mind), "Come into my parlour, said the spider to the fly." Lloyd gave a sickly grin, feeling very much like the fly. (CLICK OFF) No point in Sergeant Gablehaus hearing about Paul's apartment. *It would just be a waste of battery power,* Lloyd thought. *I'll turn the pen on again when we are in Paul's office. More likely to be something useful said in there!*

Paul's apartment was larger than the small house they lived in before Lloyd and Lacey's normal childhood fell apart. Beautifully furnished, there was a good-sized entryway, a powder room, a large living room/dining room combined, and a fully-equipped kitchen that looked like it had rarely, if ever, been used. At the far end of the apartment, there was one very large master bedroom, complete with full bath, including a jacuzzi bathtub. To the left of the master was a spare bedroom, almost as large as the master suite, but less showy. This room, also, had a full bath, but with only an ordinary soaker tub, no jacuzzi. *Not that it mattered though,* thought Lloyd. *I'm not going to live here anyway*

"So, kid," Paul yawned and stretched, flexing his muscles ostentatiously before he asked, "what do you think of the East Van Devils' clubhouse? Pretty impressive wouldn't you say?"

(CLICK ON) "It's something," Lloyd said. "A lot of stuff and a huge amount of space. It also seems to me that you must have a horrific workload. You'd never dream, looking at the outside, just how expensive this place is, how big it is! I sure hope I'll be of assistance to you, cut the workload down a bit for you. I have to say, though, that right now, I'm feeling pretty overwhelmed."

And sick, he thought to himself. *Father or no father, he makes me sick.*

"Don't worry about it, Lloyd. You'll do good. You know, there's something about you … (Lloyd stuck his tongue between his top and bottom front teeth and bit down hard to stop himself from gasping for air or passing out!) … that makes me think that even if you weren't my son, I would trust you implicitly. I think I might have told you that before. If I never have, I sure should have."

"Thanks!" Lloyd said numbly.

"Okay, the tour is over. Let's grab a sandwich in the kitchen. It's fully stocked with groceries and drinks. After we have a bite, we'll go into my office and I'll start training you. We'll also check out the room that will be your office and then we'll go to an office furniture store and you can pick out what you want. Now, off to the kitchen," Paul said. (CLICK OFF)

Once lunch was over, they went to Paul's office. It was large enough for two full-size ornate desks, an entire wall of alternating filing cabinets and bookcases that matched the desks, a credenza behind each of the desks, and two large, comfortable leather chairs in front of each desk. There was still room to walk between the chairs even when they were pushed out from the desks. An ornate wall, panelled to match the rest of the wooden furnishings, housed a nearly invisible door that opened into a bathroom. The bathroom even had a shower large enough for two. Lloyd refused to even consider the need for a large shower attached to an office!

(CLICK ON) "Dad," Lloyd asked hesitantly, "this office is more than big enough for two people. Why can't I share it with you?"

Paul nudged Lloyd in the ribs, grinned and winked conspiratorially. "The second desk is for my 'secretary' if you get my drift. She only works part-time, on different days each week, so if you come to talk to me about something, be sure to knock." Lloyd felt like belching but managed a weak grimace instead. He had rapidly come to the conclusion that either his father was just showing off, or he really was a dirty old man!

Paul said, "Now, before we get to work, let's take a look at your office and you can tell me what you want in there." (CLICK OFF)

As they walked, Lloyd was busy memorising the layout of the place, trying to guestimate the distances between what he felt were focal points. He didn't yet understand why he felt the need to compute and retain all this information in his head; he only knew it was something he seemed to be compelled to do.

They entered the empty room. Lloyd said, "This room is big enough for a whole team of people!"

"Well," Paul stated, "you can never have enough space. Now, what do you require for furnishings?"

"Not much, do I?" Lloyd really didn't care about the decorating because he didn't plan on being around all that long, but he decided to feign interest so as not to arouse any suspicion about the real reasons he was there. He paced off the approximate size of the room; he opened a door at one end. It was a washroom – no shower, thank Heavens!

After what he deemed a reasonable time to be thinking about something as unimportant to him as furniture, Lloyd turned to his father and said, "a desk, a credenza, a comfortable chair for me to sit in, two comfortable chairs for guests or clients, a bookcase, a filing cabinet, maybe an area carpet. That should do it. Oh, and a hand towel for the washroom. I hate paper towels."

"Sounds reasonable to me, Lloyd. Ready to go and pick everything out?"

"Dad, would you mind doing it? You have excellent taste. I have a heavy-duty exam tomorrow evening, worth 50% of my final mark, as well as a term paper due. I was hoping that you would let me leave early so I can prepare and then tomorrow morning, bright and early, we can put in a full day."

"I guess that would be okay, Lloyd. But do you have a particular style of furniture you would like? I really don't know you, kid; therefore, I don't know your taste."

"Whatever you choose will be just fine with me, Dad. Nothing ornate or very expensive though, please. After all, I am 'low man on the totem pole' here, and I'm here to work and to learn. I just need basic stuff."

"Gotcha!" Paul said in a bad imitation of a teenage colloquialism. "Give me a sec and I'll walk you out."

"It's okay, Dad, I know the way out. I need to go to the bathroom first, though. Okay if I use the one in my soon-to-be office?"

"Go for it, kid! See ya tomorrow." Lloyd winced at his father's syrupy, phoney tone. He knew his dad was probably just trying to make up for the past, but he really didn't seem sincere.

Lloyd waited in the bathroom long enough to ensure that Paul had left for the furniture store, and then he came out and into the hallway. Looking in all directions to ensure nobody was around, he clicked on his pen and, in a stage whisper, spoke into the pen as he quietly walked to the end of the hall. Checking over his shoulder once again, he opened the door of the laundry chute. He stuck his head inside, used the flashlight feature on the amazing pen to have a look. Satisfied that he would fit in the space, albeit with not much room to spare, Lloyd quickly climbed in, pulling the chute door closed behind himself. Until he adjusted to the size and the straight downgrade of the chute, he chose to press the sides of his feet against the walls and push his shoulders and arms against the walls in order to hold himself steady. He found it easier to hold his rubber-soled and overlapping rubber sides of his shoes against the wall rather than his hands, which were slippery with sweat. His shoulders reached the walls but just, so he really needed his arms and hands to help steady himself. Once positioned and holding steady, he then moved his feet down as far as he could reach, balanced himself with his feet and moved the rest of his body downwards carefully. He felt rather like a spider with only four legs instead of eight, but after alternating between feet, shoulders, arms and hands several times, he got the hang of it and made better time.

He reached the second floor and balanced himself, listening for any sounds coming from beyond the chute. All was quiet. All was also very dark! He thought about turning on the flashlight on the pen but was worried about the battery power. Also, he wasn't sure that the bright LED light would not be seen by someone in the hallway. Lloyd decided to try and let go and slide down. It would be quicker and so long as he didn't get stuck on a rough piece of tin liner, much easier than the 'spider-man crawl' he had just tried to perfect. He would just pretend he was on a slide at a children's playground. The worst thing that could happen was that he might get stuck!

"Here goes nothing, Sergeant!" He spoke into his pen. "If you don't hear from me further, I will be buried in a laundry chute." He was only half-joking. (CLICK OFF)

Taking a deep breath and closing his eyes, he willed himself to let go.

The chute had been built in a vertical straight line between all the floors, from the third floor down to the basement. It had been carefully and smoothly lined with tin to ensure that, as much as possible, no pieces of clothing would get hung up between the floors on their way to the basement laundry room. What Lloyd had not thought of was how he would land when he exited the chute in the basement. It would be a terribly hard landing on the cement floor. Depending on the distance from the chute exit to the floor, he could easily break a leg or worse, his back.

Luck was with him. Because it was a fairly tight fit, Lloyd didn't slide very fast. Just before he reached the basement level, he was able to jam the sides of his feet against the sidewalls, slowing himself down. He was not, however, able to stop himself completely and so when he reached the basement level, he noisily crashed through the door and fell about a metre on to the floor.

Winded, he lay there, gasping for air, listening in case his noisy entrance had attracted any attention. Heedless of the fact that a light on in the basement might attract some unwanted attention, Lloyd stood up rather shakily. Satisfied that he wasn't about to tumble back down on to the cement floor, he turned on his penlight just long enough to find a light switch. Flicking it on, he noticed that he was in a large old laundry room. This room was separate from the rest of the basement so there was no danger of anyone knowing there was a light on unless they came looking for something. He opened the laundry room door, thought to himself, *oh heck, I am going to live dangerously,* and turned on another light, this time in the main area of the basement. From the number of spiderwebs and dust on various pieces of furniture stored there, Lloyd was pretty sure that no one had been down for a long period of time.

This basement had very high ceilings, at least, Lloyd guessed, three and a half metres (twelve feet). He looked for the coal cellar entrance and spotted it high up on the outside wall. A very deep bin was placed directly beneath the entrance. Although black and dusty inside, the bin had not been used for many, many years. The entrance was too high for Lloyd to reach. He scouted around the storage area. Finally, he located a ten-foot ladder resting behind a modern furnace. Hauling it out as quietly as possible, Lloyd set up the ladder in the coal bin, leaning one end on the wall beneath the coal chute, placing the legs tightly against the inside, rear of the bin. He climbed up a couple of steps, testing the sturdiness of the ladder. *So far, so good,* he thought and continued to climb. One rung from the top, Lloyd was able to place his hands on the outside coal chute doors. He pushed hard but the doors wouldn't budge. *Drats! They must be latched from the outside,* Lloyd thought. Climbing down from the ladder, he left it set up. Walking back into the old laundry room, Lloyd turned on his pen. He described everything from when his father had left him to go buy furniture to the secured coal chute doors. Speaking quietly, he asked the Sergeant to have BeeBee release the outside latches so that if the time came when Lloyd, for whatever reason, had to make a fast exit, he would not be stuck on the wrong side of the doors!

He also told him that he was heading home to study for an exam and finish a term paper. If the Sergeant needed him, he would be at home all evening and would be back at the clubhouse tomorrow for the entire day. He then shut off his pen and went searching for the staircase that would take him up to the main floor. He hoped that the door leading into the main entrance would not be locked! It was not.

Fortunately, there was no one near the door when Lloyd left the clubhouse. When he got home, he went to the bathroom. As he was washing his hands, he looked in the mirror and saw a very black-faced ragamuffin staring back at him. He felt like Santa coming out of the chimney – '*his clothes were all tarnished with ashes and soot'* Lloyd's clothes, though, were all tarnished with coal dust and spider webs! He had a hot shower and then threw his clothing into the washing machine and turned the machine on. He certainly would not be able to explain to Mona Grace why he looked like a chimney sweep!

Lloyd hadn't invented his excuse that he gave to his father so that he could come home early. He managed to review and complete his term paper and study for his exam for an hour.

He hadn't realised what a stressful day he had just completed until he sat down at the kitchen table with a grilled cheese sandwich and a bowl of tomato soup for his supper. Mona Grace was at another meeting. He was so exhausted he could barely force down his soup and sandwich. When he finished he looked at the clock. *Only 7:10 pm! To heck with everything,* he thought. *I'm going to bed. Tomorrow will be another stressful day but I am going there rested and ready to face whatever comes my way.*

He left Sergeant Gablehaus a brief message to let him know he was home safe and sound and was going to sleep! The Sergeant sent him a message back saying good luck tomorrow and telling Lloyd how pleased he was with what he had sent today.

The last thing Lloyd did before he crawled into bed was to plug his pen in to recharge the battery. He was very impressed with the latest technology, he had to admit. It was super easy to use! Less than a minute after his head hit the pillow, he was sound asleep.

He slept the entire night without waking, and without troubling dreams for once. He awoke feeling refreshed and eager to begin training.

Mona Grace was still asleep when he snuck quietly out of the house so as not to waken her. She had been putting in some serious overtime lately and needed all the rest she could get. As much as Lloyd loved talking with her, he was grateful that they wouldn't be seeing much of each other while he was involved with the East Van Devils. This way there was no explaining to do. He would hate to have to lie to her.

Lloyd had not yet received a building key from his father, and so he had to knock on the clubhouse door.

While he waited for Brutus to come and open the door, he looked around. There were supposed to be plainclothes officers watching the clubhouse at all times, but he didn't see a soul. Choosing to believe that they were doing their jobs nearby rather than sitting in Tim Horton's drinking coffee instead of protecting him, Lloyd quit gawking around and knocked on the door one more time.

The door was jerked open rudely. The Tattoo Man stood glaring at Lloyd.

"What da ya want? I haven't even had my coffee yet and you come pounding on the door? What the hell, Lloyd?"

What? Brutus knew his name already when they hadn't even been introduced! Lloyd found this very disconcerting, to say the least; however, he 'manned up', squared his shoulders and said calmly, "Brutus, I'm Lloyd Jordan. I now work here with my father. He hasn't given me my key yet. I'm very sorry to have disturbed you so early in the morning. I'll make sure to get a key today so I won't have to bother you again."

Brutus's reputation as the guard dog of the clubhouse was in danger of cracking as he actually smiled at Lloyd! "Well, come on in then, don't stand around all day. Welcome to the clubhouse of the East Van Devils, boy. You'll like it here. There is never a dull moment, believe me."

That said, he turned around and walked away with not another word, leaving Lloyd standing in the front entrance with his jaw dropped.

He ran up all the stairs to the third floor. He walked quickly and opened the door to his new office. Wow! Paul had done an amazing job, not only in picking out very beautiful furnishings for Lloyd's office but in actually having them delivered and set up for the same day! With tongue only partly in cheek, Lloyd thought to himself, H*mmm, there could be a lot more advantages to being a gang member than I ever knew!* Then, feeling guilty for even having such thoughts jokingly, he nevertheless sat down in his brand-new desk chair, leaned back, put his feet on the desk, and took his term paper out of his backpack for one last review. He intended to drop it off at the school on his way home from work today.

He was deep into his review when suddenly he heard the sound of throat-clearing coming from his office doorway. He looked up and guiltily removed his feet from the desk.

"Good morning, Dad," Lloyd said sheepishly. "I was just waiting for you." (CLICK ON)

Paul grinned. "Your office, your furniture to do with as you wish. If you want to use your desk for a footstool, who am I to tell you differently? What do you think of your new digs, by the way?"

After Lloyd issued an invisible grimace at his father's expression 'new digs', he said, "They're wonderful! I couldn't have done as well myself. Thank you very much. You must have pulled a lot of strings to get all this done on the same day!"

"Actually," Paul explained, "the Devils 'own' the owners of the furniture store. That means, if the Devils want something yesterday, they get it yesterday."

"I see," said Lloyd in a weak and timid voice. Unfortunately, he really did see what Paul was intimating. The only difference between the furniture guys and Shelby was that Shelby didn't pay up, and look where it got her.

"Well, son," Paul said, "you've got a lot to learn so 'pitter-patter let's get at 'er!" Lloyd cringed openly this time as his father 'did his thing' with the English vernacular. As much as he kept telling himself to ignore it, Lloyd was having more and more difficulty tolerating his father, the ex-con.

As soon as they got to Paul's office, Paul told Lloyd to take a seat. He gave him a sheet of paper to peruse while Paul made a phone call. Lloyd took the paper and read what appeared to be code entry numbers.

He heard his father laughing into the phone, setting up an appointment with someone named "SUZIE Q". *Give me a break*, Lloyd thought *He's making an appointment with a hooker? He threw away a law-abiding life and a loving family for this?* He turned his back on Paul, put the paper on the spare desk, turned on the desk lamp and studied the chart.

Page 1 of the Chart was a simple cardboard cover page. It read:

COMMON ILLEGAL DRUGS

(See Chart – Next Page)

COMMON ILLEGAL DRUGS

Entry Code / Substances	**Commercial & Street Names**	**How Administered**
#1 Amphetamine (Stimulants)	Biphetamine, Dexedrine bennies, black beauties, crosses, hearts, LA turnaround, speed, truck drivers, uppers	Swallowed, snorted, smoked, injected
#1(a) Anabolic Steroids	Anadrol, Oxandrin, Durabolin, Depo-testosterone, Equipoise roids, juice, gym candy, pumpers	Injection, by mouth, pellet implant under the skin, application to skin (e.g. gels or patches)
#2 Cocaine (Stimulants)	Cocaine hydrochloride Blow, bump, C, candy, Charlie, coke, crack, flake, rock, snow, toot	Snorted, smoked, injected

#3 Flunitrazepam (Club drugs)	Rohypnal (date rape drug) Forget-me pill, Mexican valium, R2, roach, Roche, roofies, roofinol, rope, rophies	Intravenous, swallowed, snorted
#4 GHB (Club drugs)	Gamma-hydroxybutyrate G, Georgia homeboy, grievous bodily harm, liquid ecstasy, soap, scoop, goop, liquid X	Swallowed
#5 Hashish (Cannabinoids)	Boon, gangster, hash, hash oil, hemp	Smoked, swallowed
#5(a) Heroin (Opioids)	Diacetylmorphine Smack, horse, brown sugar, dope, H, junk, skag, skunk, white horse, China white	Injected, smoked, snorted
#6 Ketamine II (Dissociatives)	Ketalar Catvalium, K, Special K, Vitamin K	Injected, snorted, smoked
#7 LSD (Hallucinogens)	Lysergic acid diethylamide Acid, blotter, cubes, microdot, yellow sunshine, blue heaven	Swallowed, absorbed through mouth tissues
#8 MDMA (Club Drugs)	Methylene dioxymethanphetamine Ecstasy, Adam, clarity, Eve, lovers' speed, Molly, peace uppers	Swallowed, snorted, injected
#8(a) Marijuana (Cannabinoids)	Blunt, dope, canja, grass, herb, joint, bud, Mary Jane, pot, reefer, green trees, smoke, sinsemilla, skunk, weed	Smoked, swallowed
#8 (b) Mescaline (Hallucinogens)	Buttons, cactus, mesc, payote	Swallowed, smoked

#8(c) Methamphetamine (Stimulants)	Desoxyn Meth, ice, crank, chalk, crystal, fire, glass go fast, speed	Swallowed, snorted, smoked, injected
#9 Opium (Opioids)	Laudanum, paregoric Big O, black staff, block, gum, hop	Swallowed, smoked
#10 PCP and Analogs (Dissociatives)	Phencyclidine Angel dust, boat, hog, love boat, peace pill	Swallowed, smoked, injected
#10(a) Psilocybin (Hallucinogens)	Magic mushrooms, purple passion, shrooms, little smoke	Swallowed

Lloyd became so engrossed in the chart that he didn't hear Paul finish his telephone conversation. He did, however, hear his father leave the office. (CLICK ON) Lloyd quickly took a photo of the drug chart. He left the pen activated as he waited for his father to return.

After only a few minutes, Paul returned to the office with a cup of coffee in his hand. Lloyd heard his approaching footsteps and hurriedly put his head down, ostensibly perusing the chart. Watching his son intently, he finally walked over and tapped him on the shoulder. Lloyd jumped wildly. "Hey man, you startled me!" He spoke in a louder voice than he intended. Paul thought it was hilarious, and laughed long and hard.

When he quit laughing, Paul asked, "Are you familiar with computers, Lloyd?"

Lloyd said, "I don't have a computer but I have taken computer classes as an option in my night school classes. I don't know much about accounting programs, but I would like to."

"That's not a problem," said Paul. "I can get you a tutor to help you learn the accounting program that we use here in the clubhouse. He can be here this afternoon to get you started."

Lloyd asked sardonically, "And do the Devils 'own' the computer company and their trainers too?"

"You guessed it!" said Paul. Then he suggested, "Why don't you take a quick break? There's pop, juice, bottled water and coffee in my kitchen. Go help yourself; the door isn't locked. In the meantime, I'll arrange for the computer guy to come here right after lunch. After your break, come on back here and I'll show you the filing system and explain what you will be doing once you are trained in the office accounting system."

"Thanks, Dad, I could use a Coke." As soon as he left the office, he switched off the pen, switching it back on when he returned.

They spent the balance of the morning going through the filing cabinets. Occasionally, Paul would extract a file, read off the 'client's' name and proudly show Lloyd how much money the gang was receiving each and every month in the form of protection services. He explained to Lloyd that protection funds were received from a great number of businessmen. In addition to protection, the Devils acquired funds from the avails of prostitution, illegal gambling, drug sales, fencing stolen goods, and chop shops. "All in all, there is no easier way to make money than to be on the payroll of a prosperous gang," Paul explained.

Lloyd asked, "When is the computer trainer coming?" He couldn't stomach hearing anything more from his father about all the money being gained from so many illegal methods and kept trying to think of things to talk with his father about in order to change the subject.

"Oh!" Lloyd said. "Have you got a key for me to get into the building, Dad? Brutus was none too happy having to let me in this morning before he had his first cup of coffee."

"Screw Brutus," said Paul, "But yes, just a minute and I'll get you a key. In fact, we should go back to my apartment and have some lunch. The trainer will be here promptly at 1:00."

They headed back to Paul's kitchen for lunch. When they finished eating, Lloyd received his keys; one for the outside door, one for his new office, one for his filing cabinets, one for his father's office filing cabinets and one for his father's apartment. Paul handed Lloyd a small box containing key fobs and coloured plastic toppers for the keys. "Pick whatever you need out of here, Lloyd. Everyone has their own ideas of key organisation."

(CLICK ON) "Thanks, Dad. What are you going to be doing while we are training on your office's computer?"

"First of all, you will be using your own new office computer. The trainer is bringing it with him. I don't know when I'll be back in my office, but likely not until tomorrow. I have a young lady coming for an 'interview' you might say. We'll be in my apartment for most of the afternoon, if not all of it, (here Paul poked Lloyd in the ribs and gave a lascivious chuckle!) I would suggest you take a Coke or two with you. If I'm not in my office when you are ready to leave, please make sure the cabinets and the door are locked, and I'll see you tomorrow morning. That is, unless the young lady wears me out. Heh, heh!" (CLICK OFF)

Lloyd was revolted. He wished he could tell his father not to be so disgusting, that if he insisted on paying for sex, he could at least keep it to himself and not yip-yap to Lloyd about it! What kind of a sicko father would share that crap with his son?

The computer trainer arrived promptly at 1:00 p.m. He introduced himself simply as 'Jerome'. No last name. He was a good trainer; clear and concise, open to any and all questions. By late afternoon, Lloyd felt he had a good handle on the accounting program used by Paul to keep the East Van Devils' books.

By 5:00 pm there was still no sign of Paul. Lloyd felt relieved. The last thing he needed to hear was all about how the 'interview' went!

He carefully locked everything up, including his own office. When he reached the main area, there was still no one in sight so he quickly opened the door to the basement and went downstairs. He had noticed several old mattresses stored down there. He reached for the one standing behind several others and hauled it to the old laundry room area. *There!* he thought. *That will make my next landing, if there is a next landing, a bit easier on my carcass!* Walking back to the storage area, he carefully straightened the remaining mattresses so that they looked undisturbed. Then he ran up the stairs, pausing to listen through the door before exiting the basement, and leaving the clubhouse for the day.

Chapter 19
A Chance Encounter

It was a beautiful late afternoon. As often happened, lazy, lightly scattered clouds reflected the sunlight, filling the sky above the Pacific Ocean with spectacular hues, combinations of brilliant blue, soft pink and gentle peach. Lloyd was never tired of the view. Some people thought it was just the 'same-old, same-old'. Not Lloyd. Each time he saw the combinations of colours, there was something different, if only slightly. Every time he watched that sky, he wished he could paint, freeze that perfect moment in time in his mind's eye forever.

Most of the office towers in downtown Vancouver had emptied out their occupants and the sidewalk traffic had slowed considerably from the early morning crowds, crowds that rudely jostled and impatiently pushed their way through the throngs on their way to work.

On impulse, Lloyd decided to take a detour on his way home. He hadn't even begun to do any bookwork, yet he felt uncomfortable. Even though he felt grubby, inside and out, he needed a shower, he needed firstly to see something beautiful rather than something shady. He headed for Stanley Park.

Reaching the 'Burgers 'N Dawgs' site, he noticed that the police tape had been removed. It did not appear as if anything else had either been done or was being done to fix the place up and re-open it. He walked by, purposely not looking back. *Sorry, Shelby,* he thought to himself, *I wonder if you would approve of what I'm doing now? Somehow I think you would.* He raised his hand and blew a kiss over his shoulder towards the trailer.

It had been some time since he'd had the opportunity to visit the park. The minute he walked through the entrance he felt the weight being lifted from both of his shoulders as well as his heavy, aching head. Breathing deeply, he smelled the numerous plants, the pleasurable dampness of the rain forest, the slightly salty air along the sea wall, even the distant smell of meat grilling on someone's bar-b-que across the water.

He chose a favourite spot along the wall and sat quietly watching several sailboats being readied for an evening sail. It was so quiet Lloyd could hear the soft hum of the sailors as they readied their vessels, not any words, just a gentle murmur on the evening breeze.

"What the ---?" After several minutes of unwinding, someone suddenly put their hands around his head and covered his eyes! He hadn't heard anyone approaching! He reacted. Wildly, instinctively, he scrambled to his feet. His eyes were still covered! Whoever was after him was strong and persistent, never letting go. Lloyd could not even begin to imagine what was going on. He quit struggling, stood stock still, simply waited. While he waited, he reviewed some of the self-defence training moves BeeBee had taught him. *Wait!* he thought. *It's probably BeeBee, testing me to make sure I learned the moves she taught me!*

"BeeBee?" His voice came out weaker than he would have liked.

"Who's BeeBee?" asked a somewhat familiar female voice behind him. His eyes were still covered. He said nothing, waiting for the voice to speak once more, straining to hear it.

There was a deep sigh and suddenly his eyes were uncovered. A soft giggle sounded behind him. Turning slowly around, he looked at his captor and gasped!

"Susanna? Oh, my Lord, is it really you?" Lloyd was so stunned he couldn't catch his breath. Susanna put her arms around him, gave him a gentle hug. "Just breathe, Lloyd, just breathe."

Lloyd couldn't control the large teardrops that rambled down his cheeks. Not letting go of his hand for a second, Susanna grinned and said, "What? You're not happy to see me?"

"Of course! I'm SO happy to see you, Susanna! I just can't believe it, that's all."

Susanna stared at Lloyd. "You should believe it, Lloyd. You knew I was going to University in Vancouver. Which, by the way, is a heck of a lot more than I can say about you. Why didn't you call me? We could have seen each other long before this."

"I didn't have your cell phone number," Lloyd stammered.

"That's no excuse, Lloyd. You could have got it from Dad if you even thought about it. Anyway, we have a lot of catching up to do. What were you going to do after you left the park today?"

He chuckled weakly. "I can't remember, but I know what I'm going to do now."

"What?"

"I'm going to invite you to my place and I will introduce you to my landlady/counsellor/friend, Mona Grace Ford, and I am going to cook all of us supper."

Susanna's smile was a mile wide, revealing perfectly straight, perfectly white teeth. "I accept!"

"What, I haven't even invited you yet," Lloyd chortled.

"Tough! I'm coming. We have years of stuff to catch up on. Lloyd, somebody up there (she pointed towards the heavens) likes us."

Lloyd was having a hard time talking. When Susanna asked him a question, he turned to her and said quietly, "Susanna, can we talk when we get to my place? I just want to hold your hand as we walk, enjoy the evening walking with my girl. Once we start to talk, we will be so busy talking we won't have a chance to enjoy this walk."

Susanna said nothing, just squeezed Lloyd's hand, reached over and kissed him on the cheek and enjoyed the rest of the walk.

Lloyd was a little worried about what she would think when she saw the poor area in East Vancouver that he lived in. He needn't have worried. As they approached Mona Grace's tiny house, he tried to see it through Susanna's eyes. *Not bad,* he thought, *it's painted, the windows are sparkling, the lawn is mowed and there are hardy flowers blooming in every flower bed. There aren't even any weeds to spoil the view.*

"Oh!" Susanna breathed, squeezing Lloyd's hand tightly in her own. Her eyes were bright as she viewed the scene in front of her. "It's so cute! Lloyd, you and your friend have a little castle among the rough here. I love it."

Lloyd smiled broadly with relief. "Come on in and see the inside, Susanna. I can't wait for you to meet Mona Grace. You'll love her." He opened the door and held it. "Mona Grace?" he called, "are you home? There's someone here I want you to meet."

Chapter 20
So Near Yet So Far

Lloyd felt as if his life was passing before his eyes with the force and speed of a tidal wave.

He and Susanna spent most of their evenings talking to each other, either on the telephone or in-person, at a library that was mid-way between their residences.

When Lloyd asked about Lacey, she told Lloyd that the last time she had anything to do regarding Lacey was a few years back when she had put a letter in the Mailbox for her. Sadly, Susanna had never received any reply. One time, when she was home from University visiting Uncle Henry, she took a trip to the Mailbox. The only item in there was the same letter that Susanna had put in the stump the last time she visited the secret spot. She had heard nothing from Lacey, and neither had her father.

Susanna asked Lloyd why he was in Vancouver. Had he seen or heard from Lacey? He told her, leaving out his involvement with the police and the gang, how, a couple of years ago, he couldn't stand the suspense any longer. He talked about hitching a ride in the pumpkin truck, running off to Vancouver to find the missing girls. He also told her that Mona Grace was Charley's birth mother. This made Lloyd want to find the missing girls even more. He asked Susanna not to speak to Mona Grace about Charley though because it upset her greatly.

He told Susanna all about Shelby Sidor, about the food wagon, about his job there. He also told her about the East Van Devils, how they had demanded protection money from Shelby and when she wouldn't pay it, they trashed her business, bought off the insurance company so they wouldn't pay Shelby's claim, and beat Shelby within an inch of her life.

"In fact," he said bitterly, "as far as I'm concerned, they killed her. While she was still in the hospital recovering from the beating, she suffered blood clots; the final one attacked either her heart or her lungs and she died." He emitted a deep sigh before saying, "Susanna, you would have loved Shelby, and she would have loved you. She was as beautiful as your mother. Actually, Shelby reminded me a lot of Aunt Harriet." Emotional, he sat silent for a few minutes.

Straightening up, he told Susanna about finishing high school, that he was just a few weeks away from writing his final semester Grade XIII exams.

"What are you going to do then, Lloyd?"

"I'm going to look for my mother and the missing girls in earnest. That's what I came to do." He purposely didn't tell her that he had found his father.

Susanna asked Lloyd why he never contacted Lacey to let her know he was okay. "Because I had nothing to tell her," Lloyd morosely replied. "I made a promise to myself that when I got to Vancouver, I wouldn't go back to Alberta until I did what I came here to do. That included contacting Lacey with news, any news. Now, it has been such a long time, that she has probably forgotten about me, or is so angry with me that she won't even talk to me. It's too late to contact her now. In fact, I don't even know where she is. The last foster home we were in was number 5, and it was not a good one. I left Lacey there in that unhealthy environment without so much as a backwards glance. She probably hates me for that, and I wouldn't blame her. I didn't stop to think. I just got the idea in my head that I wanted to find my parents and my foster siblings and I took off. No stopping to think about anything. No plan. No consideration for anyone other than myself. I just took off. How immature was that?"

Susanna didn't reply. Finally, she looked over at Lloyd and said, "Are you done wallowing now?"

Lloyd looked at her. "What?" he choked. "I'm not wallowing. That's a terrible thing to say."

"Think about it, Lloyd," Susanna said kindly. "It doesn't help to fabricate excuses for something that should have been done two years ago. It's never too late to make up for a mistake. You should probably try and get hold of her NOW! Not when you find your parents, not when you find the missing girls, NOW!"

Lloyd said, "Just let me get through my final exams, Susanna. Then, after I get my results back, I will at least have something positive (hopefully) to say to my sister."

Susanna gave Lloyd a hard, long hug, whispering in his ear, "Take the time you need, Lloyd. I'll be here if you need me. I'm not going anywhere!"

Overcome with gratitude, all Lloyd could do was hug her back and whisper, "Thanks."

He was so happy with Susanna, so grateful for her company. How he hated keeping the gigantic secret about his part in the infiltration of the East Van Devils from her.

The days passed quickly, the nights passed slowly. Mona Grace seemed to have meetings almost every night. Maybe twice a week she was home for supper, but then she would leave again, mumbling something about a meeting, but offering no other explanations. On the evenings that he and Susanna didn't see each other, Lloyd was lonely.

One evening when he was feeling particularly alone, he threw on his running clothes and went for a run. When he got to Oppenheimer Park, he ran over to 'his' arbutus tree, sat down at the back of it, out of sight of anyone walking by. Suddenly, a voice in the darkness came from the other side of the rock! "Lloyd, what are you doing?"

He recognised the voice instantly. "Hey, BeeBee! I'm just going for a short run. Nobody home at my place and I needed some air. How much longer am I going to have to keep working for the Devils? It's been a couple of months. You must have enough evidence by now!"

“Hush!” BeeBee hissed. “We don’t have any idea if we are being watched or followed. Lower your voice for God’s sake! As for how much longer, I’m not sure. You are doing a great job of sending the stuff to us, and we appreciate it. What we still need, though, is something to show us that your father is crooked. When that happens, that will be the icing on the cake, so to speak. You, of course, will be the first to know what, when and where things will be going down. Now, go home and quit tempting fate! But wait until I’m outta here.”

“I will, BeeBee, thanks. Sorry, but I just had to get out.” But BeeBee was already gone. She had disappeared, as invisible as a shadow on a coal-black night, without another word. Lloyd listened to her advice. He went home.

Paul had passed on to Lloyd the responsibility of accounting for all incoming funds. Paul still did the physical collection of the monies. When he got back to the office, he usually gave the funds directly to Lloyd. Lloyd then matched the amounts with the outstanding invoices for each ‘client’, posted the information into the accounting computer program.

Once everything was posted, Paul would take the funds to the bank and deposit them into the East Van Devils’ various accounts.

While he was out of the office, Lloyd would take his trusty pen and forward copies of all of the invoices and the relevant files to Sergeant Gablehaus. He didn’t dare use the computer to forward the information. He didn’t trust that his computer entries were somehow being monitored through the computer, likely by Domingo or one of his henchmen.

One day, he asked his father if he could move the files to his own office because he was doing all of the postings and he needed the files much more often than Paul. Paul said he would think about it. A couple of days later Lloyd arrived for work. Standing against his wall of cabinets were all of the accounting files, transferred from Paul’s office to Lloyd’s, cabinets and all.

Mid-morning, Paul stuck his head in Lloyd’s door. “Well, son, does that work for you?”

“Thanks, Dad, it’s great. It’ll save me a lot of time running back and forth between the two offices every day. Will I see you at lunch?”

“Yeah, sure,” Paul answered absentmindedly. “I probably won’t be in my office this afternoon though. I have another ‘interview’ and this one has a lot for me to ‘interview’ if you get what I mean.” (Nudge, nudge, wink, wink!) Lloyd nearly retched. He resolved never to ask a question again that would prompt a stupid answer.

“See you at lunch, then. I have something I need to discuss with you, but I don’t think it will take up the entire lunch hour.”

Lloyd wasn’t sure his father even heard him because he was already partway down the hallway on the way to his apartment, whistling as he walked.

Arriving at Paul’s apartment right at noon hour, he sat at the kitchen counter waiting for Paul to come out of the shower. He smelled lunch baking in the oven. When he heard Paul get out, Lloyd took the lasagne out of the oven and dished up two plates. There was a salad in the fridge. Lloyd dished up the salad, put a bottle of beer next to Paul's plate. He got a bottle of water for himself and sat down, nervous but determined to get the answers he needed.

"Ah! Thanks, kid," Paul said as he came out of his bedroom, reeking of too much aftershave. "Appreciate you serving lunch. (CLICK ON) So, what's so important that you had to tell me you have something to discuss with me? I assume it's about work. Don't tell me you're quitting!"

"No, I'm not a quitter," said Lloyd earnestly, "but I am persistent and so I need to ask you again, where is my mother? And don't tell me you don't know," Lloyd hastened to add. "You know where she is or what has happened to her. Please, Paul," he pleaded, "don't keep me in suspense any longer. If you don't tell me, I'll have to go digging on my own. If I have to do that, I will need to quit because I can't fill two full-time positions."

Paul stood up, motioned for Lloyd to come into the living room and take a comfortable chair.

"You're right, I guess, Lloyd. You deserve to know what happened to your mother."

"The truth, Dad, don't sugar-coat it, please!"

Paul gave a dramatic sigh, leaned back in his chair, and began:

"I lied to you before, Lloyd. I told you that your mother walked out and that I hadn't seen or heard from her since. That was a lie. I heard from her many times. She would phone me, crying and begging me to take her back so that we could find you and your sister, become a real family again. I kept telling her that was not going to happen, to please quit phoning me. I tried to be nice to her, I really did, but she just didn't get it, Lloyd! Finally, I quit taking her calls. One day she showed up here at the clubhouse. Don't ask me how she knew I was here, but somehow, she found out.

"'What are you doing here, Anna?' I asked her. I was calm at that point. I took her into my office to keep her away from prying eyes. She looked like hell, Lloyd. She smelled bad, her hair hadn't been washed for some time, her clothes were stained. She looked nothing like the wife and mother I remembered.

"She sat down in my office and started whining. I watched her. Something wasn't right. Her pupils were dilated and her hands were shaking uncontrollably. She slurred her words. I got out of my chair, walked over to her and grabbed her arm, pushed up her sleeve. Her arm was full of bruises, full of needle marks. I didn't bother checking other places for needle marks. I knew they would be there. She was a goddam junkie!

"I had been prepared to give her some money to get her started in her new life, but be damned if I was going to support her drug habit. I told her to stand up. She got down on her knees, threw her arms around my legs and wouldn't let go. I tried to pry her arms free but her desperation made her as strong as an ox! Finally, I had to cuff her a good one upside her head to make her let go. Now, Lloyd, I'm not a woman beater but I had no choice.

"I pushed her back into the chair and I phoned down for Brutus to come and take her out of my office, out of the clubhouse. Told him if she came back another time, he was not to let her anywhere near me. He had to carry her out forcefully, scratching, kicking and screaming like a banshee all the way. I was so embarrassed. In fact, when I saw Brutus later, his face was as clawed up as if he had been attacked by a tiger! I bought him an expensive bottle of booze to make up for his injuries.

"Everyone in the building poked their prying eyes out of their doors to see what the hell was happening. I put her out of my mind. She wasn't the woman I fell in love with in high school, nor the woman I married, nor the mother to you kids."

Lloyd's vision blurred. "When was this, Dad?"

"Not long after I got out of prison. I had started to work here. As I said, I don't know how she found me. Druggies have their own tom-toms, their own ways of tracking people down. It's like they have some bloody sixth sense. They sure stick together, and they sure share more than just needles. They share information too.

"Anyhow, just before you and I met up, I got a telephone call from St. Paul's Hospital. Crazy woman overdosed. They tried to save her but it was too late.

"The nurse found a piece of paper in her pocket with my name and phone number written on it. I told them she was my estranged wife, heavy on the 'strange'. When she asked if Anna had any relatives, I told her no."

Lloyd stared at Paul with total loathing. "You didn't tell that nurse that she had two children? You didn't even see that she got a proper burial. What kind of a monster are you, Paul? You make me sick!"

Paul looked severely at Lloyd. "Shut up, Lloyd," he said, "I'm your father, you have to respect me.

"You didn't see her. You would have thought the same things that I did. That woman was not the mother you remembered. She was just a filthy street druggie. I didn't know her any more, I took no responsibility for what happened to her after she was carried out of my office."

Paul glanced at the clock. "My 'interviewee' should be here any minute. I need to get ready. You go back to work. I'm sorry, Lloyd, but you wanted the truth. Well, you got it. Nobody ever said life was fair. Too bad you had to learn in such a difficult way."

(CLICK OFF) Lloyd went back to his office, shut and locked the door, put his head down on his desk and cried until there was nothing left inside him.

Finally, he raised his head up from his desk. He honestly didn't know how he was going to be able to continue working with Paul. The man was the incarnation of evil; the devil himself couldn't be as brutally cold and uncaring as Paul Martin Jordan. However, what he had told Paul earlier was true, Lloyd was not a quitter. He would be back in his office tomorrow, packing a lunch. He would not be eating lunch in Paul's apartment anymore, and he would only answer a direct question. He had no intention of speaking to Paul ever again once this assignment was completed.

Although it was only 3 o'clock, Lloyd couldn't stay in his office another minute. He called Susanna but got only her voicemail. *She must be in class,* Lloyd thought, so he left a message, asking her to come to his place for supper.

He said he really needed to talk with her. He hung up and headed for home, exhausted and numb.

He was so near but yet so far from completing his business with Sergeant Gablehaus and with the East Van Devils' dirty criminal activities. Lloyd resolved that he was going to work harder and faster in order to get Domingo Sanchez and Paul Martin Jordan behind bars.

Chapter 21
Shocking Exposures

When Lloyd arrived at home, there was a telephone message from Susanna. It seemed as if they were going to play telephone tag, so rather than call her back right away, he lay down on his bed and waited for Susanna to try and call him again.

Before he could even collect his thoughts, however, the doorbell rang. "Yeah, yeah, yeah, hold your horses, I'm coming!" Lloyd grumbled crossly.

"Hey, Lloyd," Susanna said when he opened the door. "You sounded really upset, so I thought I should come over rather than try and phone you again."

"Oh, my gosh, Susanna, but you are a sight for sore eyes!" He grabbed Susanna, squeezing her tightly. No sooner did she hug him back, then the floodgates opened.

Alarmed, Susanna lead the hysterically sobbing Lloyd over to the couch, pushed him gently down, then sat beside him, waiting for him to settle a bit before she asked any questions.

Finally, he tried to stop crying by holding his breath, clenching his jaw, biting his tongue. While he calmed himself, Susanna went into the efficient little kitchen and made some tea. She added a fair amount of sugar to Lloyd's, even though he took his tea black. He was so shaky. She hoped the sugar would help him, although she didn't have a clue if it would work. She had never felt so helpless in her life as she pondered what she could possibly do. There must be something she could do, anything to ease his agony.

When the tea was ready, she went back to the front room and sat down. "Drink this, please," she directed Lloyd. "There are two heaping teaspoons full of sugar in there, just to give you a heads-up. You look to me like you need a boost. Take a drink, and then tell me what's going on." Susanna deliberately kept her tone dispassionate. There would be time for empathy once Lloyd had released all the pain and suffering that she could almost see bubbling within him. The best thing she could do now, she figured, was simply to be there and listen.

Meekly, Lloyd did as she requested, although he turned up his nose at the sticky sweetness on his tongue. He had to hold the cup with two shaky hands, but after a second big sip, he was able to steady himself somewhat.

Lloyd finally was able to talk. He spoke so rapidly that his words tumbled over each other like dice on a craps table in his haste to get the whole squalid story out of his mouth and into his beloved Susanna's ears. Susanna did not try to slow him down. She just struggled to follow his rapid recount of the horrible events in Lloyd's life.

He knew he was betraying a solemn oath that he had given to Sergeant Gablehaus and to BeeBee, but he couldn't have stopped talking even if it meant standing in front of a firing squad. He told her everything, including his involvement with the police operation designed to bring down the East Van Devils' gang. In between breath-catching sobs, he managed to tell her about Paul's reprehensible actions and attitude towards his wife.

By the time he finished, his face was snow-white, interspersed with large red blotches covering his cheeks. His nose was red, runny and swollen, his eyes also red, runny and puffy. In fact, they were almost swollen shut.

Embarrassed, humiliated and ashamed, Lloyd stared vacantly at the floor instead of at Susanna.

Susanna went into the bathroom, returned with a facecloth dipped in cold water. She pressed the cloth against his eyes, grabbed his hand and placed it on the cloth.

"Look at me, Lloyd." When he did not, Susanna soothingly placed both her hands onto Lloyd's flaming cheeks, turned his head so that he had no choice but to look at her.

"Thank you for sharing, Lloyd. I know what it cost you to tell me all of that. I also know what it could cost you if Sergeant Gablehaus and BeeBee were to find out that you told me about the covert operation. You know, though, that whatever you tell me will always stay only with me unless you instruct me otherwise.

"Just so you know, I am proud to bursting of you and your willingness to help the law fight the bad guys. It breaks my heart that your father turned out to be not only an ex-con but a practising criminal. It also breaks my heart that your mother died in such a terrible way. I guess the only thing that might give some comfort is that she is now free of her drug habit, and her soul will no longer be in pain. She must have loved you and Lacey with such an intensity that she couldn't stand being away from you. I think her drug addiction must have been a desperate attempt on her part to soothe her savage pain at not being able to help her children when they needed her most.

"And Lloyd?" She held up her hand, stopping any attempt from Lloyd to interrupt. "I know you. You're a great guy, honest as the day is long. If you never listen to me again, listen to me now. There is no way on the face of this earth that either you or Lacey could have helped your mother. You were both just very young children. It was not your fault that your mother couldn't help you. She tried. You know how hard she tried.

"Listen carefully to this: YOU WERE KIDS! IT IS NOT THE DUTY OR THE RESPONSIBILITY OF YOUNG CHILDREN TO LOOK AFTER THEIR PARENTS. IT IS THE PARENTS' DUTY AND RESPONSIBILITY TO LOOK AFTER THEIR CHILDREN FROM THE TIME THEY ARE BORN UNTIL THEY ARE ADULTS!"

Waiting for her words to sink in, Susanna sat back, tears glistening in her eyes. She wouldn't, couldn't let them fall.

Devoid of words, Lloyd simply sat, wooden and drained, more exhausted than he could ever remember being. Finally, Susanna stood up, took Lloyd by the hand and lead him towards his bedroom. She pulled back the covers, pointed at the bed, said simply, "Lay down, Lloyd, you need to rest."

Like a tired child, he crawled beneath the sheets, fully clothed. Susanna removed his shoes, covered him with the quilt. She then took the facecloth, once more rinsed it in cold water and laid it on Lloyd's burning forehead. She sat down on the floor beside his bed, held his hand as she waited for him to fall asleep.

After a few minutes, Lloyd opened one eye, saw her sitting on the floor. He patted his bed and said, "Don't go just yet. Please, don't leave me." Susanna smiled at him. She lay down beside him, whispering, "Sleep now, my love, I won't leave you until you are asleep, and then I'll talk to you tomorrow. Don't worry, I'm never going far away from you. I love you, and you, buddy, are stuck with me forever!" She looked over at Lloyd. He was sound asleep, still clinging to her hand. Susanna smiled ruefully, unsure when she would next get up the nerve to repeat what she had just told Lloyd.

When she was certain that he was sleeping soundly, Susanna got off the bed. In the kitchen, she found a paper and a pen. She sat down and wrote him a note. After placing the note on the pillow beside him where he couldn't miss it in the morning, she kissed him softly on his lips, quietly left his bedroom and slipped out of the house. She had no key to lock the door. Looking at her watch she saw it was only 9:00 p.m. She had no idea when Mona Grace might be home. She didn't want to leave Lloyd sleeping with the door unlocked. Just as she thought she would just have to go back inside and wait, an expensive, sleek, black BMW pulled up in front of the house. In a minute, Mona Grace stepped out. The car roared away immediately.

"Hi, Susanna! Are you leaving already?"

"Afraid so, Mona Grace, I have an early class tomorrow."

"How come Lloyd's not walking you to the bus?"

"I'm afraid Lloyd had some very bad news about his parents today. He's extremely upset. He has just fallen asleep. I'm sure he'll tell you about it at breakfast tomorrow. In the meantime, please try and let him sleep."

Puzzled but too polite to ask Susanna about it, Mona Grace answered, "No problem, Susanna. Get back to the dorm safely. Hope to see you soon for longer than three minutes next time." She walked up to the front door, then turned around, calling Susanna back from the sidewalk. She opened her purse and withdrew a key. "Here, Susanna, I think you should have a house key. You seem to spend a fair bit of time here. I think Lloyd is very lucky to have you in his life. He trusts you, therefore so do I. Come and go as you will. Good night."

Susanna's head was whirling so strongly that she nearly forgot to climb on the bus when it arrived! The driver whistled, hollered at her, "Are you coming or not?" jarring her rudely back to the present. She climbed the steps, apologising to the transit driver as she found a seat.

Lloyd awoke the next morning feeling like he had been run over by a giant truck. For a minute he lay in his bed, puzzled about how he got there and why his clothes were still on. He crawled out of bed and went to turn on the shower. Standing under the stream of comforting warm water, his head began to clear, his thoughts became more lucid. An enveloping sadness penetrated through his foggy morning brain as yesterday's events came to the forefront; however, he had a job to do. He was going to do it to the best of his ability, in memory of his mother. With a new determination, Lloyd climbed out of the shower and went to get dressed for work.

It was only when he returned to his bedroom that he saw the small piece of paper on the other pillow. Picking it up Lloyd read:

> *'Sleep now, my love, I won't leave you until you are asleep, and then I'll talk to you tomorrow. Don't worry, I'm never going far away from you. I love you, and you, buddy, are stuck with me forever! Love always, Susanna XOXOXOXOXO*

Lloyd smiled as he read the note several more times. Then he tucked it carefully away in a special pocket in his backpack.

Walking into the kitchen, he was surprised to see that Mona Grace was already up, dressed and had breakfast nearly ready.

"Wow! Mona Grace, to what do I owe this honour?"

"Haven't seen you for a while, kid," she said, "and I ran into Susanna last night as I arrived home. She was waiting on the step. I gave her a house key, by the way, so she is welcome to come and go as she pleases. She said you have something to tell me, something that distressed you greatly?"

Stoically, Lloyd recounted the events of the previous day, omitting, of course, the parts about his involvement with the police and the Devils. At the end of his diatribe, he bitterly finished with "So at least I don't have to find my parents, do I? I just hope the story of the missing girls has a better ending."

Mona Grace strained not to go over and hug Lloyd. He was dressed to go somewhere and she knew if she displayed any affection he would fall apart.

She did, however, simply state, "I'm so, so sorry to hear all of that, Lloyd. Life is tough sometimes, isn't it?"

Lloyd snorted. "So far, about 90% of my life has been tough, Mona Grace. The best part of my life is you and Susanna. I don't know what I would do if it weren't for the two of you. Have I ever thanked you for counselling me, for helping me out when I arrived in Vancouver, and ever since then?"

"All the time, Lloyd," she said. "All the time, little brother. That is who you are to me, and don't you ever forget it!" She cleared her throat. "Now, eat this breakfast that I got up early to slave over, and then get out of here!"

Sometime during the previous night, in amongst the tortured dreams, a question had niggled at Lloyd's brain. He hurried to work. He needed to check something before his father came out of his apartment and settled in his office.

He quickly ensured that his pen was in working order, then shut it off.

Pulling out a few test files from the previous two weeks, he opened the files one-by-one. Each one of the files contained an amended invoice. The differences between the original invoices and the amended ones amounted to a total of $32,000.00!

Lloyd thought back, remembered the first invoice that Paul had handed him to amend. Squinting, he was sure he remembered Paul opening one of his desk drawers and stuffing something in it. Now he was positive that Paul was skimming money from the 'clients' who were paying the largest protection amounts. He would take the cash from the collections, and have Lloyd alter the invoices so that the cash Lloyd received matched the invoice amounts! Come to think of it, Paul no longer handed the invoices to Lloyd. He just put them in Lloyd's basket with the lesser amount of cash attached in an envelope and left it to Lloyd to figure out the amount to change the invoice to.

Lloyd felt really sick. It dawned on him that when Domingo caught on to Paul's thievery, Lloyd would be a suspect also; in fact, he would be the primary suspect because the changed invoices dated back to the date that Lloyd started working for his father! Lloyd checked and determined that he had already been working in the clubhouse for four months. Paul had been skimming a minimum of $2,000.00 a week for the past four months.

He quickly went back to the first week he worked for his father and made a list of the client, the protection payment due, the original invoice amount, and the amended invoice amount. He then clicked on his pen, took a photo of his list and sent it off to Sergeant Gablehaus with a one-word, terse code word – "SHADOWS!"

Determined to confront Paul as soon as he arrived in his office, Lloyd found it increasingly difficult to concentrate. As the morning wore on and there was no sign of Paul, Lloyd could stand it no more. (CLICK ON) He telephoned Paul's apartment number. After the fourth ring, just when Lloyd was about to hang up, his father answered the phone, snarling, "What the f--- do you want, Lloyd? I'm busy 'interviewing' and don't appreciate being disturbed."

Lloyd just said, in a very undisturbed tone, "Well, when you are finished with your 'interview', I need to see you. I'll be in my office posting payments and reviewing invoices. I will *not* be amending any invoices." He hung up the phone before Paul could say anything. (CLICK OFF)

Lloyd's call had the desired effect. (CLICK ON) Within fifteen minutes Paul stormed into Lloyd's office, kicking the door shut behind him. Lloyd hoped that he hurt his foot when he did that! After a few minutes of swearing a blue streak, Paul suddenly sat down and became eerily calm.

"So, kid, what's so important that you had to interrupt my interview? It had better be good."

Lloyd leaned back in his chair, clasped his hands together, placed his two pointer fingers on his chin. Looking Paul square in the eye, Lloyd said, "You owe the East Van Devils at least $32,000.00. That is the amount you have skimmed off the clients with the biggest protection payments. That is just the amount you have skimmed since the day I started working here. Heaven only knows how much else you stole when you were doing all the work yourself."

Paul leaned his head back and laughed, one jeering bark. "What's it to you, young man?"

"I want you to return it to Domingo, every single dollar of it," Lloyd replied.

"Or what, Lloyd?"

"Or I go to Domingo and tell him what's been going on. That's what, Paul."

"Damnation! Would you quit disrespecting me, Lloyd! I'm 'Dad' to you, not Paul."

Lloyd remained calm. "You are not my father. Unfortunately, you are my biological sperm donor. Maybe I should call you 'Cajones'. You have a lot of ball I'll give you that much!"

Paul was positively apoplectic. He started to stand up. His fists were clenched. He looked around him as if searching for something to throw.

"Don't try it, Paul," Lloyd said, still outwardly calm. "I think we're done here. I have a lot of work to do. I will continue working for you, but you will not skim any more funds, and you will pay back the funds you did pilfer. If you decide you can't live without embezzling, then you had better fire me immediately." That being said, Lloyd turned his computer back on and started posting payments. (CLICK OFF)

Paul got up and left Lloyd's office. Trembling so violently that his teeth actually chattered, Lloyd followed behind him, making sure that Paul was not heading to speak directly with Domingo. He was not.

With a deep sigh, Lloyd went back to his desk. He was pretty sure he would be hearing from Sergeant Gablehaus as soon as Lloyd got home from work, one way or another.

Lloyd had a distinct feeling that he was being watched. He never saw anyone physically, but there was definitely a presence wherever he went in the clubhouse. He wondered how long it would take before he was brought before the big boss man, Domingo. He didn't think it would be today, maybe not even tomorrow or the next day. He only knew that something would explode before too many days went by. He also knew that Paul would mull over Lloyd's ultimatum for quite some time before doing anything about it. He wasn't the brightest ring in the Cracker Jack box. *Yes,* Lloyd thought, *I have a few days while Paul tries to figure out what to do with me.*

By mid-afternoon, the lack of sleep caught up to him. He had himself all 'nerved up'. *To heck with this noise,* he thought to himself, *I'm going home.* He swallowed a lump of sadness as he thought about his mother. The expressions 'all nerved up' and 'to heck with this noise' had originated with her. Lloyd remembered them from his earliest childhood. He had used them without thinking, and it made him very sad.

When he arrived at the house, he couldn't help but notice that the garage door was part-way open. Inside sat a sleek black BMW. *I wonder who that belongs to,* Lloyd thought. *Maybe one of Mona Grace's clients was having her store it in the garage. But then, why would the door be partly open?* He took a closer look. The car was slightly longer than the little garage was deep. The door would only close part of the way.

Not giving it any other thought for the moment, Lloyd unlocked the back door and went into the kitchen. He went to his bedroom and dropped off his backpack, then returned to the kitchen to make himself a glass of iced tea.

Behind him, he heard a strangled moan. He spun around. Mona Grace stood outside her closed bedroom door, wrapped only in a sheet. "What are you doing home?" she choked.

Lloyd shrugged. "More to the point, Mona Grace, what are you doing home, why are you wrapped in a sheet, and whose fancy-dancy Beemer is in the garage?"

"What's going on, MG?" came a deep voice from her bedroom. "Tell whoever is out there to bugger off. Come on back to bed."

"MG?" Lloyd looked at her quizzically. "I didn't know anybody called you that. I've only ever heard you called Mona Grace. Hmmm, I think you are hiding someone from me, someone that is sharing a little 'afternoon delight' with you." Lloyd grinned at her, but the terrified look on her face wiped his grin off immediately.

Before Mona Grace could explain, her bedroom door opened. Standing there, buck naked in her doorway, was Domingo Sanchez! "Hey, Babe, I said get rid of…" Catching sight of Lloyd, Domingo sputtered, "What the f---, kid, what the hell are you doing here at my girlfriend's house?" He grabbed Mona Grace roughly by the arm, gave her a shake. "You cheatin' on me, bitch?"

Lloyd spoke in a tone of voice that could have melted a piece of steel. "Don't you touch her, Domingo. She's done nothing to upset you. I pay room and board here. Mona Grace needed the money; I had to get out of the shelter; the arrangement suits us both. Nothing is going on between us. She's not a cougar. I'm way too young for her. Besides, she's my therapist. I just came to pick something up before going to see my girlfriend. Anything else I can tell you before I get out of here and leave you two lovebirds alone?"

Mona Grace looked ready to vomit. Domingo smiled at Lloyd and said, "I think you've said it all, kid. Have a good time!" He turned and went back into the bedroom, pulling Mona Grace with him.

Just before Domingo shut the door, Lloyd said, "One more thing!" He said, "Your expensive car is probably safer parked on the street in front of the house rather than in a small garage where the door won't completely close. This is your neighbourhood, but it's not all that safe. Just sayin' is all."

He changed into his jogging clothes and left the house, worried sick about Mona Grace. *What the heck was she doing? Not thinking, that's for sure,* Lloyd thought. *Should be an interesting evening when I get home.*

Suddenly, he had a horrible thought! He had sent the password to Sergeant Gablehaus, who would almost certainly try and contact him after work. He pulled his hood up to hide his face, changed direction, and started jogging towards the police station.

Nobody was at the front desk, so he slapped the call bell. The door to the back opened and BeeBee stepped into the reception area. "Can I help…" Suddenly seeing Lloyd, she grabbed him by the arm, hissing at him, "What the f--- are you doing here? Come with me, hurry while nobody's around!" They ran up the stairs to Gablehaus's office. Not waiting for an answer to her knock, BeeBee literally dragged Lloyd in, quickly shut the door and locked it behind them.

They were greeted with 'This bloody well better be good!'

"Sergeant Gablehaus, sir, it couldn't wait. I had to contact you before you tried to get hold of me at home." As succinctly as he could, he told both the Sergeant and BeeBee about what happened when he got home about forty minutes ago. He also told them about what happened at the clubhouse in his office that morning, why he had sent the emergency code word. He asked if they had listened to his conversation with Paul. They had. He asked if they thought he was just being paranoid, thinking he was being followed. They did not.

"Sir," he pleaded with the Sergeant, "It's time! I need to get out of there. It's too dangerous. Paul is going to blame everything on me. He'll tell Domingo that the funds only started going missing when I started there. They'll kill me!"

Sergeant Gablehaus said calmly, "Settle down, Lloyd. As I told you when we trained you, we've got your back. Now, listen to me. Arrangements are being made with the Vancouver Police Department's Emergency Response Team, ERT for short, to assist us when we go to the Devils' clubhouse to arrest Domingo, Paul and Brutus on a great many charges. Thanks to you, Lloyd, we are going to be able to put those guys away for a long, long time."

"When is this going down, sir? Am I done there now?"

"Almost, Lloyd. You need to go back there tomorrow, make sure your pen is turned on and then, as difficult as it will be, act like nothing negative has happened between you and Paul. Get him to believe that you have no intention of reporting him to Domingo. Tell him that for a small cut of the action, you and he can make a whole lot of money on the side. This will be the acting performance of your life. Get him excited about the idea of working with you instead of against you. When you are certain he is on side with your idea, use the code word. We will be armed and ready. Once you use the code, get the hell out of there through the clothes chute and out the coal chute doors. BeeBee will make sure that the coal chute doors are open. When you are clear of the clubhouse, go straight home and wait there. Don't go anywhere else and no matter how long it takes, wait for me."

Lloyd said, "Sergeant, I have one more thing I need to tell you."

"Can it wait?"

"I guess it can, sir."

"Alright then, tell me tomorrow when the mission is completed. Good luck!"

Lloyd said fervently, "And the same to all of you, sir. See you tomorrow. Bye, BeeBee."

BeeBee looked at the Sergeant and said, "That boy will make a mighty fine policeman one day, sir."

"Umm-hmm," mused the Sergeant. "Get some rest, BeeBee, tomorrow is going to be a busy day."

Lloyd ran the entire way from the detachment to Susanna's dorm. Susanna wasn't as close to Mona Grace yet as Lloyd was, having only met her a few times. She could probably put things in perspective for him. Lloyd certainly couldn't figure this out by himself. Also, he had the (not so) little matter of her 'pillow talk' to speak about as well. Smiling broadly, he sat down on the bench that was situated outside the women's dorm, called Susanna and then waited for her to come out and join him.

By the time Lloyd and Susanna had talked and they had a burger at the nearby A & W, it was starting to get dark. Lloyd asked if Susanna would like to come home with him, be there when he spoke with Mona Grace. She declined, saying that Mona Grace would be uncomfortable enough speaking with Lloyd, let alone having an almost-stranger in on the conversation.

He stood up. "Guess I better get going then."

Susanna stood up and hugged Lloyd fiercely. "You be careful tomorrow, please. Call me as soon as you get back to your house, no matter what time it is, no matter how late. Hear me?"

"Aye, aye Captain," Lloyd said as he hugged her just as fiercely. "Don't worry, nothing is going to happen to me!"

When Lloyd arrived at home, he first checked the garage to make sure Domingo was no longer there. Then he let himself in the back door.

Mona Grace was sitting alone on the couch in the living room, in the dark. Lloyd didn't see her at first. In a small voice, she said, "You can turn the light on, Lloyd."

Flicking the switch that turned on a floor lamp, Lloyd sat down in the armchair across from her. For a long time, he just stared at her, saying nothing, just waiting for Mona Grace to explain herself.

"I know what you're thinking, Lloyd," she said.

"No, you don't, Mona Grace. You haven't got the faintest clue about what I am thinking, so I guess I better tell you. I'm thinking, *What in the Sam Hill is this crazy woman doing? What in the name of all that's Holy is her daughter going to think about her when she is found and meets her mother for the first time since she was a child?* I'm also thinking, *Is this the same woman who counselled me when I first came to Vancouver, who offered me a place to live when I couldn't stay at the shelter any longer? The same woman who helped me get my head on straight, convinced me that I should and could finish my high school?* Lloyd stopped talking. Sunk his head into his hands and sobbed.

Finally, he lifted his head and stared woefully at his landlady, his counsellor, his friend, heck, his mentor.

"Will you listen to me, Lloyd?" she asked. Lloyd nodded his head, said nothing.

"I know this makes no sense to you. It doesn't make much sense to me either, but…" Mona Grace shrugged her shoulders, momentarily at a loss for words. "One day, after a very strenuous number of appointments, an extremely stressful day at work, I walked over to Oppenheimer Park and sat down on a bench, trying to get myself together. Some days the weight of the entire universe, not just the world, seems to settle on my shoulders. I get so tired of trying to solve other people's problems when I have problems of my own. This was one of those days, maybe even my worst day ever.

"Someone sat down on the bench next to me. I was deep in thought, didn't even notice, or for that matter care, who it was. Suddenly this voice says, 'Holy shit! Mona Grace, is that you?' Startled, I looked over and Domingo Sanchez was sitting right beside me. My first urge was to just get up and walk away, but I figured that would be just too cowardly. So, I coolly said, 'Well, as I live and breathe, if it isn't the Big Man himself! How's the head of the East Van Devils doing these days?' I just sat there and waited for his response.

"He had the grace to blush as he said, 'I never stopped thinking about you, MG, even after all these years. I kicked my own ass regularly over the years, wondering why I had left you like I did, why I left our baby girl without a daddy. It wasn't right, leaving you all alone like that. I thought so many times about calling you to see how you and the baby were doing, but I was too chicken. I was afraid, afraid that you would tell me to take a hike, tell me you were married. But you know, sometimes fate takes a hand in things and here we are! I am so happy to see you, MG, you have no idea.'

"I couldn't help myself, I was curious. 'Domingo, are you married?' I asked him. 'No,' he said, 'I couldn't find anyone to replace you. It's as simple as that, MG.' A couple of minutes later, he asked if he could take me out to dinner. You know, Lloyd, if he had shown up on a normal day when I wasn't so down, so depressed, I would have told him to take a hike and never thought another thing about it. But I was so lonely, and he was so sincere. He appeared to be genuinely sorry. Against my better judgement, I said okay, I would go to dinner with him. I said I had to go home and change clothes first, so he could pick me up in an hour. An hour later, to the minute, he was parked outside in his fancy big car. He came to the door with a big bouquet of beautiful red roses. Domingo bought me lots of expensive presents in the old days, but he never bought me any flowers. I was flattered. I put them in water and we went out to a fancy, expensive restaurant down by the water. The weather was so warm. There was no wind, so we sat at a table outside. He pulled out my chair for me. The *maître d'* called him by name. He introduced me, ordered a bottle of champagne, even ordered steak and lobster for the two of us. It was so different from when we were young. He treated me like a queen. Reached across the table and took my hand. 'Isn't this nice?' he asked. 'I have missed you, MG. Are you warm enough?' he asked me. He took off his dinner jacket and placed it around my shoulders, giving me a squeeze as he did so.

"At the end of the evening when he drove me home, he asked if he could come in for a nightcap. He came in and well, seduced me. It wasn't hard, and I didn't object. He left in the middle of the night. You were home by then, but asleep."

"When was this, Mona Grace?" Lloyd queried.

"About five months ago," she said, "Why?"

"Just curious, please continue."

"Not much more to say. It's been five months. He picks me up from work, takes me to nice places, still treats me like royalty. Takes me to the clubhouse often; I never stay overnight. He always drives me home and waits until I am safely in the house. He wants to marry me, Lloyd! Can you imagine that?"

"Does he take you places with any of his friends? Your friends? Does he monopolise all your time, or can you spend time with your friends, without him with you?"

No answer from Mona Grace, who just folded her hands together, and stared down at her lap.

"Has he ever once asked about Charley?"

No answer. Mona Grace looked ashamed.

"Does he always grab you by the arm and haul you away from other people, like he did last night?"

Silence.

"Are you afraid of him, Mona Grace?"

No words, but an almost imperceptible nod confirmed what Lloyd was thinking.

"Why don't you tell him you don't want to date him anymore?"

"I tried," she whispered.

"What happened?"

"He said we were meant to be together forever. That I didn't know what was good for me so he would just have to look after me."

"What did you say?"

"I said I could look after myself, that I didn't want to marry him."

At this point, Mona Grace looked terrified. She trembled as she said before Lloyd could ask, "He put his hands around my throat and squeezed, but not hard. He said if I tried to leave him, he would kill me."

"When did he say that, Mona Grace?"

"Yesterday, after you left."

Lloyd turned red, but he held himself in check.

"You're going to be okay, Mona Grace. It's almost over. Trust me. I can't tell you anything, but it will be okay. If he calls you tonight or shows up at your door, tell him you are ill. Tell him you don't want him to get the terrible stomach flu you have contracted, that you'll see him in a couple of days. Can you do that?"

With a visible shudder, she said, "Yes, I can do that."

Lloyd had been debating whether or not he should share with Mona Grace the fact that Domingo was far from monogamous, that he was sleeping with hookers who were working for him, for the Devils. Not sure just how to go about telling her, he finally just blurted out, "Mona Grace, you should get tested for sexually transmitted diseases. I know for a fact, having seen him myself, that Domingo is screwing around with the prostitutes that are working for him."

"Okay," she said meekly. "I can do that."

Lloyd's heart ached for the broken-down woman sitting in front of him, but he knew that she was the only person who could put an end to this relationship. Well, that wasn't quite true – Domingo would be in prison for a very long time after tomorrow, but of course, he couldn't tell her that. She would find out soon enough. In the meantime, he resolved to stay at home for the evening in case Domingo should show up. He would ask Susanna to come over to keep both himself and Mona Grace company.

The gods were with them. Domingo didn't show up, nor did he call Mona Grace. The three spent a pleasant evening playing Scrabble. Mona Grace and Susanna handily slaughtered Lloyd. He decided that if he hadn't hated Scrabble before, he certainly did now! It was one way, though, he decided, to keep his mind off the events of tomorrow!

Chapter 22
Captured

Lloyd showed up at his office the next morning, prepared to speak with Paul at the earliest opportunity. He was early, as he always was; therefore, he was surprised to see that Paul was already in his own office.

(CLICK ON) Knocking on the edge of the door frame, he said, "Good morning, Dad, can I come in?"

Paul shrugged his shoulders nonchalantly.

"Suit yourself."

From his words and body language, Lloyd surmised that Paul was not going to make this easy. He wasn't surprised, but he wasn't intimidated either. He was prepared for this leading role. *Good thing I got Honours marks in drama in school,* he thought. *Whoever would have thought in a million years that I would have a starring role in a real-life event. I just hope I remember all the acting tips!* He stooped his shoulders, pasted a contrite expression on his face.

"I need to apologise for my behaviour yesterday, Dad," Lloyd said meekly. "I was out of line. You were right, I haven't been respecting you. I was awake all night last night, thinking about how wrong I was, how I was going to be able to get you to forgive me and trust me again. I know I threatened to go to Domingo. It was only an idle threat. You're my father, I could never turn you in." *Not like you,* Lloyd thought acridly, *who turned your own children over to Family Services to be used and abused for many years.*

Paul stared at his son, growing curious in spite of himself. "And?" he asked.

"I didn't know a great idea from a hole in the ground, even when the shovel hit me over the head." Lloyd continued, "What I'm thinking is that if you and I work together, we can make a ton of money, and Domingo will never be the wiser. Instead of us fighting and accusing each other, let's make a pact to form an alliance and make some serious money. I have some ideas. I know you learned a lot in prison about how to successfully 'rip people off', for lack of a better or more polite term, no disrespect intended."

Lloyd stopped, watched his father for any sign that might indicate which way he was leaning. No clue. Stoneface. *Heck,* Lloyd thought nervously, *this guy's one cool actor!*

"Dad, I am truly sorry. I know you can teach me so much about the ins and outs of making money. Please, won't you forgive me so we can move forward instead of being stuck in the muck?"

The silence was deafening. Lloyd finally broke it. "Dad? What do you think?"

"Just keep quiet for a few minutes, son, I'm still thinking. In fact, why don't you go back to your office and start posting payments while I keep thinking? I'll let you know as soon as I figure things out."

"Sure thing, Dad!" Lloyd said excitedly. "I am excited about you and I working as a father-and-son team. I hope you can see it my way. I can certainly see it your way."

"Yeh, yeh, yeh!" He waved his hand impatiently towards the door. "I'll give you my answer before lunch. Just take off would ya?" Paul stood up, said noncommittally, "I'm going to my apartment to think in peace."

(CLICK OFF) Lloyd was antsy. It was almost impossible for him to concentrate. He knew he sounded sincere. He also knew that if he had been more technical, given some real ideas about how to make his proposal workable, Paul might have had an easier time trusting Lloyd. However much his imprisonment had taught him about how to be a crook, it hadn't taught him much about acting (or so Lloyd desperately hoped!)

As the morning dragged on, Lloyd became rather suspicious. Brutus had walked past his office at least three times. Lloyd had never seen him do that before. He decided that if Brutus walked by again, Lloyd would confront him, in a friendly fashion, but confront him nonetheless.

A short time later, Lloyd heard footsteps starting down the hallway. (CLICK ON) He stood up, stretching and yawning until Brutus approached.

"Morning, Brutus!" Lloyd said, giving one last mighty faked yawn. "What brings you into my neighbourhood first thing this fine morning?"

Brutus was no actor. "Uh, uh, just setting gum exercise, I mean getting some exercise," he said, tripping over his own tongue. "Pretty slow in the clu-clu-clu-clubhouse today. I had to walk or fall asleep. Domingo don't like it if I fall asleep." He was obviously lying about why he was walking up and down past Lloyd's door so many times.

"Well," Lloyd said, "Good luck. I'd hate to see you get in trouble with the boss, Brutus, and that's a fact. You're a great guy. I consider you a great friend. See you later!" Lloyd turned back towards his desk. His hair at the back of his neck stood at full attention. Finally, though, he heard Brutus walk away. (CLICK OFF)

Lloyd detected more footsteps. (CLICK ON) They stopped at the end of the hall and he heard Paul speaking with Brutus, although he couldn't make out what they were talking about. His stomach was churning. However, after a minute, that stretched like an hour, he heard Paul say, "Have a good day, Brutus. Nice chatting with you."

Lloyd quickly sat down at his desk, nose to the grindstone, or so it appeared.

A quiet tap on the door frame. Lloyd pretended not to hear. A louder tap, more like a knock this time. "Can I come in, son?"

Lloyd lifted his head, allegedly startled. "Of course, Dad, come in, please."

Paul came in, sat down in the comfortable chair across from Lloyd's desk.

"I'm interested, son, in your proposal. I don't mind saying, however, that it kind of worries me, after the way you behaved yesterday."

Lloyd said, "I don't blame you. I acted like a spoiled brat when I had no call to. I'm better than that. Let me prove it to you, please, Dad."

"One question, Lloyd. What kind of a cut are you expecting?"

"Now, this is something that I'm sure you're more familiar with than me, Dad. But I'm thinking that it's only fair for you to get the bigger cut."

"How much bigger?"

"Well," Lloyd drawled out, seemingly uncertainly, "I was thinking 60% for you; 40% for me seems fair."

Paul couldn't help it. He grinned amicably, and said, "Boy, you ain't just a whistling, you don't know a damn thing about the knife and fork part of negotiating."

"Told you that!" Lloyd said amiably, grinning right along with his father. "What do you think is a fair split then?"

Paul paused, probably for effect, "Well, kid, I was thinking more like 10% for you and 90% for me."

"You're kidding, right, Dad?"

"Not really. I've got the experience. You're still wet-behind-the-ears. I figured 10% for you until you can prove to me that I can trust you, that you can come up with some new and good ideas."

Lloyd pretended to be heavily disappointed, dropping his head into his hands; however, he suddenly raised his head and looked at Paul directly.

"I guess I don't have much choice, do I, Dad? After all, it was my own doing that caused you to lose faith in me. I have to earn your trust back."

He stood up, stuck out his hand. "Can we agree on one thing? That is, after three months, if you feel you can trust me and we have 'made' enough money that I have proved my capabilities, you will bump my cut up to 25%. I know I need to earn my way here, but you'll be making a ton of money right from the get-go. What do you think?" Lloyd shut his mouth. He was starting to realise that he was babbling. He didn't want to arouse his father's suspicion of him. He sat silent, waiting for Paul's reply.

"Sounds fair to me, Lloyd."

"Dad, what exactly will we be doing? I just want to be clear in my own mind what each of us is doing. I don't want to screw up, make you disappointed in me again."

Paul thought to himself, *This kid is dumber than I thought. Guess I'll spell it out for him.*

He sighed.

"It's simple, Lloyd. I'll pick up all the money just as I do now. I'll check the invoice against the money I received. Then I'll figure out how much we can safely skim without attracting Domingo's attention. I'll put that money aside; you'll amend the original invoice so it matches up with the lesser amount of cash. When we get that running smoothly, we can add on other stuff, like a cut of the drugs delivered, a cut off the hookers' tips, stuff like that."

"Sounds like a dream, Dad," Lloyd slapped his hands together with glee. Once again, he stuck out his hand. This time, Paul shook it, then held on very tightly for a few seconds. Lloyd took that gesture for the implicit warning that it was intended to be.

"I won't let you down, sir," he said. His father's chest puffed up upon hearing the sign of respect his son awarded him with the use of the single word, 'sir'.

"Oh, one thing more, Dad, nothing to do with our conversation but I just wanted to let you know that I have a Grade XIII final examination this afternoon at the school. I'll come in early tomorrow morning to make up the time if that's okay with you. I just want to be sure. It's my last exam. If I pass, I'll have my High School Matriculation. I have been studying fiendishly at night because I want to make top grades and make you proud of me." (Lloyd swallowed hard, not wanting to throw up on his new furniture!)

"Good luck on your exam, boy. I'm going to be interviewing this afternoon again anyway. I'll see you tomorrow, bright and early." Paul walked away more jauntily than when he had arrived.

Before Lloyd had a chance to click off his pen (thank goodness!) the sound of heavy footsteps echoed once again down the hallway, stopping at Lloyd's office. Lloyd stood up, said "Hey, Brutus, you again? You must be really bored. You're wearing a hole in the hall carpet, man!"

Brutus stared sadly at Lloyd. "Boss wants to see you, Lloyd, right away."

"Oh," Lloyd said, trying to appear unaffected by the news. "Did he say what about?"

Brutus shrugged his very wide, muscular shoulders. Lloyd thought, *Good! There's no way that Brutus will fit in the clothes chute.* The 'Tattoo Man' said, "Boss never tells me nothing. I just pass the word. Come with me, I'll show you where to go."

Lloyd was sweating with panic, a cold sweat, emitting a sour stench, but he tried his best to appear unconcerned. "No problem, Brutus, I know where to go. Can you please tell Domingo that I'll be there in about ten minutes? I need to go to the bathroom. I'll try not to be long."

Knowing he had no time to spare, Lloyd, while looking at Brutus, said 'SHADOWS!'

"Huh?" Brutus asked Lloyd. "What did ya say?"

"Nothing. I just said I have to go to the john before I come and see Domingo. I'll be right there; in fact, I'll probably get to his apartment at the same time as you. I'll see you there in a couple of minutes."

For good measure, once the big man had left, Lloyd whispered the code once more, 'SHADOWS!' He heard Sergeant Gablehaus loud and clear – "GET OUT OF THERE, NOW!"

Lloyd poked his head out the door. Brutus was standing at the end of the hallway, looking perplexed and unsure of how he should handle this. The boss had told him to deliver Lloyd to his office, but Lloyd had to go to the can. He couldn't deliver him to Domingo if he had to piss, could he? Of course not. He decided to go to Domingo's place and just wait for Lloyd outside in the hallway. He started to walk towards the boss's place.

A sudden sound caught his ear. He turned around, hollered, "What's going on? Who's there?" He started to walk back towards the hallway where Lloyd's office was.

Damn! Lloyd thought, *I have to go, NOW!* He ran to the end of the hallway, opened the clothes chute. As he started to climb in, his suit jacket caught on a rough edge of the chute door. Rather than wasting time trying to unhook it, he slipped it off his shoulders, left it dangling half on the floor, half caught on the corner of the chute. *No time to worry about that,* he thought. Lloyd crawled in, gave his jacket a mighty yank. It pulled free of the snag, leaving only a tiny piece still caught on the tin on the outside of the laundry chute door. He quickly threw the suit jacket down ahead of him. He heard Brutus coming closer and closer, hollering, "Hey! Where are you, Lloyd? You need to come with me, now!" He had reached the end of the hall. Noticing the tiny piece of material stuck on the door, Brutus thought to himself, *Jeeze, didn't Lloyd realise that they don't use this clothes chute anymore?* The laundry room was on this floor now. He started to open the door.

Lloyd let go, lay back with his arms tucked close to his sides, and flew down the chute, all the way to the bottom, landing hard on the mattress, flat on his back. Winded, he struggled to catch his breath. He still had to get out of the basement. He could hear Brutus yelling for him.

Thank heaven I left the ladder in position, he thought as he finally struggled to his feet. Although still gasping for air, Lloyd managed to climb the ladder and push on the heavy wooden coal chute doors with both shoulders. When the doors opened a crack, he peeked out. Brutus wasn't there yet.

Pushing with all his might, Lloyd shoved the doors open fully and took off, running at top speed, always mindful of his surroundings. He heard the clubhouse door crashing open, Brutus thumping down the steps of the clubhouse, hollering all the while, "Lloyd, get back here!" but he couldn't catch up to Lloyd.

Lloyd turned the corner, leaned against a building wall, gasping for breath.

No one was chasing him. Risking a peek back around a tiny piece of the wall, he saw Brutus standing in the middle of the entrance into the alley, scratching his fully-tattooed bald head.

No sirens sounded, but flashing lights were converging on the clubhouse. There were police cars, an ERT vehicle, a fire truck and an ambulance, all heading for the alley. One car pulled alongside Brutus, two policemen jumped out. Brutus offered no resistance, just meekly put his hands behind his back. Lloyd thought that Brutus was probably relieved to be caught. He wouldn't have to explain to Domingo why he hadn't produced Lloyd when he was ordered to.

What he wouldn't give to be a fly on the wall when all of the arrests were made. However, it was time for Lloyd to follow orders. He kept running until he reached home, went into the house and settled down to wait for Sergeant Gablehaus to come and see him once the operation was complete. (CLICK OFF)

Drenched with sweat from all of the tension and exertion of the morning, Lloyd took a shower.

When he came out of the bathroom, he went directly to his room and put on clean clothes. He threw his soggy, sweaty clothes in the washing machine.

He grabbed his textbook and sat down to study for his final exam. It was not today, like he had told his father, but it was tomorrow.

Mona Grace came home from work just after five o'clock. Lloyd still had heard nothing from Sergeant Gablehaus. Mona Grace told Lloyd to keep studying while she made supper. He was grateful for her company but kept on trying to study.

He couldn't tell her anything yet, not until he heard from the sergeant. Hiding behind the textbook he was studying from made it slightly easier to keep his mouth shut.

The knock came at 7:00 pm. When Lloyd opened the door, Sergeant Gablehaus, BeeBee and Susanna were all standing on the step. "Come on in, everyone," he said. "Quite the day, huh?"

"Let's all sit around the table. Mona Grace, do we have any coffee made? Lloyd asked.

"Coming right up," she said. "Everyone, take a seat. I'll make the coffee and then I have some ironing to do."

Sergeant Gablehaus said, "Actually, Mona Grace, I think you'll want to sit in on this meeting too."

Startled, she said, "Oh? All right, just let me get this coffee."

The two policemen sat patiently. Susanna looked like she was choking on the blower from a kid's bubble-making machine. When Lloyd tried to catch her eye, she wouldn't look at him.

Finally, the coffee was ready. When everyone had a cup, Mona Grace sat down.

BeeBee looked at the Sergeant. "May I?" she asked. Sergeant Gablehaus grinned and nodded.

"Well, ladies," she said, "just thought you would like to know that you are looking at a full-blown hero." Lloyd looked stunned, Susanna and Mona Grace only slightly less so.

BeeBee continued, "Well, we had quite a day, with Lloyd's help." She went on to explain about the covert operation, expounding on Lloyd's part in the operation.

"Thanks to Mr Jordan here, we were able to get appropriate warrants and raid the clubhouse of the East Van Devils. We arrested the leader of the gang, Domingo Sanchez; we arrested Domingo's money man, Paul Martin Jordan, and we arrested the gang's enforcer, Bernard Belcourt, also known as 'Brutus' or the 'Tattoo Man'. With the evidence that Lloyd was able to unearth and record, these three men are going away for a very, very long time."

Embarrassed by all the attention, Lloyd looked over at Mona Grace. She sat still, unsuccessfully trying to hold back tears. All she could manage to do was look at Lloyd, mouth silently in his direction, "Thank you!"

Lloyd said simply, "You're welcome, Mona Grace. I told you everything would be okay, I just couldn't tell you why or how or when."

Susanna, in the meantime, was squirming like an earthworm trying to climb out of a ditch. Sergeant Gablehaus patted her on the shoulder and said, "Okay, Miss Greshner, your turn."

Susanna stood up, cleared off the table. "Close your eyes, Lloyd," she said. "Just for a second."

Lloyd was totally mystified but did as she asked. A minute later she said, "Stand up and open your eyes!"

He did as she asked. There was a newspaper spread out on the kitchen table. He glanced at it and then looked at Susanna. "You bought me a paper? Thanks?"

Susanna could barely contain herself. "Lloyd!" she shrieked, "Look at the paper!"

"Okay, okay, although I can't begin to imagine what –"

"Just read it!" This time the Sergeant, and BeeBee, and Susanna, and Mona Grace (who had snuck a peek at the paper before Lloyd opened his eyes) all shrieked at once, "JUST READ THE DAMN PAPER!"

The front page of the VANCOUVER SUN contained two large, major headings.

The first one read:

GANG LEADER, MONEY MAN, AND ENFORCER
ARRESTED IN COVERT OPERATION

The second headline read:

CASE OF THREE MISSING FOSTER
GIRLS SOLVED

Epilogue

The next few weeks flew by.

Lloyd finished writing his Grade XIII exams. Although he had to wait for his test results, he was not worried. He had studied hard for every exam and was pretty confident he had done well.

He had several meetings with Sergeant Gablehaus and BeeBee to finalise his statements for the police. Because BeeBee would be testifying on some of the charges, her real identity was not revealed. She would remain simply BeeBee until all of the trials were complete and sentences handed out.

At their first appearances in Court, Domingo Sanchez, Paul Martin Jordan and Bernard ("Brutus") Belcourt each plead not guilty to all of the counts rendered against them. With the justice system severely backlogged, their trial dates were scheduled for more than one year down the road. Lloyd would have to appear as a witness in all of the trials resulting from the covert operation. Closer to the trial dates, he would meet with the crown prosecutors to review his statements and be briefed for each trial.

Mona Grace vacillated between anxiety and elation as she waited to be reunited with her daughter Charlotte (Charley).

Lloyd kept putting off getting in touch with his sister, saying he was too busy to contact her yet.

Susanna gently prodded Lloyd on a regular basis, suggesting he contact Lacey to arrange for him to meet with his foster sisters. His response was always the same, "I don't have time yet."

One evening, while Susanna was not with Lloyd, she got a phone call. After that call, she phoned her dad.

A couple of weeks later, Lloyd received his final Grade XIII marks – he had passed with an average of 94%. He was so relieved that he broke down crying for several minutes, at the same time reassuring Susanna that they were 'happy tears'.

Susanna made plans to go home and visit her father and her stepmother on an upcoming long weekend. She invited Lloyd to come along with her. He declined, saying, "I don't have time yet."

Two weeks after that long weekend, Susanna asked Lloyd out for dinner. He looked at her like she had rocks in her head. "What for?" Susanna rolled her eyes and told him he was about as romantic as a fish! "To celebrate our first year of dating and because I will be going home for the summer and we won't see each other for four months."

"Oh, okay then, Susanna," Lloyd said. "Where are we going?" Susanna reminded him that he had mentioned a particular restaurant called The Fish House which had great views overlooking English Bay.

"Can't think of anyone I'd rather eat there with," was Lloyd's romantic (?) response.

"It's a pretty fancy place," Susanna told him. "Dress up a bit, okay?"

Lloyd didn't have anything to dress up in, but he did have some money. Unbeknownst to Susanna, he went shopping.

The morning of the dinner date, Lloyd called Susanna. "I'll pick you up," he said. Susanna asked, "Why? I can meet you there."

"Is this a fancy date or not?" Lloyd asked her.

Susanna giggled. "Well, yes, I guess it is. Okay, pick me up at 6:30."

"See you then."

At 6:30, Lloyd picked Susanna up. He was dressed in a very handsome, very expensive navy suit. Bowing gallantly, (he hoped!) Lloyd handed her a beautiful orchid wrist corsage. This ignited a spark of suspicion that he might have somehow found out the details of their dinner. Her suspicions were put to rest, though, when Lloyd suddenly dropped down on one knee in front of the girls' dorm, snapped open a ring box displaying a beautiful diamond engagement ring.

"Susanna Greshner, will you please marry me?" he asked. Susanna couldn't speak. "Susanna!" Lloyd said, "Can you please say yes so I can get up off this hard cement sidewalk?"

Susanna pulled him to his feet. "Yes, my love, I will marry you. And, just for future reference, you will never again be able to convince me that you are not a romantic!" Lloyd smiled enigmatically and mentally patted himself on the back. Susanna thought that it was way past time that he felt pleased with himself.

When they arrived at The Fish House, Susanna excused herself, saying she needed to go to the ladies' room. She was back in a very short time and they followed the hostess to the very back of the restaurant and in through a door to a private banquet room. Lloyd was so busy staring between the fantastic view of English Bay and his beautiful fiancée that he didn't even notice where they were going, or wonder why they weren't eating in the main dining room.

A whirling dervish appeared out of nowhere, launching herself into Lloyd's arms, repeating over and over, "You said you'd contact me. You said you would and you didn't!" Lloyd looked helplessly at Susanna, who just smiled gently at him, then walked over to her father.

Lacey Jordan-Sutton clung to her brother, alternately punching and hugging him, tears of frustration and happiness clouding her vision for most of the night. She did manage to introduce her brother to her husband, Parker, and to her foster mother, Hilda Somers. Lacey and Parker were living on Stumpy and Hilda's farm. Hilda was in a nursing home close by. Lacey picked her up every Sunday and brought her home to the farm for supper.

The no-longer missing Charley was there. Susanna put her arm around Mona Grace and gently lead her over to Charley and introduced them. Ever thoughtful, Susanna had spoken with Charley at length, preparing her for the meeting with her birth mother. After an initial awkwardness, the two of them sat and held hands the rest of the night and talked non-stop.

The no-longer missing Amelia was there. Finally, fully recovered from her ordeal, she was nonetheless still very fragile. She told Lloyd how grateful she was to have survived the ordeal, and how indebted she felt to Lacey for finding her. She told him how therapeutic it was for her to find out that Lloyd's purpose had been to try and find his missing foster sisters. When Lloyd protested that he had been unable to find them, she put her fingers over his mouth. "Hush," Amelia said, "it's the thought and intention that counts." She gave him a gentle hug and then went and sat with Hilda.

Uncle Henry and his wife Cora were there. Uncle Henry introduced Lloyd to Cora. "I'm delighted to see you so happy, Uncle Henry," Lloyd said. Then he spoke to Cora, "Thank you for making him so happy, Cora. It is great to meet you."

Sergeant Gablehaus and BeeBee were also there, at Susanna's invitation. Both he and BeeBee mingled, beaming as broadly as if they had been Lloyd's parents.

Sometime or another during the evening, Lloyd and Susanna went to the front of the room. Lloyd clinked his knife on his water glass, demanding attention. He leaned over and kissed Susanna. The entire room cheered heartily!

Lloyd adjusted the microphone. "I'm not a public speaker," he began, "but there are a couple of things I need to say. First of all, thank you to Susanna for arranging this amazing evening. She practically had to drag me kicking and screaming here tonight. Thank Heaven for her perseverance! But I did get a surprise in for her as well. Friends and family, this evening, before we came to this fantastic restaurant, I proposed to the love of my life, Miss Susanna Greshner, (much loud cheering and clapping from all the guests) "and (Lloyd held up both hands in a plea for quiet), AND she accepted!" Lloyd waited until the noisy cheers and whistles died down before continuing once again.

"This evening is such a celebration. For so many years, Lacey and I have struggled. You all know our story so I don't have to go into any past details, but as I look out at all of you, my heart is full to overflowing. Thank you so much for coming to what has turned out to be a beautiful celebration of love, life, reunions and faith.

"Each and every one of you here tonight is special, but there are three people sitting here tonight that I feel the need to single out.

"The first is my sister, Lacey. Without her determination and strong will, we wouldn't be here this evening. Her bravery in doggedly pursuing the mystery of our missing foster sisters, pursuing that mystery until she solved it, well, I just don't have the words to express what that means to me, and I'm sure to all of us in this room. Thank you, sister!

"Charley and Amelia, you are no longer 'the missing'. May we all have many happy years and many special occasions to share from now on.

"Charley, Amelia and Lacey, please come up to the front and stand with me while we pay tribute to the memory of one of the missing, our foster sister who, unfortunately, we knew for only a very short time before she disappeared. Our hearts weep because our foster sister is not here in person to celebrate with us, but I feel her spirit here among us. Please raise your glasses in a toast to the memory of Miss Annie Barcley. To Annie; you are missed."

As the young women started to go back to their seats, Lloyd grabbed Lacey by her sleeve. "Lacey, can you stay up here with me for this next tribute, please? I don't think I can get through it without you by my side."

The two siblings stood arm in arm. Lloyd cleared his throat several times before he was able to speak. "Now, please raise your glasses and toast with Lacey and I to the memory of Anna Marie Jordan, our beloved Mama. Both Lacey and I are certain that she is looking down at us tonight and smiling. To Anna Marie Jordan."

Sometime late in the evening, Uncle Henry took the young couple aside and steered them out onto a side patio. Henry had planned on discussing this matter on a less hectic occasion, but he couldn't wait. He offered Lloyd a wonderful opportunity to join him in his wood-working shop. He would send Lloyd to the Northern Alberta Institute of Technology (N.A.I.T.) in Edmonton, Alberta to learn the carpentry trade. In addition, Lloyd would complete his apprenticeship under Uncle Henry's tutelage. Once Lloyd completed his training and graduated a fully-qualified finishing carpenter, Lloyd would take over the business.

The senior Greshners would then spend their winters in Arizona, and their summers on the acreage. Uncle Henry said he would like to build a cabin for Cora and him to live in during the summers. He asked that if Lloyd and Susanna didn't mind, could he build it somewhere on the property.

"Of course, we don't mind, Uncle Henry!" Lloyd looked at Susanna. "What do you think?" Susanna looked at Lloyd, asking him, "Do you want to live there and become a finishing carpenter?"

"More than anything in the world," he said. Lloyd turned to Uncle Henry and said, "I would be honoured to train under you, Uncle Henry. Thank you!"

***

A few months after Susanna's surprise party at The Fish House restaurant, Lloyd and Susanna were married. Lacey was Susanna's Matron of Honour, and Parker was Lloyd's Best Man. No one else was invited to the small wedding. After all the pandemonium of the past year, neither Lloyd nor Susanna wanted a big wedding.

Within a few weeks after the marriage, the newlyweds moved back to Alberta, into the magnificent house that Uncle Henry had built himself so long ago.

One of the first things that Lloyd wanted to do was to take Lacey back to Mountain Goat Lake. That lake had been their favourite spot when they were young children. Although they invited Parker and Susanna to come along, both declined, knowing how much the brother and sister needed time alone with each other before there could be any kind of closure.

As soon as they arrived at the lake, Lloyd leapt out of the vehicle and sat down at the water's edge. Patting a spot next to him, Lacey joined him. They sat in companionable silence for a long time, savouring both the view and the memories that came with this tranquil lake.

Climbing into the canoe they had brought, the first thing they did was to paddle quietly to the spot where the Trumpeter swans nested. The large, graceful swans ruffled their wings as if welcoming Lloyd and Lacey back to their fold.

Drifting lazily on the small lake, Lacey said, "Funny, isn't it, Lloyd, how much smaller the lake seems now? When we lived with Uncle Henry, it seemed so big." Lloyd agreed.

"You know, Lacey, while I was in Vancouver, I had a dream. I dreamed the same dream over and over. I would wake up shaking and sweating."

"Tell me about it, Lloyd," Lacey said. "I'd really like to hear it. Maybe if you describe it aloud, you won't be bothered by it anymore."

"Actually," Lloyd said, "I wrote about it. I hoped you would be interested and so I brought a copy of what I wrote. May I read it to you?"

"Yes, please," his sister said. She waited patiently for Lloyd to dig the paper out of his pocket. Then he read:

"A man and two women, one of the women no longer young, stood at the edge of the water. The late morning sun glistened brightly on the gently dancing waves of the emerald green lake. Their craft waited expectantly, tied to the jetty.

The man helped both women settle comfortably in the canoe before he climbed in and picked up his paddle. They glided smoothly along on the cool water, headed for the small island that beckoned in the distance. Reaching the land, the man positioned the canoe alongside an old jetty. While his wife held the canoe steady against the side of the jetty, the man helped the older lady out of the craft. He then turned to assist his wife, but she was already out. He reached in and removed a wicker picnic basket and four folding lawn chairs from the canoe.

It was beautiful on the shore of the island. A cool autumn breeze heralded the coming winter, but today the sun shone brilliantly and warmed their cheeks as they sat on the beach. The man pointed skyward. 'Look,' he softly said. 'See them? There are only five. One must have lost its love. Trumpeters mate for life, just like you and me.' His wife smiled and patted his hand.

Some time passed. His wife fretted. She said worriedly, 'He should be here by now. He promised he would be here.'

'We can wait a little longer,' her husband said. 'We'll wait as long as we can.'

They waited for two more hours. Finally, the man gently told both women that they would have to return the canoe to the rental agent. If they didn't leave now, it would be dark and the rental booth would be closed. They quickly packed up the remains of their picnic and returned to the jetty. The husband reloaded the canoe, then helped the women back into the craft.

Reaching the centre of the small lake, the man stopped paddling. His wife leaned back and he put his arms around her. The older woman trailed her hand in the cool water, watching the ripples grow larger until they disappeared. All three quietly watched in the distance as a young deer drank from the water's edge, in the same spot where they had sat only a few minutes before. After one last lingering look at the island, with tears wetly rippling down her cheeks, the elderly woman reached to the bottom of the canoe and brought up a wooden container. She kissed the box and then gently lowered it over the side of the canoe.

Utter silence. Not even a bird trilled. The five Trumpeter swans floated in place, their beauty reflected in the stillness of the water. Time stood still. Each lost in their own separate thoughts, the three people deeply appreciated the peace and the quiet. They fully realised that all too soon their busy lives would drown out their memory of this blissful silence and this beautiful lake.

'I'm sorry he didn't show,' the man gently said. After several minutes more, the man picked up his paddle and continued rowing back from whence they had come…

His heart pounded. The blood and sweat poured down his forehead, stinging fiercely when they reached his eyes, blinding him as he raced at full speed, stopping only when his feet hit the water. It was not a long distance, probably no more than five hundred metres, from the main shoreline to the small island. Gasping for breath, he dunked his head beneath the water to clear his vision. He then began to swim towards the shore of the island.

Exhausted, he reached the rocky beach. He swore as he slipped while trying to throw himself up on to the jetty. He caught himself but not before his knee banged painfully against the side of the ancient wooden structure.

He attempted clumsily to untie the equally ancient wooden canoe but his bleeding fingers were stiff with cold. Finally, the knot broke free. He lunged into the craft, picked up an oar, prayed that the canoe would float. He began to paddle hard. Rounding the end of the island he spied the other canoe in the distance, already nearing the far end of the lake. He called out, but the wind direction and the exhaustion in his entire being made it impossible for his voice to carry that far. Tears of frustration, heart pounding with anxiety and disappointment, he turned the canoe around and headed slowly back to the jetty. He collapsed on the shore and, chest on fire, he breathed raggedly until his breathing evened out.

He fell asleep. When he awoke, it was dark but he knew he had to keep going. Leaving the canoe, he walked into the water and began a slow swim back to the mainland. A few strokes later, he felt something sucking him down towards the bottom of the lake. He tried to kick harder, to swim faster, but still, he kept on sinking."

Lloyd looked over at his sister. Lacey was staring at him, wide-eyed, startled.

"What's wrong, Lacey?" Lloyd asked.

She said, "That dream is almost exactly like the dream that has haunted me the entire time you were away."

"What do you think your dream meant, Lloyd?" Lacey asked.

"I always thought that the people in the canoe were you, Mom and Susanna. I thought the box that they lowered into the water contained Aunt Harriet's and

Uncle Henry's ashes. I thought the person crashing helplessly through the bush was me. I would run and run and run, trying to attract your attention. You never heard me. I felt it meant I was going to die."

Lacey stared at Lloyd once again. "In my dream," she said, "the people in the canoe were you, me and Mom. The person crashing through the bush was our father. He had breached his parole and was trying to get to us, to hold us hostage. In my dream, our father turned around and left us. The box we lowered into the water contained his ashes."

"Well, Lacey," Lloyd said. "Now that we know the truth, we don't need to dream bad dreams any more. I think our mom would be the first to tell us that we have done pretty well, considering all the events in our lives."

"Agreed," Lacey said.

She reached into a bag she had placed on the floor of the canoe and lifted out two beautiful yellow roses. Handing one to Lloyd, she said, "These are in memory of our beloved Mama. Let's drop them into the water to honour her and to banish our dreams. It is time to get on with our lives."

Lloyd picked up his rose, dropped it gently into the water. Lacey did the same. "Rest in Peace, Mama," she said. "Yes, Mom." Lloyd said, "Rest in Peace."

The shadows of the missing were no more. All of the friends and relatives had years of catching up to do. Now that everyone was reunited, each was safe in the arms of love!

...OR WERE THEY?